French Kissing
IN NEW YORK

ALSO BY ANNE-SOPHIE JOUHANNEAU

Kisses and Croissants

French Kissing in New York

ANNE-SOPHIE JOUHANNEAU

DELACORTE PRESS

Text copyright © 2023 by Alloy Entertainment
Jacket art copyright © 2023 by Andi Porretta

GetUnderlined.com

Educators and librarians, for a variety of teaching tools, visit us at
RHTeachersLibrarians.com

Library of Congress Cataloging-in-Publication Data is available upon request.
ISBN 978-0-593-17361-9 (trade pbk.) — ISBN 978-0-593-17363-3 (ebook)

The text of this book is set in 11.3-point Adobe Garamond Pro.
Interior design by Cathy Bobak

Printed in the United States of America
10 9 8 7 6 5 4 3 2 1
First Edition

To Aggie,
my favorite New Yorker

PROLOGUE

The night was always going to end, but that doesn't mean I'm ready to let it go.

To let *him* go.

Streetlamps flicker for a brief instant before switching off in unison, rows of them going dark after hours of lighting our way through the city. The soft pink glow of summer dawn rises over Paris. Without discussing it, Zach and I have been wandering back toward Champ de Mars, the long, manicured park leading to the Tour Eiffel, where we met last night. The sidewalks have been almost solely ours until now, but I spot a few passersby, their eyes still half-shut with sleep, the early morning mist like a thin blanket over them. The signs are all around us. Paris is waking up, which means our time is almost over. For now.

Reading my mind, Zach pulls out his phone to check the time. I lean over to see it for myself: 5:36 a.m. Reality stares back at me, too bright.

"Less than an hour," I say, trying to keep the dread out of my voice.

We arrive at the edge of the park—deserted but for a few people walking their dogs—and Zach wraps his arms around me. I bury myself deep into him, getting a whiff of his scent, musk

1

mixed with cut grass, his hoodie like a pillow, on which I'd be too happy to fall asleep, even though the strap of his backpack rubs against my cheek.

"I'm going to miss you," he whispers in my ear. "Next year feels so far away."

My heart knocks against his chest. I know what we agreed, but my mind runs wild with hope anyway. What if he stayed an extra day, an extra week? We've gone over this all night long. My summer course at Le Tablier, the most renowned culinary program in France, has just wrapped up. Soon I'll be getting ready for my last year of high school in my hometown outside of Tours. Meanwhile, Zach will be backpacking around the world for a year and having the absolute best time of his life. Paris was his first stop, and he's hopping on a train to Berlin this morning. I'm super jealous, *obviously*, but also . . . our timing is so terrible it makes me want to scream. Why did we have to meet on his last night here?

"I'll miss you, too," I say. "What if—" I look up, stare into his eyes.

He runs a hand through my thick, wavy hair, lifts my chin, and kisses me. It gives me the best kind of shivers. We stayed out all night long, wandering the city, past the Arc de Triomphe, down the winding little streets of Saint-Germain, and even up to Montmartre, stopping to sample food along the way.

We ate fries with ketchup from a food stand. Bought a block of goat cheese and a baguette from an all-night grocer. Then there were chocolate crêpes, which Zach hadn't even tried since he'd arrived in Paris a few days ago. Two hours later, his lips still taste sweet.

I've never had a night like this, let alone in Paris. I live two hours away, in a small town southwest of here, but it might as well be a world away. It has none of the restaurants and shops and cafés and music, crowds to lose yourself in, that feeling of being somewhere truly special. Like a good daughter, I took the train home every night of my summer course, sighing at all the fabulousness I was leaving behind.

This was the one night I'd made plans to be in Paris, to stay with my friends in the school dorms so I could join for an end-of-summer picnic. But I never even made it to the gathering.

"Are you changing your mind?" Zach says.

My heartbeat gets even wilder—the lack of sleep combined with feverish want. "Are *you*?"

"No!" we both say at the same time, way too loud for the quiet early morning.

I chuckle but quickly feel the seriousness of the situation wash over me again. "A year from now, I'll be done with high school. *Finally.* Done with my small town, my boring life."

Paris is beautiful, exciting, amazing even. But it's not New York. *Nowhere* is New York.

I've dreamed about living there ever since I left it, when I was two. The Big Apple is not just where dreams are made of; it's where I was born. Where I *belong*.

"We'll be together," I add. "We *will*."

It's fate. There's no other way to put it. Some people dream of getting into a prestigious college, but all I want is to pack up my chef's knives for a life of adventure. The kind my parents had until my mom carted me off to France to become a country mouse.

When Zach told me he was American and had a job lined up as a cook in a renowned New York restaurant after his trip, my heart flipped back and forth a dozen times. What were the chances? We were meant to be.

We *are*.

But that's a whole year away. We walk in silence for a bit, and I notice a young couple kissing on a bench in the shadows. It only makes my heart sink further. This was us last night. I was there admiring the view before heading off to the picnic, when Zach came to sit down next to me. We started talking right away and never stopped. Maybe this couple will get to be together for the next year, while I can only dream of holding Zach in my arms again.

"Long-distance is the worst," Zach says. "If we spend the next year texting and just trying to . . . I don't know . . ."

"It won't work."

Of that, I'm sure.

We've had this conversation throughout the night, and the answer has always been the same. I'd never done it myself, but I'd seen some of my friends desperate to stay in touch with guys they'd met during ski trips to the Alps or beach vacations on the Côte d'Azur. They texted furiously for weeks, made all these wild plans to be together, and then, things just petered out.

"We'll ruin it. Better to wait until we can be together. For real. We met for a reason. This can't be a coincidence."

He nods, the look on his face serious. I know—and he knows— that this thing between us is special. "Yeah, but until then . . . ," he says, his voice catching.

"I'll wait for you," I whisper.

"Margot," he replies with a heavy sigh.

There's a current coursing through both of us that makes me feel like it doesn't even matter if we're apart. We're already tethered in a much deeper way.

"Tell me, again, your favorite things about New York," I say to lighten the mood.

"Everything. The energy, the people, the feeling that anything is possible. The amazing food . . . although I know French food is pretty great, too."

"French food *is* great," I say, even if it's not exactly how I feel. "I mean, it's fine. It's famous for a reason, I guess. But it's also *all* I've eaten my entire life. It's what my mom cooks in her restaurant—only the most traditional dishes—and at this point it just feels so . . . old-fashioned? Kind of blah?" I grin up at him. "I'm ready to taste something new."

He kisses me in response. "New York is unlike anywhere else. You will love it so *so* much. I can't wait to share it with you."

His body is abuzz as he talks about his favorite places, his life there—skateboarding in Central Park, attending indie rock concerts in Brooklyn, the best things to order at a famous diner that was used as a movie set. I can't wait to feel the thrill of it all.

Back at the Tour Eiffel where it all started, Zach and I both know that it's time to say goodbye. But neither of us can bring ourself to say it, to accept that we won't see each other again for a whole year. Each heartbeat feels like another second ticking down on the clock.

He takes a deep breath. "And you're sure you don't want to join me on my trip?"

I laugh. Wouldn't it be absolutely wonderful if I could drop everything tonight and follow him to the ruins of Athens, the souks of Marrakesh, or the sandy beaches in Croatia? But . . . school. But . . . Maman. But . . . money. I'm a dreamer, but even I can be a tiny bit reasonable sometimes.

It's just not going to happen.

I shake my head, and he shrugs sadly. "Hey, I had to try."

I pull out my phone again and Zach frowns. "I thought we weren't going to swap numbers?"

That, I admit, was my idea. Exchanging phone numbers or Instagram handles meant texting, me seeing his amazing adventures and feeling even more sorry for myself from the back of my chemistry class. I'm attached to my phone as much as the next seventeen-year-old, but come on, technology and romance do not mix. If Zach and I are going to be together—and we will—it has to be epic. A story we'll be telling for the rest of our lives. Together.

"We're not," I say, more convinced than ever. "We just need to set a date. And a place."

"You pick," he says with a smile. "And I'll be there, waiting for you."

I open my calendar—which, unsurprisingly, is wide open for next summer. "Let's say August first."

After school finishes I'll need to work at Maman's restaurant for a bit to save money before leaving.

Zach types in a few characters into his own phone. "Okay. Two p.m.?"

I take a deep breath. A time a year from now. "Two p.m. doesn't feel so romantic. How about midnight?"

"You're right. Midnight it is. Now, a place."

The pressure hits me. "You know New York way better than me," I say. "Shouldn't you pick a place?"

He ponders this for a moment. "I think it's more fun if you decide. What's the one spot you want to see the moment you arrive?"

To be honest, there's not just one. I want to see it all: the Empire State Building, Central Park, Chinatown, the Met Museum, the charming little streets of the West Village . . . "Times Square," I finally blurt out.

Zach chuckles. "Um, okay? But Times Square is huge and extremely busy, night and day."

I close my eyes and see the neon lights, the bustle, all the scenes from movies that portray the famous square like it's the only place to be. The center of the world. I imagine Zach pulling me into his arms, twirling me around, and kissing me for all of New York to see. It feels right. "August 1 at midnight in the Times Square bleachers, bottom right."

A plan is made. It's definitive, and Zach can probably read it on my face, because he leans down and kisses me. Electricity shoots up and down my body. We're doing this.

He pulls back, letting out a deep sigh. "What if you decide not to come to New York after all? What if you get a great job at a restaurant in Paris and decide to stay here?"

I can tell he has more what-ifs, so I cut in. "What if *you* decide not to come back to New York? What if you meet another girl during your trip? What if you break your leg on the way to Times Square and never make it there?"

We stare at each other in silence, the Tour Eiffel standing tall over us.

Then I continue. "Here's the thing. I've been dying to get out of my tiny town in nowheresville for forever. I *need* this to happen. Doing this course the last few weeks has made me realize how much I'm ready for my life to begin. So there's no way—*no way*—I'm not coming to New York next summer. I'm going to be there, August first at midnight in Times Square, even if the world is collapsing around me."

Zach's chest rises and falls as a huge smile takes over his face. "And so will I." He pulls me closer. "Goodbye, Margot."

His lips are only inches from mine, lingering. A year is only a blip in the grand scheme of our lives. The way he looks at me now, that twinkle in his eyes, makes me feel like anything is possible.

"*À bientôt,*" I reply. At his confused expression, I translate, "See you soon. Very soon."

He kisses me and, just like that, our fate is sealed.

Chapter One

A year later

I've been dreaming about this forever, but I'm still a little stunned that it's happening. I'm in New York. I live here now. This is real. This is weird. This is . . . amazing.

The airport terminal looks like a city-sized shopping mall, with everything from luxury brands to coffee shops lining the halls, and so many people. More people than I feel I've seen in my entire life. In my earbuds, Taylor Swift sings an anthem I've selected for this very moment, the upbeat melody drowning out the cacophony of the terminal. *Welcome to New York! It's been waiting for you.*

Not as much as I've been waiting for it.

After going through customs, I'm looking for the signs for baggage claim, when my heart stops. At the end of the conveyor belt, there's a tall guy with blond hair, square shoulders, and skinny legs. I immediately recognize him as the one. The one I've been thinking about nonstop, the one I meet every night in my dreams, the one and only Zach.

Our meeting is in just *two* days, but right this minute I feel sweaty, my skin dried from the air-conditioning on the plane, my breath stale from the gross industrial food. It's not at all how I hoped our reunion would go after a whole year of fantasizing about it, but I have no choice. Zach is here now. So.

I zigzag past the other passengers between us, and before the nerves get to me, I put on my best smile and tap him on the shoulder. He turns around. I stare at him, my brain a little slow to process reality. This is not Zach. In fact, he doesn't look anything like Zach. Up close, he's not even blond. I made this up in my head. Silently cursing, I blame the jet lag.

"Um, yeah?" He sounds annoyed.

I have to say something now. "Hi! Do you know when our suitcases are coming out? My dad's waiting for me."

The guy opens his eyes wide and, without responding, points a finger at the screen above the conveyor belt. The one everyone has been looking at, which indicates the exact time—four minutes from now—when our luggage will start feeding out onto the belt.

"Perfect!" I say extra-cheerful. Deep down I'm mortified. "I'm going to text him!"

My cheeks burning, I fall back into the crowd. How many minutes is two days?

All is forgotten when I spot Papa's and Miguel's happy faces beaming back at me from just outside the sliding doors to the terminal. Papa throws his arms in the air in a motion that I think is supposed to be a wave but that actually makes him look like a blown-up marionette shimmying in the wind, the kind you see outside used-car dealerships on American TV.

As soon as I'm within reach, we give each other *la bise*—one kiss on each cheek, the French way. Then, he pulls me into an American hug. That's what he always told me as a child: when you have two cultures, you get to have the best of everything. Sometimes that means double of a good thing, like a toasted cheese sandwich on a baguette. Or *tarte aux pommes* with crust on top, which, yes, *I know*, is just apple pie.

Papa's boyfriend—I mean, his *fiancé*, Miguel—hugs and kisses me: he's learning fast.

Papa has lived in Manhattan most of his life. He visits his company's headquarters—a wine distributor—in Paris several times a year for work, and spends most of his vacation time hanging out with us in France. Miguel has even tagged along a few times. I've never had the opportunity to visit them in New York . . . until now.

Miguel hands me an oiled paper box marked "DOUGH." "Your dad wanted to bring welcome balloons," he says, glancing at the ones floating high around us, "but I had another idea."

I start salivating as soon as I open the box. Six giant donuts stare back at me, all glazed in different colors. And by "giant," I mean that each of them is basically the size of my face. I'm not even sure how I'm supposed to fit one in my mouth, though I'm definitely willing to give it a try.

"I know it's not *croissants*," Miguel starts. Papa gives him the side eye, like they've had the donut-versus-croissant debate many times before. "But that's the point. *Bienvenue*, Margot! You're not really American if you're not always carrying food with you."

I laugh. "Challenge accepted."

My stomach groans and I pick up the first donut that catches my eye, glazed hot pink, and take a bite. The texture is incredible—dense but not dry, fluffy but crackling, thanks to the layer of sugar on top. The subtle scent of hibiscus surprises me, in a good way. It tastes like summer, indulgent but light all in one bite. I'm in love.

"Quick question for you," I say, turning to Papa. "How would you feel if Miguel suddenly became my favorite dad?"

When I originally made plans to move to New York, I knew I'd be living with Papa and his boyfriend while I searched for an apartment, but I didn't expect they'd get engaged by the time I got here, after four years together. Now Miguel is my future step-dad and the wedding is in just over three months. I couldn't have hoped for a better start to my life in the big city.

Papa grimaces. "Excuse me, *ma fille,* but remind me who convinced your maman to let you come live here with us?"

"Good point," I say, taking another bite of the donut as he grabs the handle of my suitcase.

At the mention of her, I pull out my phone, rereading the text that was waiting for me when I landed.

> Bien arrivée? J'espère que tu ne vas pas te
> perdre dans l'aéroport. C'est vraiment grand.

> Arrived safely? I hope you won't get
> lost in the airport. It's really big.

Ugh. It still annoys me now, even though I *did* feel like I could get lost in there for a minute. Of course I won't tell her that. I don't want to add to her long list of reasons why I should never have done this. Such a big city! So ruthless! And loud, too. Probably too much for an eighteen-year-old country girl like me. Maman hasn't tried to hide the fact that she thinks me moving here is a terrible idea.

But I was determined. For the last few months, as school was winding down, I sent my résumé to an ever-growing list of restaurants. I'd heard nothing, when Papa mentioned he'd read an article about a new restaurant called Nutrio, helmed by renowned chef Franklin Boyd. Imagine my surprise when I discovered that Maman actually worked with him while she lived in New York all these years ago, and that they'd been friends.

I asked her if she would email him, but Maman resisted every step of the way. She had so many excuses. *We haven't spoken in years. I really don't see you working for him. Margot, trust me, you won't like cooking in a New York restaurant.* She kept going on and on about how different the restaurant business was in the big city. It was so annoying.

Of course it's not like in France. That's why I'm here. Maman has been cooking the same small menu of classic French fare in a restaurant where the basic decor hasn't changed since I was a child. I know *she* loves it, but I want more. Something different.

It wasn't until my flight was booked and Maman realized I was actually going that she agreed to get in touch with her former friend. Not only did he respond quickly, but what he said made me leap with joy.

Bien sûr, Nadia! I'll give Margot's details to Raven, one
of my sous-chefs, and she'll be in touch when something
opens up, which happens all the time. And Margot should
feel free to reach out when she gets to New York.

How amazing is that? I kept sending résumés afterward, but I
knew in my heart that this was it, my new kitchen. I've read everything I could find about Nutrio, and it seems like a wonderful
place. It's a modern vegetarian restaurant in the Flatiron District,
just got a glowing review in the *New York Times,* and is walking
distance from Papa's apartment. In my head, I'm already working
there. I'll be in touch with the sous-chef on Monday, as soon as
I've settled in. My fabulous New York life is almost here!

Miguel follows us out of the terminal. "And, Bella"—this is
Miguel's nickname for me—"I'm not sure I'm ready to be anyone's dad."

I do my best contrite face. "Okay, so no donuts for you, then?"

Outside the air is thick. Steamy. Heavy in a way that makes
me feel the weight of my clothes, jeans and a T-shirt, right away.
I did not expect that.

A few minutes later, the three of us squeeze into the back of a
yellow cab, me in the middle with the box of donuts on my lap.
I've finished the hibiscus one, but I want more. Maybe the plain
glazed will be a good palate cleanser. Miguel looks longingly at the
box and I turn it toward him, letting him choose. Come on, we
know why he bought these donuts. It's like when I bake a birthday
cake for my best friend, Julien. I'm doing it for him, but I'm also
doing it for me.

Everything is bigger in America. That's what people say. But I'm not sure I fully understood what they meant until our taxi merges onto a jammed highway with more lanes than I can count. I clutch my fists as the car navigates left and right, trying to shave a few seconds off our trip.

"How were your last days at home?" Papa says with a guilty expression. He's no stranger to Maman's displeasure about my moving here.

"You know how Maman is," I say with an eye roll. "Not emotional, but also not *not* emotional."

He laughs awkwardly, making *me* feel guilty now.

"She'll be fine. I'm here now, she's going to have to get used to it."

"I know, but she felt so strongly about—"

"About me not going through with my dream, yeah, I know. But I'm eighteen now. And *this* is what I want. I would have made my way here even without your help."

My parents were never a couple, but they love each other deeply. Just not romantically. It all started when, fresh out of culinary school in Paris, Maman moved to New York herself. Hypocrite much? It didn't take long for her to meet other French people in the Big Apple—apparently they're everywhere in the city—including Papa, who grew up here. His parents are French, but they lived in the States for thirty years, where they had their two sons. Papa was raised on the Upper East Side, learning French at home and English at school. He always wanted to spend time in France, but he got a job right out of college and stuck around.

At the same time, Maman had spent her twenties doing every type of job under the sun, before finally deciding to pursue her passion for food. My parents became friends a few months after she moved here and quickly became inseparable. I heard stories of wild parties and last-minute trips to the Hamptons or Chicago, where my uncle, Papa's brother, lives.

Months became years. Maman felt like she'd never have a serious boyfriend, but she wanted a baby. Papa had always thought he'd have one, too. Eventually, they agreed to do it, together. I don't like to think of myself as a turkey baster baby—if that's even how it happened—so I never asked the exact details of how a gay man and a straight woman made *moi*. It wasn't exactly an epic love story, but here's something I've known from a very young age: I was wanted. They didn't care one bit about making a slightly different family.

Before Papa can bring up Maman again, I change course. "On my last night I had a party with my friends, Julien and some of the others from school. They gave me a photo album with pictures of all of us, and we did karaoke for hours. It was bad in a great way."

"Now you're finally here," Papa says with a relieved smile.

"And Zach Day is upon us!" Miguel adds.

Oh yeah, we're this kind of family. Not oversharers, exactly, but loose with information, especially when it's juicy. Like how I met a guy one night in Paris and made a pact to see him a year later at a set time and place in New York. Maman was livid when she found out I'd stayed out all night with a stranger, but, hey, I came back in one piece. I was still so high on my Zach-induced endorphins that I didn't care about being grounded for a month.

I let out an exaggerated sigh. "I'm nervous."

Papa shoots me a look. "Nervous happy because you're going to see him so soon, or anxious about what might or might *not* happen?"

I only need to think about it for a second. That night Zach and I had, what we promised to each other, it was real. I knew it in my bones then, and nothing has changed in the past year. I'm ready for love. The life-changing kind. The can't-breathe-without-you kind. Romance, with a capital *R*. There was a moment that night when Zach stared deep into my eyes and said that he'd never been in love *before*. I still remember how my legs almost gave out from under me, thinking about what he was implying.

"Nervous happy," I say. I check the time on my phone. "It's actually just a day and a half now."

Miguel lets out a laugh between two bites of his donut. "You two better not steal the spotlight at our wedding."

"I wouldn't bet on that," I say with a devilish grin.

"Look," Papa says.

We're driving over a bridge—the Williamsburg Bridge, he tells me—and the city comes into view. I spot the Empire State Building first, the most recognizable skyscraper in the most famous skyline. Soon we're going past creamy-white and brick-red buildings, most of which have top-to-bottom metal stairs attached to the facade. Fire escapes, Miguel explains. Cars, taxis, buses, and bikes surround us. And the people! The sidewalks are swarming with them, all walking at the same pace, like salmon swimming upstream.

My throat tightens with excitement.

I. Am. Here.

At last!

"It can be a lot at first," Papa says. "Toto, you're not in Touraine anymore," he says with a wink. Touraine is the region Maman is from. And me, too, I guess. He's right. This is a far cry from the rolling hills and quiet life I grew up living.

"I *love* it," I say. "Give me the buzz, the crowds, and all the thrill. This is what I signed up for."

The city that never sleeps, where the lights shine brighter and dreams are made. Cooking at one of the hottest new restaurants. With Zach by my side, forever. This towering place already feels like it's mine: full of possibilities and adventures. And love, obviously.

Finally, my life begins.

Chapter Two

There's something terribly wrong with my dad's apartment. Or, rather, with his kitchen. Let's start with the fridge. It's a gigantic metal thing, the size of a small car, with *two* doors. Three if you count the enormous freezer section—which is complete with an ice maker. Speaking of the doors, they're so heavy that I have to push against the wall with one hand to create enough force to open one, the rubber seal making a pained suction noise as it resists the effort. When I manage to do so, it's only to discover that this monster of a thing is tragically, bizarrely, unacceptably . . . empty. Well, almost empty.

Last night, Papa gave me a quick tour of the apartment, on the fifth and top floor of a walk-up building in the West Village. There's an entire wall of floor-to-ceiling windows that look onto neighboring buildings, so close that you can see other people going about their business. The living area is cozy, with a large velvet sectional in a deep blue, and contemporary paintings in shades of white and beige on the wall behind it. The kitchen is what French people call *une cuisine américaine*. It's a corridor open on one side, and overlooks a dining nook. The two bedrooms are at the other end of the apartment, each with their own windowless bathrooms.

I was so tired after my flight that I took a long shower, rummaged around in my suitcase for my nightie, and was in bed by nine p.m. local time, three a.m. in France. I don't even know what the guys did for dinner. Maybe, like me, they were still full from the donuts. I woke up a few times throughout the night, wondering where all this noise was coming from. Cars. Sirens. People squealing down the street. New York is *not* quiet.

When I opened my eyes for good, light was filtering through the thin curtains. I got up slowly, feeling woozy and a little disoriented. My mouth was as dry as a piece of parchment paper, and I felt so very hungry. I tiptoed to the kitchen, bottomed-up two glasses of water, and started rummaging around for something to eat, something to *make*. My first breakfast in New York; it had to be special.

After a thorough inspection of the kitchen cupboards, I feel even less inspired. I give the fridge another chance. There's a carton of oat milk that's almost empty, a squeezed-out container of ketchup, and a bottle of soy sauce. The only thing that counts as food is the half-dozen eggs in their cardboard container, but who eats eggs for breakfast? I know. *I know.* Americans do. When it comes to breakfast, there's nothing American about me: it's irrevocably, unapologetically sweet, and, even then, the options are plentiful.

The most obvious choice is, of course, *tartines*. You slice a long piece of baguette in half, slather each side with butter, and top it off with the jam of your choice. And none of that "toast" nonsense. Baguettes are eaten fresh, just picked from the bakery, preferably still hot from the oven.

Then you have croissants, a classic among classics, one that rises above all the other *viennoiseries* on name recognition alone. Other bread-like baked goods include *pains au chocolat, pains aux raisins, brioche,* or even *pains au lait.* All of which can—and should—be dipped in a piping-hot bowl of black coffee or chocolate. And yes, the liquid *will* drip down your chin as you inhale the soaked piece of pastry. That's how you know you're doing it right.

I'm still daydreaming about breakfast options when I hear the front door open. A moment later, Papa appears behind the kitchen counter. He's wearing gym clothes, his graying hair thick with sweat, his cheeks flushed.

He checks the clock behind him. It's 10:33. "You're up!"

"You have no food." My judgmental tone is deliberate.

"I had a feeling you'd say that." He unzips his duffel and produces a greasy white paper bag. "Something from home," he says with a smile. "In case you miss it already."

"I don't," I say, snatching the paper from his hand. The smell of butter gives the contents away before I even take a peek: Croissants. The golden, flaky, puffy kind. The happiness kind. "*This* is my home now. I want to try bagels. And Cronuts. And those iced coffees served in giant cups that look like they'll make me pee all day."

Papa frowns. "But you love croissants. You always say that there's no breakfast like a French breakfast."

That is so *not* the point, but it'd be a crime to let croissants go to waste. What's a girl to do? Of course I take a bite. And to my surprise, the flakes melt on my tongue the same way they do at home. These are *good.*

"Not bad, huh? That should tide you over until Luz arrives."

I squeal, even though my mouth is still full. Luz is not just Miguel's niece. She's my sister from another mother—family and one of my closest friends combined into one. It's just a small detail that we haven't met in real life. Yet.

"I have to get ready!"

I shuffle back toward my bedroom, my bare feet almost slipping on the glossy wood floor.

About six months into their relationship, Papa traveled to Miami with Miguel. He called it a sunshine break, but we all knew what he was doing. He was going to meet the family: Miguel's parents; his sister, Amelia; and her daughter, Luz, who's a year older than me. Miguel, Papa, Amelia, Luz, Maman, and I got on FaceTime one day, a virtual meeting of the nearest and dearest. Luz and I haven't stopped talking since, between our regular video chats and our constant DMing on Instagram. We've been as close as two people can be across the Atlantic Ocean. When she told me that she'd be studying design at Parsons—she's now one year in—it gave me another reason to move to New York, as if I needed it.

"Tu es ici!" she scream-laughs the moment she walks through the door. It sounds bright and sparkling, so very Luz. "You're actually here!"

"Estoy aqui!" I say, jumping off the couch to meet her. "You're here. We're both here!"

I did six years of Spanish at school and Luz did four of French, so we'll sometimes pepper our conversations with *un poquito de español* or *un peu de français.* We each keep saying we want to learn more, but we always revert to English.

Throwing ourselves into each other's arms, we jump up and down while holding on tight, practically screaming into each other's ears. Miguel and Papa have retreated back to the other side of the room, looking slightly frightened of us.

After we pull apart, I study her. She's taller than I expected, though still a little shorter than me, and her hair looks even glossier in real life. She's also definitely more tanned than the last time we video-chatted. Next to her, I look like I have a *teint de navet,* the complexion of a turnip.

We spend the rest of the afternoon and evening catching up. Miguel has an important work dinner and Papa offers to stay back—it's my first night in New York!—but the truth is I'm really tired. Between my last weeks of school, working at our family restaurant to save money, packing up to move over here, and the flight, I've been running on fumes. And of course, I need to look and feel my very best for tomorrow, Zach Day.

Luz and I order in pizza and pore over the subway map, making sure I'm well aware of all the different lines that can take me there. She warns me that the crowd in Times Square will be thick—what were we thinking, meeting on a Saturday!—and insists I should let her come with me. But I don't need her to. This rendezvous is one year in the making.

Zach and I are meant to be. Now he's so close I can practically feel him.

Chapter Three

The next day, the four of us head out for a late brunch at Cafe Cluny, which is a few blocks north. It looks like France inside, which I suspect is why Papa chose this place. He's always been supportive of me, but he doesn't like going against Maman's wishes. Mirrors line the walls, with intricate moldings above them. The chairs are wicker, the tables tiny, the lighting cozy.

We meet three people in the space of a few minutes: the hostess, who leads us to our table; the waiter, who drops off menus before we've even sat down; and yet another man, wearing black, who inquires about our water preference. I know he's just asking if we want still or sparkling, but it sounds fancy.

Before I can decide, though, my phone rings. Papa sorted out a U.S. phone number for me, but aside from Maman, all the people who have it are here with me.

I hold my breath as I answer. "Hello?"

"Margot Lambert?" the woman on the other end says, pronouncing the *t* in my last name even though it's silent.

"This is Raven Jones. I'm the sous-chef at Nutrio. How are you doing?"

"Good. Great," I say, trying to compose myself. *It's the restaurant,* I mouth to my family, *Nutrio!*

"Well, um, *great.* I'm calling everyone on our roster because I have an urgent situation." She sighs and then adds, quieter, "Again."

"This is perfect," I say, putting on my most professional tone. "I was going to reach out to you on Monday. I would be so excited for the opportunity to work at Nutrio. I know Chef Boyd must have very high expectations, but I've been working in a kitchen my whole life. I'm ready to show off my skills. In a good way, I mean. I'm a total team player."

Luz gives me an approving nod. Miguel and Papa clasp their hands enthusiastically.

"We love to hear that!" Raven says, with an exaggerated chirp. "So, what's your availability like this afternoon?"

Um, what? I know she said "urgent," but I didn't think she meant *that* urgent. My plan for this afternoon is to get ready to meet Zach tonight. That's it.

"Hold on a sec," Raven says before I can respond.

There's clattering behind her, people shouting, moving around, a bustle of activity. My heart swells. The largest staff Maman has ever had is six, and that includes her and me. It hits me again just how much I want to work there.

Raven is back on the line. "Can you come in for an interview? Say four p.m.? And then if all goes well, you'd be staying on for tonight's shift."

No. *No no no no no.* Not tonight. This isn't possible.

"I'm really sorry, but tonight—" I start. Papa frowns, and the expression on Luz's face reads W. T. F. I pause. But what else can I say? This is too much, too soon. I need a minute. "Unfortunately—"

Luz puts her hand on my arm, telling me to stop. "Are you trying to ruin your life?" she whispers.

"Margot," Papa says kindly. "This is your dream job."

I cover my phone. "But Zach—"

"We'll figure it out," Luz says. "We'll get you to Times Square on time."

"Luz is right," Miguel says. "This is New York. When opportunity calls, you answer, and you figure out the details later."

They don't get it. "I've been here five seconds. I'm jet-lagged, and this humidity—"

"*Oui, oui,*" Luz says, cutting me off. "But time moves faster here. The city waits for no one."

I take a deep breath. Papa, Miguel, and Luz stare at me, silently telling me to do the right thing. Zach and I are meant to be together. This will all work out. I wanted an adventure, well, here it is. Excitement bubbles up inside me. I'm going to get the dream job and the dream boy all in one day.

I bring the phone back to my ear. "Four p.m. I'll be there."

"See you soon," Raven says, but it sounds like her mind is already elsewhere as she hangs up.

Luz beams. "You got this, *ma sœur.*"

I return her smile. "*Gracias, bonita.* You're the best sister I never had."

The name lettering on the front of the building is stark and modern, **"NUTRIO"** in big, bold letters. Inside, oversized glistening chandeliers dangle from exposed pipes painted white. Squinting through the window, I make out a few late brunch patrons hanging back after their plates have been cleared out, their glasses empty as they keep chatting away. I can also see a hint of activity toward the back, a few bodies moving around in the shadows. My new colleagues are getting ready for the dinner shift.

A shiver of anticipation runs through me as I head in, through the minimalist lobby, and stop at the unattended hostess's podium. I walk slowly, like I'm invading someone's home, but my intrusion must have been noticed, because a young woman in chef whites appears from the back, a smile that means business plastered on her face. She has dark brown skin and midlength, tightly braided hair held up by a colorful silk headband that matches her red lipstick.

"Margot? I'm Raven."

My guess is that Raven is in her mid-twenties, and if she's already a sous-chef, she must be pretty awesome at her job.

"Hello," I say, my voice rattling inside my throat. She holds out her hand and I shake it, even though it feels so weird. French people—especially young ones—don't really shake hands.

"Thank you for making it over on such short notice. I'm sure I don't need to tell you how it is. People come and go so much in this industry. Sometimes it feels like half my job is trying to figure out who is *not* going to turn up today."

"Well, lucky me!" I say, trying to untwist my tongue. "I couldn't wait to get started, so I'm thrilled."

I've already looked at pictures of Nutrio online, but walking through here feels different. The walls and the furniture are so spare especially within this vast expanse of raw space. A few large paintings in fluorescent colors hang from the high ceiling with nearly invisible threads, hovering away from the walls. It's so modern and cool. This place belongs ten years in the future.

"Here's my résumé," I say, handing the piece of paper to Raven. Luckily I slipped a few printed copies in my suitcase when I came over. Smart move, Past Margot.

As Raven casts her eyes over it, I launch into my speech. "My mom owns a restaurant in the Loire Valley in France, and I've worked there in one way or another ever since I could hold a knife. I basically grew up in a kitchen. And then I did this course at Le Tablier last summer, which I'm sure you've heard of." This sounds a little cocky to me, but Luz briefed me in the taxi on the way over. *Sell yourself, Margot. Give them every reason to want to snap you up. Show them how lucky they'd be to have you.*

"Yes, yes," Raven says, pausing to listen to the commotion coming from the kitchen. I'm not even sure she's paying attention to me. "That sounds good."

I smile, start again. "Le Tablier was an incredible learning experience, and—"

Raven cuts me off. "So great, Margot." Her eyes are drilled on the kitchen's double doors, behind which the clanking noises are getting louder. "Chef will be with you in a minute. Take a seat," she adds, indicating one of the nearby tables, which are already set for the dinner service.

She's gone before I can respond. As the minutes drift by, my heartbeat starts to pick up and I feel sweat trickling at my hairline, thinking about what Raven mentioned earlier. They need someone to start tonight. *Tonight,* when I'm supposed to be with Zach. But that's assuming I get the job, of course. And this place is not so far from Times Square. I have to believe that everything will be fine.

I look at the time once, twice, three billion times. There's definitely stuff going on at the back, but no one comes out of that kitchen for a loooooong while.

Starting to feel the panic, I pull out my phone and text Luz.

> Still waiting for my interview with Chef ahhhhhhh. I think I'm going to have a heart attack.

Her reply comes instantly.

> Deep breath! You're a rock star, my friend, and they're fools if they don't see that.

Taking deep breaths works, but only for the next few minutes. I can't keep waiting like this. I'll just head over there and look for Chef Boyd, that's what I'll do. It won't be weird at all. *Um, excuse me, Chef, can you interview me already so I'll know if I got this job and will still have time to go meet the love of my life? Merci beaucoup!*

Of course, now that I think of it that way, it sounds like a terrible idea. I talk myself into staying put, looking longingly toward the kitchen. And then, *finally*, a short, buff, and pale man in a tightly fitted cotton jacket comes through the kitchen's double doors. Franklin Boyd. He frowns when he sees me across the restaurant.

I shoot out of my chair and meet him halfway. "Hello, I'm Margot Lambert."

Chef cocks an eyebrow, like he can't place me.

"Nadia Lambert's daughter?" I add.

"Oh, right. Look at you, all grown up."

It feels weird to be reminded that I used to live in this city, that my mother had a completely different life, once upon a time. The kind that I want to have now, even if she doesn't like it.

"She spoke so highly of you." Though, come to think of it, she didn't really say anything. I know they worked together, but that's about it.

He raises an eyebrow. "She did?"

My smile is plastered on as I nod, sweat dripping farther down my armpits. Get the job, Margot. *Just get the job.* "I *so* appreciate the opportunity to interview here. I swear you won't regret it if you give me a chance. I read everything about you, and how you bounced back after the pandemic. It's so sad that you had to close your last restaurant, but really inspiring that you started a new one with great success so quickly. I hope I can be like you one day."

He responds with a pained smile. "Um, so Raven briefed you, right?"

My brain freezes. *Did she?* We barely exchanged a few words. "I guess . . . I'm a hard worker, a—"

"Good, good," Chef says impatiently. "We'll give you a try."

Wait, what? Oh my god! I want to do a little dance, but I stop myself because Chef is motioning for me to follow him out back.

"Thank you! Thank you so much. I swear you won't regret it."

"Welcome to the team, Margot."

There isn't much warmth to his tone, and I hesitate to ask the question burning inside of me: Will I get out in time to go meet Zach?

But for now, there's just this: I got the job. I GOT THE JOB! Luz was right. I *can* have everything I want: the great wild experience and the great wild romance.

One down, one to go.

Chapter Four

In the back of the restaurant, it's family mealtime: when the whole staff gathers to eat before the start of the dinner service. The tables closest to the kitchen have been dragged together to create an extra-long one. Two staff members are scattering cutlery sets and glasses across it.

A blink and Chef disappears behind the double metal doors while more people, including Raven, come out carrying various things—jugs of water, a basket of focaccia—and pass them down in swift, rehearsed moves. Meanwhile, I stand there, still stunned, but mostly pumped, by the day I've had so far. New city, new life, new job, and then . . . Zach. It's a lot for one day, but a lot is exactly what I've always wanted. A lot of life, a lot of fun, and a lot of love.

"So this is most of everyone," Raven says with a sweeping gesture. She's next to me at the top of the table and I wait for her to continue, to introduce me to my new colleagues, but the tired look on her face tells me that she has bigger things to worry about. I guess it's up to me to make a good first impression.

"Hello, hi!" My voice comes out high-pitched, but I soldier on. "I'm Margot. I just moved to New York, from France. My dad lives here and I was born in the city, but I haven't been back since I was two. It's so exciting to be here. *Really* exciting." Raven gives me a side-eye, but otherwise her face is devoid of expression. "I grew up cooking all the time in my mom's restaurant, and I've been dreaming of working in New York for a long time."

While I talk, the group starts to fill their plates, only glancing at me once or twice. The sensible side of me knows I should probably shut up now—seriously, how many times can I say *exciting*?— but that part left the building when I opened my mouth. I turn to Raven, hoping she, at least, will care. After all, I was supposed to be interviewed for this role, and that didn't really happen.

Now that I think about it, it's a little weird, *non?* Does Franklin Boyd trust Maman so much that he only needed to see me in the flesh before giving me the job?

"And last summer, I studied at Le Tablier, a famous culinary school in Paris. It was good but *this* is so much better."

A few people nod or force a smile. Others start eating. Someone please stop me from this ramble ramp I'm tumbling down. Luckily, one guy hears my plea and stands up. He has tan skin, shaven hair, and pitch-black eyes with a spark in them. Full lips, dimples in his cheeks, not super tall.

"Hey, Margot. Welcome. I'm Ben," he says, patting his hands back and front on his cotton pants before coming over to shake mine.

Here's the thing. I've watched tons of American TV shows. I know people here don't greet each other the same way we do. When Raven held out her hand earlier, I didn't flinch. But shaking a guy's hand feels weird. Ben must be about my age, maybe a little older, and he's . . . cute. Like, cheeks-on-fire cute. Not that I care in any way whatsoever, but it's hard not to notice when he's right in front of me.

A long time passes between the moment he offers me his hand and when I realize I really must take it. So long, in fact, that he begins to pull his back, a pained smile on his face. I feel the stares of everyone around us, my breath in a holding pattern.

Luckily, Ben comes to the rescue again. The whole interaction must have taken just a few seconds, but I'm so relieved when our hands touch. His is warm and strong. Maybe I don't mind shaking a guy's hand after all.

"I'm one of the line cooks," Ben says, his eyes not leaving mine. "On the hot station."

"Great! We'll be working together. . . ." I trail off, unsure if I should put a question mark at the end, or if there are so many cooks in this kitchen that not everyone interacts with one another.

A couple of people snicker. This is more than a staff. It's a crowd. I wonder how long it's going to take me to learn who does what. There's the front of the house, from the waiters, to the hostess, to the bus boys. And then, out the back, there are dishwashers, a prep team, cooks, sous-chefs . . . and I'm probably forgetting some.

I turn to Raven. "You haven't told me which station I'll be on yet. I'm pretty good at sauces. And salads. But I make amazing roasted vegetables, too. You have to be able to multitask when you work at a small restaurant, so, really, you can put me anywhere you like."

"Right, well—" Raven stops talking when Chef comes out of the kitchen.

"Okay, people, we have a full house tonight," he starts, addressing the table. "Ari, we still need to finalize the gazpacho special. It's too liquid, too salty. Pedro, if we get a repeat of yesterday, you'll jump in and help Ben and Martin on the hot station. I don't know why our roasted cauliflower is so popular in the middle of summer, but we have to give the people what they want."

Chef Boyd continues addressing his staff, and I deduce some of the roles based on his instructions: Diego, probably late thirties, is the *saucier;* Ari, another youngster like me, is on the cold station; and Angela, definitely older than my parents, does the salads. Two quiet guys at the back of the table seem to be in charge of prep. There's a pastry chef, whose name starts with *D.* Diane? And then I sort of lose track. Finally, Chef finishes his lap around the table, and his eyes meet mine.

"Ah—" he says, like he can't remember my name. We were literally talking ten minutes ago.

"I'm Margot Lambert? Nadia's daughter?"

Suddenly, it feels like everyone has stopped eating and is watching us. I may have been a random stranger a moment ago, but now I'm a random stranger with a personal connection to the chef.

"We all have to start somewhere," Chef says. "And, you know, everyone on the team matters. A kitchen is like an orchestra. If one player underperforms, the whole act suffers."

"Totally," I say, perking up. "You're only as good as the next cook on the line." That's something I remember from my course at Le Tablier. The instructors often said that.

Silence falls over the group. It's hard not to notice the funny looks some people exchange. Ben, the hot-station cook, shoots me a kind but sad smile.

"Didn't you brief her?" Chef says to Raven.

She glances at me wearily. It doesn't bode well for me if I get her in trouble before I've even started. "Our p.m. dishwasher quit at the end of the brunch service," she says.

I try to keep a smile on my face, even though I'm confused. Maybe it's the jet lag. Again.

"You've operated a commercial dishwasher before, right?"

I nod, speechless.

"Great," Raven says breezily. "I'm going to show you how it works anyway. Just in case."

"But I'm a trained cook," I say quietly.

I know how I must sound. Whiny, childish. Not cool. It's the truth, though. I've lived and breathed cooking my whole life.

Raven sighs. "By the end of the night, you'll be a trained dishwasher, too."

A few minutes later, I follow Raven for a tour of the kitchen, where we find the other sous-chef, a thirty-something French man named Bertrand. He barely looks up. Raven is in charge of the staff, she explains, and Bertrand has been busy working on the specials all days. He is not to be disturbed.

Every station is ready for the dinner shift: there are plastic containers with various ingredients neatly lined up on the counters, clean pots and pans resting on the nine-burner stove, and handwritten checklists dangling from the ticket racks. Other than that, it's pristine. The stainless steel glimmers and the tiled floor shines under the harsh halogen light. The place smells of bleach and chemical citrus soap. It's so big—bigger than any kitchen I've ever been in—and I feel like I'm walking through a spaceship as Raven indicates the stations—cold, hot, sauce, salad, prep, and pastry, a reasonably basic layout since there's no meat or fish to contend with.

"Here we are," she says when we arrive at the far end, in a narrower part of the kitchen by the back entrance.

There's a large sink with a spray faucet on an extended arm and, next to it, a metallic box hanging at eye level over an empty plastic crate. I stare at it, unsure what to say.

Raven grimaces, like she feels sorry for me. Still, she pushes through. There's work to do, and I'm not here to waste her time. "The bussers drop off the dirty dishes in the gray bins over there," she starts, pointing at a spot on the other end of the kitchen, toward the doors leading to the dining room. "You need to make sure the bins don't get too full, or else they'll have nowhere to put stuff after they clear the tables."

"Of course," I say, trying, and no doubt failing, to sound more upbeat.

She explains the rest at breakneck speed. Grab the bin of dirty dishes. Bring it over to my station. Rinse everything with the extended arm spray, separate plates, glasses, and cutlery into the crates with the appropriate dividers. Slide to the side. Pull down the handle of the dishwasher. Then, when it's done, move the crate off to the left to let the dishes cool down.

"You're also in charge of mopping the floors and emptying the trash cans. Basically, keeping everything clean, bringing fresh dishes to their stations, and making it easier for everyone else to do their jobs."

"Easy, got it!"

Raven taps on the metal counter twice as though to signify training is over. "Rodrigo, did you find the diced beets in the walk-in?"

And now I'm on my own at my new station.

Can I quit a job I haven't started yet?

Chapter Five

Breaking news: making everyone else's life easy is not easy at all. I quickly learn that my weak little arms can't carry the bins if they're even half full. That means I have to watch the bussers like a hawk, and make three times as many trips to their station so I can grab these huge containers when I can actually lift them. Getting there is like an obstacle course past all the cooks, who are shuffling around, left to right, back to front, as they chop, sauté, whisk, and plate. If I so much as brush past them, they grunt or yell at me to keep out of their way.

It looked so big earlier, but now the kitchen is cramped, hot, and smoky. A strange mix of odors hangs in the air, fried garlic with pistachio, red peppers with orange blossom essence. It's gross, but only if you have time to think about it.

"Hey, Bambi," Ari, one of the cold station cooks, says behind me.

He and a couple of the older staff have been calling me that ever since the start of the shift. The dumb French girl who thought she was going to come in here and be assigned on the line because her mommy knows the chef. And they're right: I actually believed that. I felt like I was on top of the world, with my dream job and my dream boy all within reach. Speaking of which, I've been dying to ask Raven when I can get off work, but it's hard to catch her in my dark corner of the kitchen. All I know is I have time; we're still in the thick of dinner.

"I need gazpacho bowls NOW!" Ari screams over the sound of Ben's glazed carrots searing on the stove.

"Coming!" I say back without thinking.

But here's the problem: I'm not entirely sure what the gazpacho bowls look like. There are so many different kinds—deep, shallow, blue . . . I haven't had a second to pay attention to the dishes as they get plated up. What's worse: only the shallow bowls are clean. Everything else is either in the machine or still dirty.

Ari comes over and stares at me, his nostrils flared. My heart stammers in my chest as I fish around the bin for two bowls that look like they just had gazpacho in them, but I see nothing with a red film, no sign of tomato anything. Which makes sense, because I studied the menu before coming here, and I'm pretty sure I didn't see it on there.

Ari inches closer. "Are you kidding me? You don't have a single clean bowl? Did you come to New York for a vacation? Is this just a bit of fun to you?"

"I'm sorry!" I say, flustered, as I keep looking through the pile of dirty dishes.

"Are you sure you've ever worked in a professional kitchen?" Ari spits.

"Pretty sure," I say, feeling more snarks bubbling up in my throat.

Ari takes a deep angry breath, but before he speaks, Ben appears next to him, wiping his hand on a towel. "Hey, Ari, cool it, okay?"

None of the other cooks pay the three of us any attention.

"She's slow *AF*," Ari says, pointing his chin at me.

"Maybe you could *show* her what you need and save everyone time? This is her first shift. Cut her some slack."

Ari rolls his eyes, but his face softens a bit. Finally, he gives in, rummages around the stack, retrieves two small bowls stained green, and throws them in the sink in front of me. They clatter loudly, making me jump.

"These are gazpacho bowls?" I ask, incredulous.

"It's *cucumber* gazpacho," Ari says. "Didn't you hear Chef call out the specials? Do you know what a cucumber is? Does your mommy serve them in her restaurant?"

He storms back to his station before I can respond. I'm fuming on the inside; a thousand comebacks shoot through my mind, but I bite my tongue. Instead, I turn the faucet on way too high and hot water sprays everywhere, all over me, in my hair, and up my nose. I think I hate it here.

The next three hours go on much the same, with an array of people whose names I don't know screaming at me or complaining about something I did wrong: the missing bread plates, the "clean" knife that still had food caked on it, the rising mountain of pots. By the time Raven comes to tell me I can take a short break, I practically run through the loading dock and into the back alley.

I'm in desperate need of fresh air, but outside the night is thick with humidity. A heavy mugginess surrounds me, along with a distinct smell of garbage and urine. It's all very disgusting, which matches how I feel perfectly.

"How's it going in there?" a voice comes from behind me.

I turn around, bracing myself for trouble, but it's just Ben, standing against the wall a few feet away. He's sipping from a metal water bottle, his phone in the other hand. I still haven't memorized everyone's names and roles, but I'm pretty sure he's the only person in the kitchen who hasn't bitched about me. Yet.

"I'm doing fantastically terrible, why do you ask?" I say, attempting a laugh.

He grimaces. "We've all been there, you know? It's a rite of passage. Tough, but necessary."

"I *have* been there. It's not like I've never washed dishes in a restaurant before, but—"

"You didn't expect you'd have to start from scratch here?"

I walk over to lean against the wall next to him, away from the garbage cans. You can barely see the dark sky in this tiny alley. It bleeds into the top of the buildings above us.

I shrug. "Well, um, yeah."

Ben takes a sip. "That's what they say about New York. It doesn't matter what you've done elsewhere. You get here and you're a nobody, no matter who you think you are."

I nod slowly. My whole body is in pain—my shoulders strained and my legs wobbly. "Lesson learned. I'm a nobody."

Ben chuckles. There's a warmth to his face, kindness on full display. "An *essential* nobody. I don't think I need to tell you that there's no serving food without clean plates."

"Hmm," I say, pouting.

Usually, I'd be the first one to agree that every step—from welcoming patrons at the door to delivering the bill at the end of their meal—is an important part of the dining experience, but shockingly, I'm not in the mood right now.

"And it's very impressive that you studied at Le Tablier. So many great chefs have gone there."

I can practically hear Maman's thoughts on that. *A summer course is barely enough time to learn how to chop onions. You need to spend a couple of years there and get proper training. To study cooking the old way. The slow way. The* boring *way. New York is not a kind place.* Translation? She doesn't think I can make it here.

Instead of saying all this, I shrug. "I only did a three-week course."

"Still," Ben says, his eyebrows raised.

I shake my head, trying to clear it. "Hey, do you have the time?"

I left my phone in my locker, per Raven's instructions, but we must be getting closer to Zach Time now. I can't believe I'm going to have to meet him like this: sweaty, with greasy hair, and smelling like dishwater.

"Sure," Ben says, checking the watch on his wrist. "It's 10:37."

"Oh," I say, breathless.

I feel dizzy, being almost there. What a day.

"Everything okay? You've turned really pale."

"It's just that I—"

I shouldn't tell this guy—a new colleague—that I absolutely must get off in time on my first day to go meet my boy . . . I mean my . . . um, Zach. But then Ben looks at me expectantly, like he really cares, and, well, I'm going to have to figure out how I can get to Times Square by midnight. Because I have to. I *have* to. I didn't come this far to miss Zach now.

"I need to meet a friend at midnight, exactly." Ben starts smiling and my throat tightens at the thought that he may have questions about that. "I *have* to be there at midnight. I can't be late."

Ben nods, still looking amused, but with a hint of confusion, too. "I don't think anyone expects the new girl to close up the kitchen on her first day. You'll be fine."

I bite my lip. Fine is not good enough.

Somehow, Ben can read my mind. "The subway is your best friend, and Google Maps is super accurate. My best tip: figure out which exit you need to get out at—east, west, north, south—and follow the signs underground before coming back up. Times Square is a bit of a maze."

I swallow hard, because I don't fully get what he's trying to tell me. Kinda sounds like I should have packed a compass in my suitcase. Luz said something similar about Times Square and I'm starting to think I don't always have the best ideas.

"Got it," I say to Ben, when it feels like it's been too long since he spoke.

He nods, then takes a last sip of his water and glances toward the entrance to the loading dock. Both our breaks are coming to an end.

"Thank you. You're so—" Ben raises an expectant eyebrow while I figure out how to finish my sentence. I settle on "Nice."

He deflates, like that's not what he likes to hear. To be honest, it's not really what I meant. There's definitely more to him than *nice*.

I want to say something else, but, out of the corner of my eye, a black shape scurries from the opposite side of the alley to ours. I jump away from it. "What the hell was that?"

"What?" Ben says, looking where I'm pointing.

The shape moves again along the wall this time, and I take another step back. Some kind of rope trails behind it. No, it's not a rope, it's a tail. The tail of—

"OH. MY. GOD. IS THAT A RAT?" I'm back at the loading dock, ready to run inside.

Ben doesn't move. "You've never seen one?" he says, looking scared of me. Of me! When there's a rat right there on the street. In the middle of the city.

"Nope." I'm almost offended. "Look! It's massive."

Ben raises his hands in the air like, *So what?* "They're everywhere, especially in restaurant back alleys, where the good stuff is. Give it a couple more weeks and they'll just feel like part of the decor."

My heart won't calm down. "They don't show that in the movies."

Ben laughs. "I wonder why."

"Bambi!" Ari calls from inside. "It's a pigsty in here. Any interest in doing your job?"

I give Ben an anxious look. "At least there're no rats in the kitchen."

"That you know of," Ben jokes.

But I don't find it funny.

New York is supposed to be magical, where even your biggest dreams can come true, and where life is larger than, well, life. Nobody said anything about the rats.

Chapter Six

By the time the clock strikes 11:35, my heartbeat goes from really fast to omg-I-can't-breathe. At 11:00, I went to find Raven and explained that I really had to leave soonish. She confirmed what Ben had implied: someone else would take care of closing, and the last few dessert orders had just gone out, so everything would be fine.

Except there was one more set of pots to wash, and then someone dropped a jug of vinaigrette all over the floor and the stickiness wouldn't go away even after I mopped again and again. I almost made it to the lockers at 11:26, but one of the bussers mentioned something about how their station needed to be stacked full for tomorrow. I couldn't tell if he meant that *I* had to do it. He just walked away and I didn't want to risk the chance of getting fired on my first day.

It's 11:42 when I drop my apron in the dirty laundry hamper, and 11:46 when, fully changed, I run out of the back alley, saying goodbye to no one.

Sweat drips down my back as I sprint to the subway at Union

Square. *Take the express train if there is one!* Luz told me earlier as she coached me. She went on to explain that express trains only run between certain hours, and that I needed to read the signs carefully. I'm already pulling out the MetroCard Papa gave me as I tumble down the stairs. I have to swipe it one, two, three times before it lets me through. T minus ten minutes until Zach Day. I can do this. It's all good. I mean it's not, but it has to be.

Once I'm down there, I'm totally unprepared. There. Are So. Many. Staircases! And they're all offering to take me even farther underground. I find the "N/Q Uptown" platform . . . *Check that it's uptown! Everyone makes that mistake once!* . . . and manage to just skip onto a train car before the bell announces that the doors are closing.

Phew. I got used to taking the métro in Paris during my course at Le Tablier, but this system is completely different, with the numbered streets and the local and express options. Anyway, I'm on now. And I really hope I got on the right one. I look down at my outfit: a white lace top tucked into a black skirt and silver ballet flats. It's the one I packed when we got home after brunch, with Luz's input of course, and I'm pretty pleased with the result. It's just missing one thing. I open my cross-body bag to retrieve a couple of gold bangles that I slip around my wrist. There, perfect for the most amazing second first date.

I search around for my lip gloss when I notice something out the window. It says "14th Street—Union Square," which is where I got on. Several minutes ago. Wait. The train isn't moving. I was so thrilled to be on *a* train—most likely the right one—that I didn't even notice.

"Excuse me, but, um, why are we not moving?" I ask the guy next to me.

He shrugs, then points up with his index finger. An announcement is coming over the speakers, but the sound is all muffled.

"I don't understand anything."

"We're stuck, is all you need to know." He seems unfazed.

"But I need to go to Times Square now!" I say to no one in particular. "Or they have to let us out!"

I get up to go look out the door, but that accomplishes approximately nothing, except that I immediately lose my seat. I shake my head, feeling the panic coming on again. I should have accepted Luz's offer to wait for me outside the restaurant. I should have let Papa call me an Uber. Like him, I was nervous about being alone late at night in the city, But I'm tired of people treating me like I'm a delicate flower in need of protection. *I* would take myself to Times Square. *I* would make sure I reunited with my great love. I would show them all that I knew what I knew.

I feel sweaty all over again, even though the air in the train car is ice-cold. My breathing gets heavy as I look around. A couple of people look a little agitated, like me, but everyone else seems extremely chill about the fact that we're trapped in a metal tin can meters and meters underground.

I pull out my phone. Five minutes until Zach Day. There's no point in texting anyone, especially since the one phone number I need is the one I don't have. Whose idea was this again? Yeah, I know.

And then the train sputters to life. We're moving. We're actually going somewhere. I think I could cry with joy, but I lost two precious minutes fixing my makeup after my shift, and I'm not willing to take a chance on exactly how waterproof my new mascara is.

Midnight in Times Square. Bleachers, bottom right. Midnight in Times Square. Bleachers, bottom right. Midnight in Times Square. Bleachers, bottom right.

Zach Day has been ingrained in my mind for a year, and it's happening now.

I'm the first out the door when we arrive at the station, climbing the steps two by two ahead of everyone else. I look up at the signs, trying to find the exit. But there isn't one. Instead there are plenty, as far as the eye can see. 40th St. 44th St. NW. SE. *That's* what Ben meant! I whip around, debating. It all looks the same underground. Gray, drab, and smelly, too. I just need to get out.

It's after midnight now. But Zach will wait. Once on the street, I'm not sure I can orient myself anywhere. The buildings are even taller than they are near the restaurant, giving the impression that the sky doesn't exist. There are people everywhere, I mean literally, on every centimeter of every sidewalk. Busy signs, food carts, people selling touristy trinkets right off the ground. I start running in one direction, but, moments later, the little arrow on my phone tells me that I'm going away from the meeting spot. This is way too confusing. I spin around, retrace my steps.

"Excuse me! Excuse me!" I call out as I try to shimmy in and around the masses. No one cares. Most people have headphones in their ears, or they're just not paying attention.

It's ten past midnight when I round the corner into what *has* to be Times Square. There are neon lights on every surface, blinking and shining. It's overpowering, almost in a scary way. Who can watch this stuff and not go loopy? There's a big illuminated American flag, tourists are taking pictures with Elmo, and five guys hand me flyers in the space of two minutes, each yelling something about a show and discounted tickets.

This place might be the *least* romantic spot I could ever imagine. It's huge and loud and dirty, and argh . . . the bleachers! Zach should have talked me out of this. We should never . . . It doesn't matter now.

I'm here. I'm here. I'm here.

Where is he?

The steps are overcrowded with people eating, taking selfies, or just scrolling through their phones. Nearby, a couple in a colorful, glittery outfit randomly performs ballroom dancing.

I scan every face, pace back and forth, up and down, ignoring the annoyed glances that come my way.

"Zach!" I call out. "Zach! Zach! It's Margot, I'm here."

But my voice can't carry over the noise. It's 12:15. There's no way he left already. I take laps of the bleachers, the whole square, drenched in sweat, parched, exhausted. My head spins every time I come across a vaguely tall, sort-of-blond guy. He's here. He has to be.

Every few minutes, I go back to the bleachers, bottom right, and look some more. A couple with two teenagers carrying bags from the M&M's store look at me painfully. I don't blame them; I'm sure they can see the despair on my face.

My phone beeps.

So?

It's Luz, of course, checking in because it's 12:30 a.m. now. She must think I'm on top of the world and I can't bring myself to tell her. Not until I know for sure. I respond with a thumbs-up and put my phone away.

Maybe it's because my legs can't carry me any longer, but I decide to stop. I'm not giving up—obviously!—but I'm going to sit right here, bleachers, bottom right, until Zach shows up. He could have been delayed. I mean, *I* was stuck on a train on the way here. Or maybe there was something with work. Do you know how often I've thought about calling that famous restaurant Le Bernardin, where he said he had a job lined up after his trip around the world? All the time. But we made a deal. We had not just a plan, but a dream. This is it.

So I sit here.

And I wait.

Zach will come. He will come. He will come.

Or he won't.

My phone beeps again, this time with a text from Maman.

Alors, ton premier service?

I texted her earlier to let her know I had my first shift at Nutrio, and promised I'd let her know how it went. But I can't bring myself to respond. Not now.

An hour past midnight, I finally let the tears roll down. Once they start, there's no stopping them. Within minutes I'm sobbing, shaking, sniffling. I've never been more humiliated in my whole life, crying in front of thousands of strangers. I'm not sure if anyone notices, but I do, and I can't stand it. I ruined everything. My dream job is a disaster and now my dream boy is lost forever. My New York adventure crashed during takeoff and I have no idea how I'm going to be able to pick up the pieces.

Chapter Seven

"So . . . ," Luz says over breakfast the next morning. "This isn't great."

"Yep," I agree, my throat in knots. "It's not great how I completely ruined my life."

Last night I ended up calling Papa, who sent an Uber to pick me up from Times Square, and waited for me until I got home. He wanted to know all about my first shift at Nutrio, but I was too upset to talk about it, or anything else. When I woke up, he and Miguel had already gone to work. There was a white paper bag on the kitchen counter with the yellow logo of Dominique Ansel, a famous French bakery in SoHo.

Papa had left a note. *Your New York adventure is only just beginning.*

It doesn't feel that way, and the famous Cronut does nothing to cheer me up, even though it's delicious, sweet and doughy with a subtle but interesting taste.

"These things are so good," Luz says, a bit of sugar stuck to her chin. "Cross-breeding a croissant and a donut was a genius idea."

She grunts with pleasure. I know I'm supposed to laugh, but I can't.

I put down the rest of my Cronut. "Have I made a terrible mistake coming here?"

"You've dreamed of this for years," Luz says. "I remember when we first FaceTimed and you told me about your plans—you wanted New York long before Zach."

This girl is always right. Sometimes I find that really annoying. "Do you know how much a dishwasher gets paid?"

When Raven told me last night, I had to get her to repeat it.

"I'm guessing not a whole lot," Luz says with a grimace.

"It's even less than that." There goes my dream of living in the West Village. I checked the available rentals during my second break last night and nearly wept at the cost.

"You're not going to be a dishwasher forever. You just have to work your way up. That's how it goes."

Luz gets up to clear her plate. I pop the last bit of Cronut into my mouth, finish my hot chocolate, and follow suit. "Maybe I should go back to France."

"You're not giving up on your dream because a guy—" I raise an eyebrow, waiting for how she's going to finish that sentence. She doesn't. "What I'm saying is, you've been here two days," Luz continues. "My sister's not a quitter. Come on, let's get ready."

We go back to our bedroom. I want to believe in Luz's positive attitude, but the thing is, I *have* only been here two days, and everything has already gone terribly wrong.

"I'm never going to know if I didn't find him, or if he just didn't show up," I say, rummaging through my suitcase.

Luz has already emptied hers and put it away, but mine is still lying open on the floor with half its contents spilling out. She'll be moving into the dorms at Parsons for her sophomore year in a few weeks, but for now we get to be roomies.

"*Never* doesn't belong in New York. Everything changes all the time. *Vale, Bella,* since you're not working today, we're going on an adventure."

I pull out a pair of denim shorts, a navy tank top, and tan sandals. Luz opts for a red dress flared at the bottom, which she wears with big hoop earrings and slip-on sneakers. She helps me tie my hair in two braids to keep it away from my neck, and we're off.

There is one thing that has worked exactly as I hoped: I finally get to hang out with Luz. I've always been quite happy as an only child—and I have plenty of friends at home—but when I met Luz via FaceTime a few years ago, something clicked. We're both the only daughters of independent mothers who work hard to give us a good life. Luz's dad remarried when she was four and he's a little too focused on his new family. But it was more than that, like the distance between us made room for everything, from our deepest secrets to our wildest dreams.

Once again, the outside feels like a steam bath, and not in a good way. It's oppressive, or maybe it's just that I ruined my chance at love. My first love. I'll never forgive myself for letting it slip away. I can't even be mad at Zach; I'm just angry with myself.

Even though I feel dead inside, I can't help but notice the bright blue sky. Apparently, it's like that throughout the year, even on the coldest winter days. Of course, it's a little hard to imagine right now, when a tank top feels like too much clothing and beads of sweat drip from my hairline.

We start walking in the direction of I don't know where, because I'm a newbie and Luz is in charge. On the way, we talk about the wedding—Papa and Miguel are having passionate debates about the song for their first dance—Luz's schoolmates, whom she's excited to see again, and my text exchanges with Julien, who wants to know if I've been to Central Park yet and is expecting detailed reports on everything. Luz also brings up Zach a couple of times—*maybe he had an accident, what if he got the date wrong*—but I'm too heartbroken to take the bait. The what-ifs won't help me now.

Soon we arrive in the Meatpacking District, with its cobblestoned streets and warehouse-like buildings. There aren't many signs that this was once where meat was being processed in the city. It's now a glamorous neighborhood with shopping galore: a Sephora, several high-end fashion brands, and an Apple store. A couple of blocks north, we stop in front of a redbrick building on Ninth Avenue. A glistening sign announces "CHELSEA MARKET" above the rail-shaped awning. Groups of people come and go through the double doors, hinting at a crowd buzzing inside. In spite of myself, I smile. It's been high on my list of places to visit ever since I first heard of it, and I've been stalking it on Instagram.

"I thought this would cheer you up," Luz says.

I don't know if that's possible, but at least it helps distract me.

"The fishmonger in there is supposed to be one of the best in the city, especially for lobster," I say, wondering where I heard that.

I ponder this some more as we pass through the large doors. Maybe Zach told me about this place, too. He named many of his favorite spots around the city, his eyes glistening at how much he loved it all, but I was too swept up in the moment to make note of everything.

The hallway is dark, the floor painted black, the walls covered in exposed rails and bricks. This industrial vibe creates an exciting mix of people and smells: roses, spices, and butter all blending together. My senses are on high alert. Everything is "more" here: bigger, brighter, shinier, louder. This is the New York I dreamed of. Well, *sans* Zach.

There's an Anthropologie store next to a cookie place, and a flower stand in front of a wine shop. A taco shack opposite a ramen counter. I want to go to all these places and try all of the things, from the gingham dress in the window to the black-and-white cookies.

We make our way through an extended area where, in quick succession, we pass by an artisanal *fromagerie*—okay, fine, a cheese shop—a Japanese-inspired Mexican food counter (which . . . what?), and even a place called Bar Suzette, *Hello, France!*, which sells sweet and savory crêpes to go. The smell of roasted hazelnuts and cocoa fills the air, bringing me back to that fateful night. Nutella crêpes were the last thing Zach and I ate together in Paris. We made a promise to each other. It meant something to me. What if he thinks I forgot him? What if he's sitting around somewhere in the massive city, devastated that I stood him up?

My heart sinks again.

"You're very quiet," Luz says, as I debate whether I'm hungry or just want to check for myself if these crêpes are the real deal. "Are you doing that thing you told me about? Cooking in your head?"

Usually, when I go to the market, I put together meals as I make my way through all the aisles. It's not just *what could I do with these chanterelles?* I actually picture every step: peeling the cloves of garlic and slipping them in the press, the smell bursting from the crushed bits; the butter sizzling in my imaginary pan, bubbles forming as the melted fat slides across the surface.

"Tell me what you've made," Luz insists. "You do realize that I've spent the last few years listening to you talk about food through a screen, and feeling extremely frustrated that I couldn't taste any of it, right?"

I hate lying to her, but I feel like I have to. "Okay, well, so far, I baked oat-and-almond granola bars, I've used an entire block of Gruyère in *gougères*—you know, the savory puff pastries?—and now I'm making a ratatouille crêpe with a decadent amount of goat cheese."

For a moment I think Luz is going to call me out, because of course what I'm really thinking about is Zach. "Well, now I regret asking," she says. "I'm starving. How do you say *goat cheese* in French again?"

"Fromage de chèvre."

Luz frowns. "I'm not even going to try to pronounce that. Never mind, let me buy you an ice cream."

There's a *gelateria* at the end of the Chelsea Market, a melon-hued counter with a pink sign indicating "L'Arte del Gelato." All the stores have these beautiful color schemes and pretty typefaces. Everything feels perfectly designed in New York.

I have a strategy for picking ice cream flavors. For the first one, I go with my favorite, the one that jumps at me from the multitude of trays overflowing with creamy, swirly concoctions. For me, on this summer day, it's peach. For flavor number two, I choose something unusual that I've never tried before or that just sounds plain weird. I've ended up with not-so-great combinations in the past, but I tell myself that being surprised is a way to train your palate. There are a few contenders for my second pick, but one in particular stops me.

"Cinnamon?" I say to Luz with a frowny face. "I can't stand the taste."

"Oh, Margot . . ." She sounds like she's about to tell me that I actually invented Zach in my head. "This is going to be a problem."

"It is?"

"Cinnamon is the national spice. We put it on everything."

"Define everything."

"You'll get used to it," Luz says as we move forward in the line to order. "Just wait until you try a pumpkin spice latte."

A what spice what now? "Latte as in the drink?"

Luz nods.

"As in coffee?"

Another nod.

"You people put pumpkin in coffee?"

More nodding. "Well, technically you're one of us, but anyway.

It's a combination of spices: cinnamon, nutmeg, ginger, cloves, and a little pumpkin purée."

"In *coffee?*" I repeat, like we're speaking a different language. In some way, we are.

"Don't knock it till you try it." Then she turns to the cashier. "I'll have strawberry and melon and she'll have cinnamon."

"And peach!" I add quickly. By the time I realize how very wrong this is going to taste, it's too late to change my mind.

Luz pays and we move to the side, waiting for our cones.

"Okay, maybe I'll try that pumpkin something latte, if it's that important," I say. "Where do I get one?"

Luz squints at me. "You can't get one for a few more weeks. It's a fall drink. We're not animals."

"You have seasonal coffees?"

I. Just. Can't.

"Margot, we have seasonal *everything*. This is who we are. And who you are now, too, *mon amie.*"

To eat our ice creams, we go up to the Highline—a former railroad redesigned as an elevated walkway that sits atop a large swath of downtown Manhattan. I've seen it in dozens of pictures before, and it's surreal to finally be here. It's narrow, manicured, and crowded, which means we have to keep up with the flow as we lick our gelatos. It's not just the sheer volume of people that boggles my mind, it's the buzz through the air, the *vibe*—like there's no place anyone here would rather be. And why would we?

I swing my arm around, indicating not just the Highline but the whole city. Okay, this is amazing.

Luz can see the delight on my face. "Girl. I told you. This place is incredible."

"You're forgetting about, like, all of yesterday?"

She shakes her head and raises her hands defensively. "Sure, you will hate it at times, but the good parts will make it all worth it. I swear."

I nod, my eyes fixed on the scenery, the glass skyscrapers, the weirdly shaped ones, the Empire State Building in the distance, and the streets below us stretching as far as the eye can see. Maman has never liked to talk about her time here, but Papa more than made up for it, regaling me with tales of the city ever since I was little. New York in real life is so much better, though. Or it would be, if only Zach and I were together right now.

We keep on walking and pass two girls about our age, also eating ice cream. One of them is wearing a completely sheer floor-length white mesh dress, over what might be a bikini or just plain royal blue lingerie. Her friend is in a poufy bubblegum pink mini number—more appropriate for the Oscars—which she's wearing with black Dr. Martens.

"That's a *choice*," I whisper as the girls approach.

Luz frowns.

"Don't you think their outfits are kinda . . . out there?" I cringe at myself because I sound like I'm judging these two girls, and that's really uncool of me. But, yeah, I'm judging them.

"If that's what they want to wear . . . ," Luz says.

"Totally." I'm trying hard to sound breezy. "But if two girls walked down the streets like this where I live, people would stare and laugh them out of town."

Luz looks *me* up and down. "Because they're not wearing perfectly ironed neutrals?" I know she's joking but I feel myself blush.

"*Chica,* this is New York. You could waltz around butt naked with a parrot resting on your head, while belting out the Star-Spangled Banner or whatever the French national anthem is—"

"'La Marseillaise,'" I cut in.

"Right, so you could sing 'La Mar*something*' at the top of your lungs and no one would even bat an eyelid."

I let out a laugh, but Luz looks nonplussed. "Like, for real?"

"For real. You're *supposed* to be weird in New York. It makes it easier to deal with all of this."

"I can be weird," I say.

"Doubtful," Luz teases.

I stop in my tracks as ice cream drips down my fingers. I take a deep breath and begin to sing as loudly as I can. *"Allons enfants de la patrie—"*

"Hey, watch out!" comes a voice from behind. I turn to see two guys almost bumping into me.

"Margot!" Luz calls through a fit of giggles. "You can't do that." She motions for me to keep walking. "You can't stop in the middle of the path without notice. That's such a tourist thing to do! You have to learn to be a New Yorker."

I catch up to her. "I can waltz around butt naked and sing 'La Marseillaise' but I can't stop walking?"

She rolls her eyes, like I'm being difficult. "That's different."

"I literally just stopped walking. That's all I did."

"Well, just . . . don't. Now, how about this ice cream?"

"Still a big nope on the cinnamon. Sorry, but I'm only about one-quarter American."

Luz pouts. "I guess this is when I admit that I don't like cinnamon ice cream either."

I flick her on the arm in mock outrage. "Excuse me?"

"Eh," she says with a shrug as she takes another bite of hers, her lips covered in melted gelato. "You have to learn how to be American. I already know."

And in that moment, I get exactly what she means. I have so much catching up to do.

Chapter Eight

"You're back," Raven says when I come in for my next shift. I can almost hear a question mark at the end, even though I'm slotted through Saturday.

"Of course I am."

There's a blank look on her face, as if she wasn't the one who set up this schedule. "Sometimes people don't come back."

I give her my most confident smile. "I'm here, aren't I?"

In fact, I'm going to pretend that my first shift didn't actually happen. I did *not* ramble in front of all my new colleagues about what a great cook I am. I did *not* act like the girl coming out of her country town who thought she was going to rule New York within a day. I'm just one member of the team. Nothing to see here.

Ben, Ari, and a couple of the younger waiters are in the locker room when I come in. They're sharing a juicy story by the looks of it, laughing as the two cooks take off their sneakers and slip on their clogs. That stops when they see me. Only Ben smiles and says a silent *Hey.* I hide behind a locker door to change into my black pants and T-shirt, and grab a clean apron from the linen closet to wear over my clothes. Unlike the cooks, I don't get a uniform. As I tie the apron around my neck and waist, I tell myself that I chose this. I *want* this. Or some of it anyway. Things change. I have to adapt. It's all part of the adventure.

I take one last look in the mirror to make sure my hair is completely off my face and then it's go-time.

A lot of life rules apply to a kitchen. Take this one for example: a place for everything and everything in its place. Organization is key. By keeping things in order, you save time. Economy is a founding principle of professional cooking. Of space. Of movement. Of ingredients. Be wasteful and everything falls apart.

As a p.m. dishwasher, my shift starts a little later than most everyone else's, which means that by the time I step inside the kitchen, activity is already rampant. Cooks reach into the lowboys and pull out plastic containers for their mise en place. Plastic covers are removed from large bowls. Knives are sharpened, the swooshing sound bringing a strangely meditative rhythm to the bustling atmosphere.

For a moment, jealousy cripples me, glues me on the spot. But the wrong job in a renowned kitchen is better than no job at all, and I have to get to the other side of the room to start doing it. I need to go through this—washing dishes, paying my dues, proving myself—to get what I want. That's what Luz said. And Ben, too. That's what I have to believe.

I decide to turn this into a game: Find dirty dishes and bring them back to my station as quickly as possible. Double points if I manage to stay out of everyone's way. Triple if they don't even notice I'm here.

Hours later, my score is pretty low.

While I saw little of Chef on my first shift, tonight he is everywhere.

"Fast doesn't mean sloppy, Ari. I need it perfect *and* now!"

"Who chopped these onions? Have you ever held a knife in your life?"

"If we get one more refire tonight, I'm throwing all of you out of my kitchen!"

Refires are when a customer sends back their plate to the kitchen because something wasn't to their satisfaction, or their order was mixed up. It has to skip the line in order to be made quickly, which delays everything else. Basically, it messes up the entire flow.

I hold my stomach in as I walk around, in the wild hope that it will render me invisible.

"Watch out, Bambi!" Ari says with a sharp tone when we almost collide. But we don't actually touch, and the contents of the plate he's holding—a roast beet salad—remain intact. Meanwhile, I'm not so lucky. I lose control of the stack of clean bowls in my hands, and the top one goes clattering on the pastry station, knocking over a jar of raspberry coulis, which, *phew,* had its lid screwed on tight.

Still, I freeze, waiting for Chef's wrath.

He stares at me coolly. "Be careful, *oui?*"

I swallow hard. *"Chef, oui, Chef."*

He walks away, but the scene is not over.

When I turn around, Ari is shaking his head. "A free pass for Mommy's girl!"

It's close to midnight when I get into the locker room. Most of the team have already changed back into their street clothes and are ready to head out. Some of the younger staffers are talking about a club, somewhere in the East Village.

"Are you coming?" Ben says as I'm kneeling in front of my locker, getting my things.

I don't respond at first, convinced he's speaking to someone else. My hair smells like fried everything, and I'm so ready to crawl into bed. Maybe even cry a little. Tonight has been a lot. Again.

"Margot?"

I turn around. He's grinning at me and I can't help but smile back. This is my chance to get to know people better. I don't want to be the new girl forever and I need to carve a spot for myself in the team, to start feeling like I belong at Nutrio. If I go out with them, the others might even learn my actual name. "Bambi" is starting to catch on.

"Ben," Ari says from across the room, motioning for him to hurry up.

"Coming!" Ben says, not taking his eyes off me. "And Margot's joining us."

"But I'm only eighteen!" I say, feeling even younger than that. In France, I'm old enough to drink and go to clubs, not that I've done much of that so far. When you live in the country, your options are kind of limited. But that's the point, I'm not in France anymore.

"And I'm not even twenty," Ben replies. "Don't worry, we have our ways. So?"

"I'm in."

After getting changed as quickly as I can, I find Luz waiting for me outside. She was having dinner with some of her school friends, and she texted me half an hour ago to say that she was still out and would swing by to pick me up.

"They're going to a club," I explain, pointing at my colleagues, who are already walking away. "And I guess we're going with them?"

Saying it out loud makes me feel a little queasy, but in a good way. I'm going to a club in New York City with a bunch of people I didn't even know a few days ago (well, you know, plus Luz). This is my life now? I mean, this is my life now!

Luz whistles approvingly. "Your first night out in the big city."

"*Our* first night out together," I say, looping my arm through the crook of her elbow.

I introduce her to Ben, and then we fall into step behind him and the rest of the group.

I still can't get over how different the city feels at night. The lights take on an orangey hue—and a breeze whisks some of the hot air of the daytime away.

"It wasn't as bad today," I admit. "I mean, it was hard as hell, but I knew what to expect."

"Progress is progress," Luz says.

As we arrive at the club, her mom calls to check in and Luz

tells me to go ahead. I do, and follow behind the rest of the group to the end of a long line outside.

"My mommy knows the chef," Ari is saying to Raven and Erica—one of the waitresses—in a puppet voice. They laugh. "Look at me, I'm a real French cook! I can make French food with my own two French hands! But now I just wash dishes the French way . . . extra slowly." He makes what I assume is a funny face, and the girls chuckle some more.

Ben and Robby—a busser—are lost in their own discussion.

"Wanna bet she doesn't last a week?" Ari says now, his voice dripping with snark.

Erica shrugs. "Most of them don't."

I inhale sharply. Luz is still on the phone, and I'm glad she didn't hear any of this.

Who do they think they are?

"Watch me!" I say loudly.

They turn around.

"I mean it. You don't know me, and you have no idea how hard I've worked in my life. I'll show you."

Ben turns around, a smile forming at the edge of his lips. I didn't realize Ben was listening, too. "Maybe you shouldn't judge people you don't know, Ari."

"Hey," Luz says, coming over. She must notice the look on my face. "All good?"

"All *great*," I say, my eyes firmly on Ari.

Just then, he gets a text and motions for us all to follow him. Around the corner we go, then down a back alley. The ground is wet and glistening in the night, even though it hasn't rained. I stare at my feet, ready to jump at the sight of rats, but I don't see any. We stand by the back door for a few minutes while Ari types furiously on his phone.

Soon after, the heavy metal door opens to reveal a young woman in a black apron. She has a rose tattooed on her neck, lots of piercings in her ears, and a wiry frame. "Ari, baby!"

She and Ari hug, and then she steps aside to let us in.

"She used to work at Nutrio," Ben tells Luz and me.

Luz frowns. "Wouldn't this place be a downgrade?"

"It depends on what you want. I like to think that, in New York, there's a kitchen for every cook," Ben says as we walk through a pitch-black corridor. "This club has a limited menu, which means a smaller team and less pressure."

My heart rate goes up a notch as I take in the scene. I feel so *adult* being here. At the far end, people are munching on small plates of calamari rings and guacamole while sipping elaborate cocktails in bright colors. A crowd gathers all the way along the bar, which wraps around the whole space. Indie pop plays on the speakers. The lighting is soft, the atmosphere plush. This might take some getting used to. Be cool, Margot, be cool.

"Let's get drinks!" Ari calls out.

Luz throws her arms in the air with excitement but I might just pass on this round. I'm not exactly in the mood to cheer with Ari and I have to keep a clear head in front of my coworkers.

"Go ahead," I say to Luz.

She goes off with Raven, Ari, and most of the group, heading for a break in the crowd at the bar. The bartender has already lined up a row of shot glasses and is filling them with a clear liquid.

"Thank you for sticking up for me," I say to Ben. It's just the two of us now, and I'm in no rush to go rub elbows with Grumpy Ari over there. "Can I buy you a drink to thank you?"

He scoffs. "On a dishwasher's salary? No way. It's on me."

Before I can protest and tell him that I'll just have a water, he's shuffling closer to our end of the bar. On the other side, Luz and Erica are throwing their heads back in laughter. Ben tries to get someone's attention. Meanwhile, I take the opportunity to scan the space around me. You'd never know it's a Tuesday night. The club is packed with people. I've heard that the East Village is a party neighborhood, especially for people our age. My breath hitches as a thought comes to me. However small, there's always the possibility that Zach is here with his friends.

"Looking for someone?" Ben says as he hands me a dripping-wet brown glass bottle.

We clink, and a little sloshes over the top of mine.

"Sort of . . . I mean, yes."

I shouldn't say more. Ben's a quasi-stranger. Worse: he's a colleague. What if he tells everyone at work that I'm silly enough to get stood up by a stranger from a year ago? Still, I feel like I can talk to him. I *want* to talk to him.

"I met a guy in Paris last summer. An American. He lives here." I take a sip for courage. "We had the most amazing night together and we promised to find each other again when I arrived. But the thing is, I don't have his phone number, or any way of reaching him."

Ben nods, drinks, and nods again. I wonder if he heard me. The music is so loud in here, I'm basically yelling.

I motion to a bench off to the side, not far from the entrance. We have to push past people to get there. After we sit down, I explain the rest of the story. The handsome stranger on the bench near the Tour Eiffel, our dreamy night of wandering the city, the promise we made, and our missed connection in Times Square. That, or he just didn't show.

"He was supposed to be my New York adventure, or at least a big part of it," I admit, sheepish.

"I don't get it," Ben says, a frown forming between his thick eyebrows. "Why didn't this guy take your number?"

"It was a romantic thing." I look away, feeling my cheeks go flush.

"It was romantic *not* to take your number? To risk never seeing you again?" His tone is incredulous.

I want to tell Ben he's got it wrong. Zach and I had our reasons. We talked them through. All year long, I kept thinking about the story we'd tell for the rest of our lives. We waited for each other. We *believed.* Meeting him again in Times Square was going to be the most wonderful thing that had ever happened to me—after that night in Paris. What we had was real. It was about seizing the moment, living it fully, and trusting the universe to guide us, after it brought us together in such a perfect way. Instead, I just take another gulp of my drink. I don't know anymore.

"I bet he was there," Ben says after we've both been silent a while. "You two sound like you're meant to be. You can't give up on him."

"You don't have to humor me. Really."

"I'm not."

I search his eyes. He seems sincere. "Yesterday I called the restaurant where he was supposed to work after his trip. They told me they didn't have any cook named Zach." I sigh. What else am I supposed to do?

Ben ponders this for a moment. "We should find him."

My heart leaps in my chest at the thought, but . . . "How?"

He turns to me and looks me in the eyes. "Margot, you moved to New York right after high school. Yes, I know, your family helped you, but that takes courage. You got a job at Nutrio, and practically told Ari to shove it. You don't strike me as the kind of girl who gives up on things."

"I'm not," I say. Ben's right, but sometimes I need the reminder. I take a deep breath. There is a way through this. I just have to find it.

"What do you remember about him?" Ben asks.

"Um," I start, pulling out my phone and opening the notes app. "He went skateboarding on Thursdays, er, in the park. I think he said 'the' park, like there's only one. And then something about getting this cookie the size of his face right after. A cookie that's like a cake. Does that even make any sense?" I jog my memory for more details I didn't write down. "I want to say it was a French-sounding bakery? A tiny little place?"

"Levain?" He's asking, but there's no doubt in his voice.

"Yes!" I say immediately, and then I stop to think about it. That sounds right. I can almost picture Zach saying that name, somewhere on a sidewalk in Paris.

"And skateboarding in the park? That'd be Central Park. My best guess is that he goes to the original Levain on the Upper West Side."

A surge of adrenaline kicks in. There must be more memories of my time with Zach buried in my brain. Soon, Ben and I are combing through each conversation, each thread from that magical night, searching for clues that could lead me to the love of my life. And Ben is like a New York wizard. He knows everything.

City's best pastrami. A diner.

"Katz's Delicatessen," Ben says.

Cat. Ping-Pong.

"The Fat Cat in the West Village," Ben adds matter-of-factly. "I love that place."

We beam at each other. Something major is taking shape right in front of us.

"See, Margot. We're going to find him."

"But New York is so big," I say. I want to believe Ben, but I'm scared. What if I get my hopes up again? Can I handle getting crushed another time?

"It is and it isn't. You have a great list there, and you told me you guys took selfies together. It's worth a shot." He sticks out his free hand. "Give me your phone."

Our fingers brush as I hand it to him, making my skin tingle. I've been in New York for just a few days, and I'm in a bar having drinks with a guy who's not Zach. I know it's not like that, but the rest of our group is still on the other side of the room, so it feels like we're alone.

Ben presses a few keys. "There," he says, sounding very sure of himself as he gives it back. "Now you have my number. That doesn't mean we have to get married and live happily ever after. It's just a phone number so we can meet up on our next day off."

Even though he's making fun of me, I laugh. "Noted."

Ben smiles, a kind, heartwarming smile that lets me know we're in this together now. Operation Find Zach is on, and I think I may have made my first New York friend.

Not a bad night after all.

Chapter Nine

The blisters on my fingers are starting to harden into calluses, I notice as I put on a pink floral dress with spaghetti straps, then my pair of cream espadrilles. The closer I get to being ready, the faster my heart beats in my chest. I'm going to find Zach. He's somewhere in this big, bold city, waiting for me.

I slip my bag over my shoulder, check my phone battery, make sure I have my wallet and that, yes, it's filled with a few American dollars, and head out the door. Luz is out with a friend, Papa and Miguel are at work. This is my first day of exploring the city alone. Well, not alone, actually.

Ben lives in Williamsburg, Brooklyn, with three roommates, but he had plans in Manhattan this morning, so we agreed to meet at West 4th.

SE side, Ben specified by text earlier.

I replied with a thumbs-up, fighting off flashbacks of my first time in the subway, lost underground near Times Square and desperate to find the best exit when I still hoped Zach was waiting for me on the other side. Something I'm quickly learning about New York: this city works entirely in codes. Most of the streets have no names, only numbers, organized like a grid. Take SoHo, for instance, the neighborhood just below the West Village. It sounded like a real name, until I found out that it just means South of Houston. Houston, the street! Why does everything have to be north or south or west or east of something?

The main entrance to the West 4th Street subway station is by a large newsstand selling more snacks and drinks than actual newspapers. As I approach, I notice the real attraction of this street corner: a fenced basketball court, covered by trees and jammed against a brownstone building. A group of Black guys is playing, all very tall and toned. Most of them are wearing nylon shorts that go past their knees, shiny tank tops, and sneakers so wide and intricate that they look like mini rockets. There are more guys still on the edges of the court, cheering them on and howling.

I'm totally absorbed in the game, when I feel a presence next to me. Ben, who immediately comes in for a hug. He smells like sunscreen and amber, warm and soothing.

"Who's winning?" he says with a cute grin. A grin, I mean. A regular kind of grin.

Ben is on the shorter side, especially compared to these guys, but he stands out in other ways. That smile, so bright and genuine that it makes you feel like you're his dearest friend. The sparkle in his eyes, like he's looking at something precious.

"I'm not sure," I say. "But these guys are good. I've only been standing here a few minutes, and I've already seen one perfect shot."

The crowd erupts in cheers and we look over to see another epic dunk.

"Now, about this cookie," I say, turning to Ben. "You seemed so certain the other night, but are you sure it's Levain?"

Ben lets out a laugh. "Margot, the clues only pointed in one direction. Are you really asking me how well I know the most famous cookie in the whole of New York?"

"So that's a yes?"

He chuckles. "That's a *oui*."

Soon we're claiming two bright orange seats on the subway train, which, in sharp contrast to last time, actually gets moving right away. Seriously. It's like the universe conspired to keep me away from Zach that night. The air is ice-cold in the train car, mixed with an unidentifiable stench. New York might be dazzling and awesome but let's get real: sometimes it stinks, literally.

Settled in for the ride, I turn to Ben. "By now you know all my career plans and my weirdly dramatic love life, and you're still a mystery to me."

It comes out more serious than I intended, but Ben, as always, responds with a smile. "What do you want to know?"

I shrug. "Let's start with, um, everything."

He taps his hand to his chest. "Benjamin Saint George, ma'am. Born in Queens, New York. Lived there my whole life, just a few blocks away from my grandparents on my mom's side, until I moved to Williamsburg this summer. I've never really been anywhere else. I'm the boring one in the family."

"I'm going to need way more details, sir."

"They've traveled so much. My mom's parents are Haitian and they lived all over: Canada, France, and then here, obviously. Mom stayed in France for school. So I grew up speaking *français,* reading *Le Petit Prince,* listening to French music, eating *bûche de Noël* at Christmas and *galette des rois* for Epiphany. I'm like the most French person who never left New York. Is that weird?"

"Are you kidding? I'm the American girl who thinks your cars are way too big, that American football is just repackaged rugby, and seriously, what's with the flags everywhere?"

"Patriotism?"

"You can love your country on the inside."

Ben laughs. "Not this one. You gotta be loud or you don't really exist."

"Okay, well, that just proves my point. I'm the least American American, so I don't think it's weird that you're the most French non-French person."

"Fair," he replies with a smile.

"I've always been jealous of my parents' adventures, too."

"How long were they together?"

"Oh, they were never a couple. But they've always been inseparable." I explain the rest of the story: gay dad, straight mom, a cozy childhood in the French countryside.

Ben nods, impressed. "They sound like a lot of fun."

"See, you and I are the same. We just want to live more exciting lives." I feel my face flush before I even finish my sentence. I barely know Ben, so why does it feel like we're friends already?

When we get off the train at 72nd Street a few minutes later, there's a change in the air. The streets are wider, the buildings taller. There's a quieter energy, couples with kids on scooters, old people strolling about. It almost feels like a different city.

Ben warned me there would be a line at this ultra-famous cookie place, but I'm still surprised to see so many people waiting in front of such a tiny shop.

"That's it?" I ask, pointing to the narrow storefront painted blue. "*This* is a New York institution?"

Ben shrugs. "Small shop, big cookies."

When it's our turn to get in, I'm again surprised by how bare-bones the place is—just a counter with ovens at the back, where two bakers are working. The menu, too, is pretty minimalistic, with a small assortment of pastries and just four cookies available: chocolate chip walnut, dark-chocolate chocolate chip, oatmeal raisin, and dark chocolate peanut butter chip. In my not-so-humble opinion, it's a crime to put raisins in a cookie. Are we supposed to count it as eating fruit? *Come. On.* Ben and I agree to split the first two. My treat, obviously, since we're here for me. Well, for Zach.

After I finish paying, I try to ignore the growing line behind us and whip out my phone. I pull up a photo of Zach and me. It's the one he suggested we take just an hour after we met. He seemed excited that his trip was off to such a great start and insisted we needed a memory already. We kissed for the first time right after that.

I show it to the girl behind the counter. "This is kind of a weird question, but do you maybe know this guy? His name's Zach. He's tall and he's a big fan of your cookies. I think he comes here often. On Thursdays, usually."

The girl glances at the screen. I half expect her to tell me off, but she just shrugs. "I dunno. We get a lot of people here."

"Right," I say, like that's helping at all. I shift my weight from one foot to the other and flash an embarrassed smile. "Could you maybe show this picture to your colleagues?" I point at a guy who's pulling a tray of cookies from the oven. Another one farther back is making dough.

The cashier hesitates for a moment, but she grabs my phone at last. It doesn't make any difference, though, because the bakers just shake their heads as she shows them the picture. Before I can think of anything else to do, the people behind us grumble, trying to nudge us out of the way. It's over. For now.

But we still have the cookies, so we sit on the bright blue bench in front of the shop, in full view of the line. I keep a laser-focused eye on it, even as the little voice in my head reminds me that a watched pot never boils, which is silly because if you turn on the stove and put a pot of water on top, it *will* boil after a few minutes, even if an entire restaurant staff stares at it.

I'm still looking in the distance when I bring the cookie to my mouth, and it takes me a second to realize that this isn't a cookie. It's fluffy, chewy, and crumbly. Like a cake, a brownie, and a cookie all mixed into one. So simple, and yet so unlike anything I've eaten before. It's love at first bite.

Ben studies me, amused. Crumbs stick to his chin and I wipe my own, feeling self-conscious all of a sudden.

"So?" he says. *"C'est délicieux, non?"*

I nod as I swallow the rest of the bite. "The long line makes sense now."

"Yeah, New Yorkers don't waste time unless they have a very good reason. Do you believe me now? A cookie like a cake, the size of your face, from a bakery that sounds French?"

I nod, but my smile is fake because, just like that, my brain is back on Zach. He's been here. He might even be on his way now. I can almost picture him, waiting for his turn to buy his weekly cookie, knowing it's worth the wait. My eyes flicker back to the line and I'm crushed all over again when I don't see him there.

"We were probably not going to find him on our first try," Ben says, reading my mind.

"Yeah." The word catches in my throat. I wasn't supposed to have to find Zach. We were going to wait for each other. August 1. Midnight in Times Square. Bleachers, bottom right. "I'm sorry for wasting your time."

Ben shrugs. "Eh, I got a free cookie out of it." And then, looking me in the eyes, he adds, "There are worse ways to spend a day off."

He's right. "So where to now?"

Ben ponders this for a moment. "Since we're up here, we could go to Central Park. It's a nice day; I'm sure a lot of guys have their skateboards out. You never know."

My whole body buzzes at the thought, not only because Ben remembered Zach might be skateboarding in the park on Thursdays, but because I've always wanted to go there.

Central Park looks gigantic on the map, so I'm not surprised when, a few minutes in, it almost feels like we've left the city. Sure, I can see skyscrapers in the distance, but the sense of peace is almost immediate. We're surrounded by trees and patches of grass, with squirrels scurrying around on the ground and jumping from bench to bench. Of course, because it's New York, there are people—and dogs—everywhere. Cyclists, joggers, skateboarders, and pedestrians wandering around, enjoying the bright sun and fresh air.

We walk and talk for what feels like hours. I tell Ben all about Maman's restaurant—especially her famous *gratin dauphinois*—and answer all of his questions about growing up in France. He's shocked to hear that kids really do get served four-course meals for lunch at school, but that we don't have anything resembling a prom or any other dances. I learn that he started working at Nutrio just nine months ago, which is like five years in the restaurant world, especially in New York, where things move so fast.

"I started as a dishwasher, too," Ben tells me as we arrive at the mall, a boulevard going down the middle of the park. "It's kind of Chef's thing. If you're really young and he doesn't know you personally, he has to put you to the test, to see what you're made of. Are you willing to do the dirty work or are you going to be a diva?"

Well, that explains a lot. I failed, and spectacularly, too.

I point at myself. "Um . . . total French diva over here!"

Ben laughs. "Don't worry, you're not the first, and you won't be the last."

I wrinkle my nose. It's a tough truth to swallow; I really did make a total fool of myself that night. But I love that he's being honest. Yes, I screwed up, but I'm going to make it up ten times over.

We're wandering down the mall, keeping an eye out for any and all skateboarders, when my phone beeps. It's Luz.

Just making sure you're not lost!

I'm not! I respond. At Central Park with Ben. Love it here.

Um, okay? Need more info when you're back.

I reply with a thumbs-up and put my phone away. What's the big deal? Is it that surprising that I'm out having fun with a friend? To our right, a man in a top hat blows up balloons. To our left, an elderly couple quietly reads on a bench. We go down some stairs and arrive under an archway, where a classical music group entertains a small crowd. The violin echoes across the dark and damp space, making my spine tingle. Past that, children run around a huge fountain. It hits me for the millionth time: I'm in New York freaking City.

"Is this place for real?" I say, trying to look everywhere, to take it all in. But there's so much, *too* much, and it's all so . . . thrilling. I know I just moved here, but also . . . how does anyone *not* live here?

Ben follows my gaze and smiles. "Yeah, it's really special. I mean, it's not Paris but it's cool."

"Paris is *magnifique,* it's true. And you know they have restaurants there, too, right?"

"So I've heard," he says with a laugh.

"I'm just saying . . . You could be a cook there if you wanted to. Or you could study at Le Tablier," I add that last part as I remember our conversation during my first shift.

"That'd be totally awesome." Ben is smiling, until a cloud passes over his face. "But that doesn't fit with my ten-year plan."

I let out a laugh. It's only when I look at him again that I realize he's being serious.

"Ten-year plan? Sounds extreme."

Ben glances over at another man making balloon animals for a group of kids. The giraffe is particularly cool. I almost want it for myself, but I'm not prepared to fight the little girl in the princess gown for it.

"Yup." I raise an inquisitive eyebrow, and Ben continues. "Three to four years on the line at Nutrio to beef up my résumé. Even if his restaurants haven't been runaway hits, Franklin Boyd has a lot of cachet. I might even make it to sous-chef, though I know that's a long shot. Then I'll move on to a franchise, something buzzy that basically prints money. That's how you meet the movers and shakers of the industry, especially investors. But the end goal, obviously, is opening my own place: moody and pared-back in Brooklyn, maybe. If all goes right, that's what I'll be doing in ten years."

I feel my stomach tighten. "I don't even know if I'll make it another week. Nutrio is pretty intense."

"It's tougher when you're starting out. The older crew are so cocky. They look at us and wonder how we're even allowed in a place like that. They don't care that we're working just as hard as them." He sighs but barely pauses. It's like he's on a roll now. "Chef has this thing, you'll see, that the more seasoned staff gets priority with the shifts. I want to work six days a week, but I'm lucky if I get five, which means the pay isn't that great."

I gulp. I guess I'm going to be crashing at Papa and Miguel's apartment for a while. They both said I could stay as long as I want to, but they're just about to get married and I want my own space, my own New York adventure. Though clearly I'm really lucky to not pay rent. If I had to support myself on a dishwasher's salary . . .

"I don't know if I could handle that kitchen six days a week."

"It gets easier, I promise."

I can't help but wince. I feel the bone-deep exhaustion just thinking about work.

"Emotions run so high in a big kitchen," Ben adds. "Most of the staff feed on the adrenaline; they're high on the pressure. People don't mean half the things they say during a shift. Personally, I tune it all out."

"You'll have to teach me how."

He shrugs then looks ahead. "Okay, let's start by changing the topic. How about another classic New York experience to finish the day?"

"Sure!" I say, intrigued.

He leads me toward a food cart with colorful pictures taped to the outside.

"Four hot dogs!" he orders.

I'd like to think I heard him wrong. "What? No! I don't know if you noticed, but that cookie was basically a full meal. I mean, don't get me wrong, it was delicious, but, wow, it was so big. Besides, there're only two of us."

"Sorry, Margot," Ben says, nodding to the man inside the cart to proceed with the order. "Hot-dog-eating contest. It's a New York thing. You gotta do it."

"Wait—"

Too late. He pays for the hot dogs and hands me two of them. "Come on, Margot."

"So, um, how does this work?"

"It's a speed contest."

I frown. "In France, we don't believe in playing with our food."

"You're not in France anymore," he says with a wink. "Whoever finishes theirs first wins."

"Wins what?"

Ben pouts. He hadn't thought of that. "Right, um, the winner gets to pick the next place on the list for Operation Find Zach, where we'll go next time."

This sounds all right, then. Operation Find Zach has only just started. He's still out there, waiting for me. "Deal."

I lose the contest. Obviously. But as I watch Ben do a victory dance, laughing with my mouth full of hot dog, I almost forget why we came here in the first place.

Chapter Ten

My New York life begins to take on a familiar pace. One in which I'm working at Raven's whim, whenever she says she needs me, which varies based on the other dishwashers' schedules. And as my third week at Nutrio comes to an end, it becomes clearer and clearer that there isn't much time to think about anything else. Wash dishes, sleep, eat, repeat.

I've also been coming in early so I can eat the family meal with the rest of the staff. The a.m. dishwasher has been working all afternoon, cleaning up after all the prep work, so my shift only starts when the dinner service does, but I want to get to know my colleagues better. I need them to know *me*, to see me as one of them, if I have any hope of being put on the line. On every phone call, Maman keeps reminding me that it's okay if I change my mind and decide to come home. It makes me bristle. She doesn't think I have what it takes—that I'm too flighty, too immature, too *delicate*—to make it in this city. I wish she could see my chapped red hands and feel how sore my legs are. The truth is, I jumped headfirst into the tornado, and, all things considered, it's working out okay. So why can't she understand that I *am* capable? That I'm making it happen. It doesn't matter; I'll show her.

Ben and Ari were in charge of cooking for us today, and we're in for a treat. There are flatbreads with zucchini and ricotta; a fried rice dish brimming with bok choy, shiitake mushrooms, and toasted sesame oil; and a modern version of a Caesar salad, with kale, Parmesan, and croutons soaked in a creamy vinaigrette that sizzles on the tongue. It's not as expertly presented as the dishes on the menu, but still the colors and textures leap off the table—like we're eating at a high-end restaurant. Which, well, we are.

This is our time to catch up and relax before the dinner rush begins, and everyone is in a chatty mood as we help ourselves. Raven went to an outdoor party in Bushwick last night and came home at six a.m. She shows us videos on her phone. It looks wild, with palm trees—in New York?—and people dressed in elaborate costumes. Ben is in the midst of an animated conversation with Ari and some of the older cooks, but I can't hear what they're talking about. Our trip to Levain was only about a week ago, but it feels longer than that. We haven't talked much since. Here we're in work mode, friendly, but all business at the same time.

We're halfway through our meal when we hear crashing in the kitchen, like someone's having a fistfight in there. The sound is a lot, but when I scan the table everyone seems to be here.

"It's Chef," Raven says, putting another forkful of salad in her mouth. "He's experimenting for the fall menu."

Curiosity courses through me. "Ooh! What's he planning?" A few ideas pop up in my head. A mushroom ragù—with red wine and paired with a thick pasta that can soak it up, like rigatoni. Or maybe a chestnut soup.

Raven raises an eyebrow at me, her telltale sign that I'm being clueless, or annoying. Probably a bit of both. "Chef doesn't share his process with us. With Bertrand, maybe, but otherwise he just does his own thing, and we'll find out when he wants us to."

Even though Raven is a sous-chef like Bertrand, the hierarchy is clear there, too. Raven gets the scraps—managing an ever-changing staff, making sure the lines of communication are always open with the front of the house—and Bertrand basks in the glory of being Chef's confidant. You can read on her face how Raven feels about that.

"Right, of course," I say, staring at my empty plate. But my wheels are spinning. I haven't had an opportunity to speak to Chef since that first day, and he's alone in the kitchen. I glance around the table again. Everyone is still chatting, but the meal is wrapping up. It's now or never.

I wait until Raven starts talking to Erica and get up. The locker room is my first stop, where I get changed and tie up my apron before heading to the kitchen. Chef doesn't see me at first. He's hunched over a steaming pot, smells of carrot, cumin, and coconut milk rising from the surface, savory and sweet. Behind him, a chopping board is covered in orange skin and onion peel. His nostrils flare as he stirs a wooden spoon, evaluating the combination of fragrances. It reminds me of Maman, even though she's not one to experiment in the kitchen. Old recipes are the only ones she cares about.

Whereas I love this process of discovery, the thoughtful assembly of ingredients, adding and removing until the perfect balance is achieved. It hits me hard, how much I want to do this, how I've been missing out since I first started working here.

I clear my throat. Chef doesn't move. *"Bonjour . . .* uh, I mean, *bonsoir."*

Before I left, Maman coached me that I should play up the French part of me a little more, that it might help me stand out to Chef. When they worked together, he used his limited French any chance he got, always slipping the fact that he studied in Paris into the conversation. You don't really know cooking unless you know *cuisine.* And hey, at this point, I'll do anything.

"Oui?" Chef says without moving, like he knew I was there but had no interest in acknowledging me until I forced him to.

"I heard you were working on the new menu—" I stop. I don't know what else to say, other than, *and I was wondering if you could give me a job as a cook already. It's been three weeks, buddy. I'm waiting.*

He pulls out a clean spoon and, without looking up, motions for me to get closer. "Try this." He dips the spoon in the pot, fills it up halfway, and hands it to me. "Don't be shy. Being able to judge a dish is a hugely important skill when you work in a kitchen."

"I know." I hope I sound a little offended. Then I gently blow on the spoonful of soup. Steam rises from it, warming my face.

He lets out a dry chuckle. "Right, your mom's a chef."

"And I grew up in her restaurant," I add, feeling silly about how boastful I'm being, but not silly enough not to do it.

Finally, I slurp the hot liquid. The flavors burst in my mouth, soothing. It's autumn on my tongue. It tastes like evenings by the fireplace, like the crunch of red leaves blanketing the ground in the forest.

"What's missing?" he says, matter-of-factly, looking at me now.

I don't hesitate. "Butter. Lots and lots of it."

"There's fat in the coconut cream." His tone is flat, giving no indication of what he thinks.

"Sure," I say, immediately feeling self-conscious about my answer. I'm talking like Maman. Adding fat is the answer to pretty much everything in France, but we're not in the kitchen of a simple little French restaurant here. Nutrio is modern and imaginative. Cutting-edge, even. Chef must have a different way of doing things.

Chef's face remains stern for a long moment, but then his eyes light up just a little. "*Ah, le beurre, bien sûr.* It's the French way."

"I was just, um—" but I don't know how to take it back. "Let me think about it. I can come up with a better idea."

As I'm talking, he rummages through the lowboy behind him and pulls out a long log of butter wrapped in wax paper. He opens it, cuts a thick slice, and drops it in the pot.

"As you would know, French cuisine has a long history," he says. "There are so many traditions and unspoken rules, but I tend to think that's why the French way is often the best way. Your mom taught you well."

Wait.

I *was* right? This is a huge win. Now I *have* to ask.

Stirring again, Chef turns to me. "How's she doing by the way?"

"She's great. I'm sure she'd like to catch up with you when she's here for my dad's wedding."

He cocks his head, as though that's a surprise. "Oh, I hope she comes to eat here. I'll give her the best table in the house."

"Of course she'll come!" *Vas-y*, Margot. Now. "There's something I wanted to—"

Just then, the swinging doors fling open and in come a few of the cooks. Ari raises a suspicious eyebrow at the sight of me, like he knows exactly what I'm up to. And now Chef barks at Bertrand to meet him in his office.

Though I'm bummed about the interruption, two incredible things happen during the dinner service. The first is that I don't make it through my shift. I mean that I don't *just* make it through: running after dirty dishes, haphazardly stacking up clean ones, my fingers burning on the still-hot porcelain. I manage to deal with all of that while being able to take in my surroundings. The arranging of romaine lettuce leaves in a perfect circle. The swish of the aioli being whisked up. The sizzle of eggplants on the grill. I see it all. I'm part of this. I *belong*.

The other amazing thing that happens is that Ari doesn't say a word to me. I'm sure he's trying to find things to complain about, but I don't give him any. Not only does he get everything he asks for, I even anticipate his needs once or twice. Those damn gazpacho bowls hold no surprise for me anymore.

"You look happy," Ben says when I sneak outside for a short break, just as he's coming back from his.

I pause for a moment, pondering. "I think I am?" He raises an eyebrow and I realize how that must sound. "No, I am. *Yes,* I am, I mean. Ari didn't call me Bambi once, so that's something to celebrate, right?"

Ben pulls on the strings of his apron, tightening it. "I don't mean to burst your bubble, but that might not have anything to do with you. Ari met a girl. At least I'm pretty sure he did. He was texting with her in the locker room earlier. He got all funny when one of the guys teased him about it."

My heart pinches. If the universe can give grumpy, snarky Ari someone to love, then why can't I find Zach? Zach, whose ears, not his cheeks, turn red when he blushes. Zach, whose entire family gets together at his uncle's house down on the Jersey Shore at Thanksgiving. Zach, who's out there in the kitchen of some restaurant in New York City, this very second. I wonder if he still thinks about me, if he still remembers all those details we whispered between kisses a year ago.

"Well, good for him," I say, not meaning a word of it. "If that keeps him off my back."

Silver lining, Margot. Just take it. Wrap yourself in it.

And I do. Because for the first time since I got here, my night is almost entirely devoid of drama. I won't pretend that I didn't come *this* close to dropping a stack of frying pans on Bertrand's feet as he was passing dishes to Chef, but I did my job, and I did it well.

By the end of the night, I even have enough brain space to remember how my shift started, my conversation with Chef. Just because that moment passed doesn't mean there can't be another one. Like, now.

You miss one hundred percent of the shots you don't take, Luz told me yesterday when I moaned about my dishwashing duties for the twentieth time. I'm not throwing away my shot.

I find Chef in the office to the side of the locker room. It's a cramped space, with a desk covered in papers, a small fridge, and boxes of samples lined up on a shelf. In a way, it's a better place to talk to him, less intimidating somehow. He's still wearing his chef whites, but they're creased and stained now, and he doesn't seem as serious as when he's in the kitchen.

The door is wide open, and he looks up when I knock. He doesn't actually invite me in, just nods. My stomach is in a knot. I still have time to reverse course and run out of here. But then I won't get what I deserve.

There's a chair opposite the desk, but Chef hasn't motioned for me to take it, so I stand by the door. Makes for a quicker exit if I need it.

"I—uhhh—I wanted to ask you something." I'm a big girl, an adult. I just moved to a new country. I can do this. "As you know—" I stop. This isn't the right way to go about it. I take a deep breath. Try again. "I'm a good cook. More than a good cook, actually." I pause, but he doesn't respond. "Your restaurant is . . . I love what you're doing. Your menu is inventive and so fresh. I want to work here, learn here, grow here. As a cook. On the line.

I was happy to help when you needed a dishwasher, and I'm definitely a team player but—"

"You don't want to be one anymore?"

Crap. Now I've annoyed him, haven't I?

He lets out a deep sigh. "I know your mom. I understand the kind of training you got. But I believe in paying your dues, in learning to climb your way up, slowly but surely. To me, these are more valuable skills than talent."

This stings, but I'm not out of arguments yet. "Raven is your sous-chef, and she's only twenty-four. Ben and Ari are on the line and—"

"My castle, my rules. I decide who does what. Nobody else."

More thoughts swirl in my mind. He needs to get to know me, but that's not going to happen while I'm stuck in a corner washing dishes. I came to New York for the adventure of a lifetime. Scraping hardened cheese next to a stinky alleyway is not it.

"But I'm a good cook. If you just let me show you . . ."

Chef looks at me flatly, like he's had this conversation a thousand times. "What I need is a good dishwasher. Someone I can trust to get the job done. I don't have a position on the line. So your options are simple: be a dishwasher in *this* restaurant, or try your luck elsewhere. But I'll warn you: every person I've hired was recommended by someone. You're nobody until you know somebody. So this is what you get for now. Is that enough?"

I nod firmly. *Fiercely.* "Of course it is. *À demain, Chef.*"

As I walk away, his words—"You're nobody until you know somebody"—hit me a little too hard. I only got this job because I knew someone. And now I can't help but wonder if I would ever have made it on my own. It took Ben three months to get off dishwashing duty. I don't know how I'm going to last that long.

For now I just have to cling to the hope that Zach is still out there, waiting and searching for me. Otherwise, I'm just a dishwasher. Otherwise, I'm nobody.

Chapter Eleven

It will surprise no one that of all the wedding-related things to be done, I'm most excited about cake. Cake *tasting,* to be precise. Luz is designing the place cards and the menu, and we're both going to help pick the flowers since Papa and Miguel have wildly different ideas—one has been talking about a tropical forest of bold blooms, while the other would be happy with a handful of white roses.

But the wedding cake is all mine. It's Saturday morning and I have a very special brunch planned. Cake, cake, and more cake! *C'est parfait, non?* The four of us are ready for a mission, organized by yours truly. I researched bakeries for weeks, contacted the ones that looked like serious contenders, and whittled the list down to just four.

Our day of cake extravaganza starts on the Upper East Side, at a place called Two Little Red Hens. It's a traditional American bakery, famous for its simple yet decadently rich cupcakes and cakes. They offer flavors I've never tried, like Brooklyn Blackout, which boasts four layers of chocolate cake, three layers of chocolate pudding filling, and fudge frosting. It's basically just chocolate in every way, shape, and form.

Two Little Red Hens is not just a small bakery, it's a hole in the wall. There's a red awning above the shop, an old-fashioned wooden door, and a few decorative hens in the window, like it's permanently Easter in there. Inside, we plan to get an assortment of cupcakes for tasting. Luz insists on the key lime, and I'm tempted by the peanut butter fudge swirl. Luz and Miguel claim one of the tables by the window, and while Papa and I wait to order, we gaze at all the cakes on display. The designs are quaint and colorful, with intricate flowers of varying sizes. Simple with a touch of whimsy, exactly like I pictured a traditional American bakery would make.

I give our order, imagining what it would be like to own a place like this, creating new designs and coming up with new flavors. It sounds a lot more fun than dishwashing.

Papa frowns at me. "You seem down."

"But definitely looking forward to having cake for breakfast, lunch, and dinner."

"You've been working such long hours."

I avert my gaze, not wanting to get into it, and then our plates of cupcakes appear. Moments later, the four of us are tucking into them. Papa and I go for the Brooklyn Blackout first.

A sigh escapes my lips. This is *good*.

"It's so rich," Papa says, licking a swirl of ganache off his fork.

"Hmm," Miguel adds, rolling his eyes with pleasure, clearly enjoying his taste of the peanut butter fudge. "Decadently perfect."

The door jingles as a woman enters, letting a wisp of fresh air into the bakery.

Miguel's smile drops. "Ugh. First chill day of the year. That came really fast."

It's only just September, but he's right, the temperatures dropped enough this morning that I went back in to grab my denim jacket.

Papa shakes his head. "We have plenty of warm weather left," then more to me, he adds, "It's typical New York. One day it's hot and unbearably steamy, and the next it's 'hello, fall!' But by the end of September it often feels like summer has started again. You'll see."

"True," Luz says, pushing away the plate with the half-eaten red velvet cupcake. She moved into her dorm two days ago, when I was working, and this is the first time we've hung out since. "And fall is really magical, Margot. You won't believe the colors on the trees. It's like they're photoshopped in orange and red."

The spark in her eyes makes me want to be there already, but I'm distracted by the funny look Miguel and Papa exchange.

Papa chuckles. "It's that time of year when Miguel starts talking incessantly about moving back to Miami."

"Where it's warm and sunny all year long!" Miguel says dreamily.

"Is that what you want?" I ask. My dad is such a New Yorker that I can't quite picture him among the palm trees.

"Our careers are here," Papa says, ending the conversation a little sharply.

Miguel shrugs and Luz subtly shakes her head at me. *Just don't,* she seems to say. Instead, I take a bite of the key lime cupcake, the acidic taste hitting me strangely. Papa stares down at his plate. It feels like I struck a nerve.

Then Papa turns to me. "I vote for the chocolate one. Great pick, Margot."

I agree with him. It's so creamy and sumptuous, an ideal combination of the sponginess of the cake and the smoothness of the ganache icing. But the vibe of our group has gone a little sour.

By the time we make it back downtown, any awkwardness seems to have dissipated. Our next stop is at Empire Cake in Chelsea, known for its creative and colorful fondant cakes on display in their windows overlooking Eighth Avenue. It ticks all of our boxes, but we can't agree on the best flavor, only that it's a toss-up between raspberry lemon and hazelnut.

After that, we go to France. Or at least, the Frenchiest place in the Lower East Side, as far as I can tell: a *pâtisserie* called Ceci-Cela. This is one of just a handful of bakeries in New York where you can get a *pièce montée*—the traditional French wedding cake. Here people know it as a croquembouche, meaning "crunches in the mouth." It's a tower of *choux,* aka small puff pastries, each filled with vanilla custard and covered in a layer of caramel glaze. Personally, I find it too old-school—not to mention that it looks a bit like the poop emoji—but, hey, it's not my wedding.

I'm surprised to feel all warm and fuzzy as we arrive in front of the *pâtisserie.* The word is written in all-caps gold lettering on a shiny black placard above the awning, just like you find throughout

France. It's strange to see something so familiar in an unfamiliar place. Inside, the soothing scent of *viennoiseries,* the nuttiness of butter, fills me, comforts me. I didn't know I needed that.

We order coffees and iced teas while we wait for our sampling of *pièce montée.*

"Margot, do you know if you could take a weekend off?" Miguel says after our drinks arrive.

I take a sip of my black iced tea, savoring the subtle bergamot flavor.

"For the wedding? Um, yes, obviously. Like I would ever miss it!"

"What about another weekend?" Papa asks.

I frown. "Raven said people sometimes swap weekend shifts with others. It's trickier for the newbies, but if you can find someone to cover for you, then you're good. Why?"

"Because we're going to the Hamptons next month."

"What?" I do a little jump on my chair, but Luz looks nonplussed. "Did you not hear him say we're going to the Hamptons?"

"Um, yeah! And did you not hear me tell you a few nights ago?" She notices the blank look on my face. "I guess you were distracted."

She's not wrong about that. I have a lot on my plate right now.

Miguel jumps in. "Our friends own a house there, and they offered to throw us a bachelor party."

"And *we're* invited to that?" I say, meaning Luz and me.

"It's not a traditional bachelor party. Everyone's invited. We're just going to hang out, have cocktails and amazing food, and you girls are free to do whatever you want."

I turn to Luz. "We're going to the Hamptons, baby!" I raise my hand up, and she meets me halfway for a high five.

For a moment, I forget about everything: Papa and Miguel's quarrel; my cramping shoulders, sore from endless days at work; and how much cooking I'm *not* doing. But not Zach. I never forget about Zach. And while I could really use a weekend away and an actual break, I can't help but note that it's just going to be another two days taken away from looking for him. Unless I find him first. I *need* to.

I feel like I'm starting to forget how warm his chest felt against my cheek; his stories about eating noodles for a month straight when he was planning his trip around the world, adding different kinds of spices every day so he could pretend it was a different meal; and how he cried in front of his entire group of friends when his high school girlfriend broke up with him. I found it endearing, picturing Zach and his first heartbreak. Every minute I spend apart from him feels like I'm throwing my future away. We were meant to be together. We *are*.

Our sampling arrives, and I'm reminded of my duties. Not just cake tasting; I also promised Maman she'd get to join in on the fun. I whip out my phone and FaceTime her.

"Are you sure you're in New York?" Maman jokes when she sees the *pièce montée* and the French-inspired surroundings.

"Hi, Nadia!" Luz says, before biting into a puff pastry. "These are really simple but *so* good."

"It's the simplicity that makes it good," I say without thinking. Do I really mean that? Simplicity and Margot don't often go together.

"See, Pascal," Maman says as I shift the phone over to Papa. "She does take after me for *some* things." Papa laughs, and before I can grumble about their inside joke, she adds, "How's work? I bet you're happy to have the day off."

Maman only speaks to me in English when Papa is there. He speaks French—his parents always spoke their native language at home—but he and Maman always communicated in English, as it was easier with their other New York friends around. Her accent has gone thicker with time, since she doesn't speak the language so much anymore. We don't get too many American tourists in our country town.

"Work is *so* great!" I smile brightly. "I'm learning so much and it's the best experience ever."

Over the top of my phone, Papa, Miguel, and Luz give me weird looks, and I make sure to keep them out of the frame. What? I'm just giving Maman the highlights.

But she frowns anyway. "Oh, that's nice."

"Really, Maman, I'm having the time of my life."

I feel the usual flare of heat spike inside me, waiting for her to say something more. I pop a second *chou* in my mouth as Papa swivels the phone to him. "Don't worry, Nadia. We're looking after her."

Then he raises an eyebrow at me, which I ignore.

Best to change the topic, especially since tough decisions await. "Guys, I think we have to be honest here. We're not going to be able to pick just one wedding cake. And we haven't even gotten to the bakery in Brooklyn that makes the most incredible naked cakes."

"Naked cakes?" Miguel says with a laugh. "It's not that kind of wedding."

"They're naked because they're not covered in icing. It's a more natural look," I explain with a smirk. "I think you'll like it. Come on, let's go."

Maman lets out a laugh. "Okay, I'm off. Sounds like you're on a mission." She blows us all a kiss. "*À bientôt!*"

We wave goodbye and she hangs up.

"Margot," Papa says, "why are we going to Brooklyn to taste more cakes when we already can't decide between all of these?"

"Because," I say, standing up, "I've just decided. We're having a dessert bar. We'll do one main cake, a mini *pièce montée*—it's tradition, after all!—and cupcakes of different flavors. Oh, and macarons. *Évidemment.*"

"And who's paying for this?" Papa says, but I can tell he's joking.

"I'll stay on budget, promise," I concede. Honestly, this cake venture is the first fun I've had in days. It's almost enough to distract me from the conversation with Maman.

"Margot knows her stuff," Miguel says, getting up as well. "If she wants us to go to Brooklyn for some naked cake, then that's what we're doing."

And *that* is exactly what Margot wants.

Chapter Twelve

The kitchen looks like a war zone. Strips of vegetable peels are scattered on the counter like wounded soldiers. Olive oil spills congregate in circles, surrounded by jars of *herbes de Provence* and other spices lined up to do their duty. Spoons, forks, and knives battle it out on the field. I'm making dinner for my family to enjoy while I'm working tonight, and this is my kind of fight. Chef can keep me off the line, but he can't stop me here.

I glance at my phone as I slice beefsteak tomatoes, the sharp edges of the serrated knife slicing through the skin and releasing small squirts of juice. I found handmade burrata at Eataly—a supersized Italian market in the Flatiron District, not too far from the restaurant—and a bunch of basil leaves so fragrant that I stood in the aisle inhaling them, feeling like I was at home, in our garden, snipping them right off the earth.

I'm bringing the vinaigrette to a foaming consistency when I see a new text on my screen.

Still meeting in an hour?

My heart hits pause. Today is our second day of looking for Zach, but Ben and I also have to be at work by four p.m. We're meeting in Jackson Heights, Queens, an area famous for its cuisines from all around the world, and it'll take me about an hour to get there. I must have lost track of time.

I put down the whisk too abruptly, and splatters of vinaigrette fly in the air before falling onto my white T-shirt.

"*Génial,*" I mumble to myself, patting the stains with a kitchen towel.

After rushing through the rest of dinner preparation, I run to the bedroom, and rummage through the closet. I extract a miniskirt and a shirt with a star print in a silky fabric, which I'll wear with my denim jacket. A cute outfit, just in case. Today might be the day.

Then I'm on the street, dodging pedestrians and quickening the pace on my way to the subway station. I feel so lucky that Ben offered to help me. Luz has been supportive about the whole Times Square debacle, but I know deep down she feels like I'll just get over it. That Zach and I weren't *really* meant to be, since we didn't end up, well, *being*.

But for Ben, helping others just seems like it's in his blood. I see him around the kitchen, always paying attention to who might need a hand. He's the first one to defuse tension, to crack a joke, to smile and make it better. Even the older cooks, who look at us like we're trying to steal their jobs, secretly love him. It's just who he is.

At least I think that's who he is. Sometimes it feels like all we do is talk about my problems and I know so little about his. Maybe he doesn't have any since he has all these well-ironed plans. For starters, I've heard nothing about Ben's love life. I can't really believe a guy like him—so sweet, so cute, so easy to be around—would be single. By the time I get off at Roosevelt Avenue in Queens, I'm bursting with a question.

Ben's already at the corner, smiling as I approach.

"I've been wondering," I say. "Do you have a girlfriend?"

He jerks back in surprise, an amused look on his face.

"Well, um, hi?" His laugh is awkward, maybe even a little embarrassed.

Now I don't just want to know. I *need* to. "Yes, hi. But you know *everything* about me," I say, looking at him sideways as we start walking down the street. "It's just not fair."

We pass by many food trucks, offering everything from Colombian arepas to Ecuadorian blood sausage and potato cakes. Smells of smoke and roasted meat fill the air while the aboveground trains rumble over our heads. New York is always such a strange blend of scents and noises, people and atmospheres.

Finally, Ben turns to me. "I don't have a girlfriend, but I'm dating someone. A girl, I mean."

It throws me off. Just a bit. How has it *not* come up in conversations before? And why did I expect, despite all the good reasons to the contrary, that the answer would be no? But then I'm distracted by something else he said. Come to think of it, Ben's statement makes no sense at all.

"If you're dating a girl, then how is she not your girlfriend?"

We pass by a few restaurants, most of which have flashing "OPEN" signs in the window, posters with pictures of the food on offer, with names listed in various languages. It's almost lunch-time, and though I tasted the food I made earlier, my stomach is starting to grumble.

"Because we're only dating."

I frown. He frowns back. Something is not computing.

"Dating and being in a relationship are two different things." His tone is kind, but there's a *duh* in there, too, like it's an indisputable fact.

Except that it isn't. "Americans are weird," I say.

Ben lets out a laugh. "Um, yeah, but about what, exactly?"

"In France, if you're dating someone, they're your boyfriend or girlfriend. It's that simple. You go on a date once, and if you like each other enough to meet up again, then that's it, you're basically a couple."

"Ahhh," he says wistfully. "Everything is more romantic in France. Okay, then by that definition I'm in a couple. She—Olivia, that's her name—and I have gone on several dates already. We met at a coffee shop a few weeks back. She's nice. I just don't think—I guess I'm not sure how I feel about her."

"So why don't you break up?"

He raises an eyebrow.

It takes me a moment to get it. "Right. You're not *together* together, so you can't break up?"

"Something like that. But wait a minute, if you think you're a couple after your first date, then does that make Zach your boyfriend?"

111

I chuckle loudly enough for the people in front of us to turn around. "I think maybe I have to find him first?"

"Yeah, I guess knowing where your boyfriend is or at least having a way to get in touch with him would be kind of helpful."

I gasp in mock outrage. He laughs. I like the sound of it, and the way his whole face lights up. It's the kind of laugh that warms you from top to bottom. I bet Olivia is super pretty.

We arrive at the Jackson Heights Greenmarket, the one that—if Ben guessed correctly—Zach frequently visits on Sundays. There are farmers' markets all over the city, each on different days of the week. What makes this one special is the diverse neighborhood it's in. Zach had raved about the treats he enjoys after getting fresh produce for his grandmother who, I *think,* lives nearby. There are tamales available near the entrance of the park, but Zach also mentioned some kind of famous Moroccan bread that I'd never heard of. Ben felt certain that these would be in Jackson Heights.

This place is amazing, from the bursting colors of the vegetables and the soothing scent of roasting corn to the one of garlic naan. After an hour or so, I can no longer ignore the familiar sinking feeling in my stomach. I seriously thought today might be the day. But now I have to face the truth: I'm not going to see Zach today. I won't hold him in my arms. Reality, I don't like her.

"He's not here," I say, defeated.

"The market is still open for a little while," Ben says, a sorry look on his face.

He's only trying to cheer me up; we can both see that several stands are starting to pack up the few remaining goods they have and dismantling their tables. Zach's not showing up now.

"I'm going to need to eat something," I say, scanning the space. Now that I've swallowed the disappointment, I realize there's another feeling brewing in my stomach. Hunger. And *that* is something I can take care of. The line at the tamales is pretty long, but they do smell delicious.

Ben has a better idea. "My friend's uncle has an amazing restaurant in the neighborhood. He sees a lot of people. If Zach is used to coming around here . . ."

I nod, feeling the hope light up again inside my heart. "I trust you," I say, meaning both the amazing food and the idea that someone, somewhere might recognize Zach.

A few minutes later, we come upon a restaurant tucked between a phone store and a computer repair shop. An electronic sign announces Nepalese food next to posters selling unlimited data plans. Weird, never seen before, and intriguing. New York in a nutshell.

"Tashi!" Ben calls when the chef comes out of the back, a short, bald man with a crooked smile and kind eyes.

He introduces me, and then keeps chatting with his friend's uncle as I read the menu. "What's a momo?"

"It's a type of dumpling," Ben explains. "They can be pan-fried or steamed, and filled with anything: meat, chives, potatoes. . . . Want to try?"

Tashi beats me to it. "Of course she does! It's why you're here, no?" he says with a laugh. "I'll put an order in for you."

"Thank you," I start. Ben smiles at me, urging me on. "I'm also looking for a guy. It's kind of a long shot, but maybe you've seen him around? Someone who works in a restaurant, I just don't know which one." I pull out my phone as I speak, and show him the picture. "His name's Zach."

Tashi frowns as he studies it. After he's had a good look, he says, "Eh, fancy white boy. He's probably at one of those chic places in Manhattan." He straightens up and mimics wearing a collared shirt. "You know the real food is right here in Queens? Made by immigrants, for immigrants."

I don't tell him that I already called some of the biggest restaurants in New York, asking after Zach. No luck there. People told me they either don't give out information about their staff, didn't have anyone named Zach on their roster, or couldn't help. I talked to maybe fifteen people before giving up. It'd take me all year to contact them all.

"Are you sure you don't recognize him?" Ben says.

Tashi's face scrunches as he looks again.

"Sor—" Ben starts, but I shake my head, stopping him.

"No one knows him, no one's seen him. It's never going to happen."

My heart feels heavy, but my empty stomach is still growling.

"You'll like the momos," Ben says as we sit down.

They arrive in a bamboo steamer basket, along with a sesame tomato chutney. My mouth is already watering, and I have to hold back as Tashi places everything on the table.

"Try," Tashi says, watching me.

I grab my set of chopsticks and get to it. "Hmm . . ." My eyes roll with glee after just one bite. *Trop bon.*

Tashi laughs. "Oh, you are French?" He turns to Ben. "I see why you like her."

The lighting is a bit weird in here, but I'm pretty sure Ben is blushing.

"This guy's obsessed with France," Tashi says. "Our Benny cooks better French food than the best French restaurants in the city."

Ben's eyes pop wide open. "Don't say that to the French girl who literally grew up in a French restaurant . . . in France."

"I am right," Tashi says like a proud father, as if Ben were his own son. "You taste his French onion soup?"

Like most French people, I'm a bit of a snob when it comes to anything to do with food. And by that, I mean that I'm a *total* snob.

"You know," I say to Ben, finishing off my first dumpling and blowing out the heat, "if you really were the most non-French French person, you'd just call it onion soup. Because that's what it is. No one here says they're eating an American burger."

"You mean they're not eating a burger with French fries?"

"Um, wrong? Fries are Belgian. We can't take credit for every famous food. Just most of it."

"Okay, well, you can definitely take credit for this. Legend has it that Louis XV invented the soup when he found himself alone in his hunting lodge with just a few ingredients, but the truth is that it's been around for centuries. Onions have always been a staple because they're so easy to cultivate."

He notices the funny look on my face and pauses.

"Oh shit, am I Frenchsplaining the most famous dish in your gastronomy? Or is that mansplaining? ManFrenchsplaining? Is that a thing?"

"You're not 'splaining' anything to me, because I didn't know that. How do you know more about French cuisine than me?"

Ben shrugs. "Apparently it was a hit at Versailles. Even if you have access to all the luxury in the world, sometimes the simplest things are still the best."

Ben has a point. I squish one of the momos between my chopsticks and lift it up. "I'll raise a dumpling to that."

Ben mimics me and then clinks his own with mine. It makes a sploshy sound, and we chuckle.

Tashi looks from me to Ben, and then back. A smile forms on his lips. "You try his Fr— his onion soup. Best in the city."

"Oh, I would love to," I say. "But be warned: I'm a tough critic."

Ben puffs up his chest. "I'm not afraid of a challenge."

"Okay, you're on."

And, just for this moment, today is no longer about Zach. It's about discovering new foods, exploring my city, enjoying everything it has to offer. It's about friendship, and the surprises life throws at you. Like American boys who know everything about France. And even though my first few weeks in New York haven't exactly panned out how I'd hoped, I feel deep inside that the future will be rich and flavorful. Especially if it involves *soupe à l'oignon.*

Chapter Thirteen

It's Christmas in September. At least, that's what it seems like from the exhilarated look on Luz's face this morning as she swings by the apartment to pick me up. She's been waiting for this moment since the news of the engagement. I'll be excited, too . . . once I'm fully awake.

"SoHo is the only place to go," she tells me as I get ready. She fixes her glossy black hair while I focus on finding a pair of shoes I can walk in for hours and which I can easily slip off. We're about to try on a lot of clothes, so practicality is paramount.

"Uh-huh," I say, looking inside my wallet, making sure I still have Papa's credit card. *Get whatever you want,* he said. *Treat yourselves, I mean it. Okay, maybe don't go into Chanel . . . but we really appreciate all your help with the wedding planning, so think of it as your reward.*

"I've been thinking about this a lot," Luz adds, poking around in my makeup bag and handing me my mascara. "We can't just go rogue. Like, sure, the grooms said we could wear whatever we wanted, but this is a wedding. We're bridesmaids. 'Whatever' is not an option."

I unearth my pair of loafers under the bed. Perfect.

"Margot?" Luz says in the mirror, staring at my reflection. "You've looked at the last inspo pictures I sent you, right?"

The thing is, there have been *a lot* of inspiration photos. One moment, Luz is "feeling" metallic, maybe something floor-length with disco drama, and the next she's showing me photos of fifties-style dresses with bows everywhere. Ever since the grooms told us we had carte blanche to pick our bridesmaid dresses, Luz has been on high alert. My biggest criterion is that the dress be comfortable so I can dance the night away. When I said that to Luz, she told me off for using the c-word.

I stand up and smile. *"Chef, oui, Chef!"* Before she can remind me of the seriousness of the situation, I add, "We have an entire day and my dad's credit card. I believe in us."

It takes us just fifteen minutes to walk to SoHo, which, as we've already established, is Luz's favorite place to shop. I understand why when we get there. The narrow cobblestoned streets, the wrought-iron stairs lined up against the cream buildings complete with fire escapes, and the tall arched windows all look like quintessential New York. The one from the movies. It's bustling with fashionable people and shops. In fact, as we make our way down Prince Street and walk up and down the side streets, I recognize many French brands.

But our first stop is a place called *& Other Stories,* which we enter through the back door on Mercer Street after going up steep metal stairs. We browse through maxidresses with subtle prints, plaid pants, flowy long-sleeved blouses, and checked blazers. It's all very appealing for the new season, but nothing feels quite right for a wedding.

We continue roaming the streets, enter every store, consider every dress. I fall in lust with a black chiffon number with cap sleeves, immediately vetoed by Luz—*it's not a black-tie wedding!* She likes a green floral wrap dress, but the fit is off, baggy in the waist and tight in the shoulders. A no go. By now we must have tried on fifteen outfits or more, all of them discarded for various reasons.

"We should go to Nolita," Luz announces. "There are so many more shops over there. We are finding our dresses *today!*"

I'm pretty sure she adds that last part based on the worn look on my face. I like clothes as much as the next girl, but Luz is a shopping warrior. We've been at it for almost three hours and she shows no sign of waning.

The same cannot be said about me. "Okay, but can we please get lunch first? I'm about to eat this curtain."

According to Luz, Ladurée, the French temple of macarons and candy pink pastries, is the obvious choice. Not only is it just around the corner, but the restaurant boasts a garden at the back, a hidden oasis behind mint green walls and covered by trees, perfect for a gorgeous autumn day. The bistro tables and chairs remind me of Paris, as do the waiters dressed in black pants and white shirts. I wouldn't say it feels like home exactly—I'm a country girl, not a chic *Parisienne*—but it seems like a dreamy, peaceful place to be.

We get a table at the back and start perusing the menu. The

simple decisions are the hardest to make, especially when it comes to food. After much debate, I settle on the egg-white omelet with spinach and goat cheese, and Luz orders the Gourmand Avocado Toast, with smoked salmon.

"Have you made a decision about your date?" Luz says, after we order our food.

Papa and Miguel told us we could each invite someone, and when I picture myself on the dance floor, I'm in Zach's arms, the same ones I've been wanting to curl myself in since that night in Paris. There was a moment that night when we came upon a street performer playing the accordion: Zach had launched into a waltz right there on the street, showing me the steps while I tried not to crush his toes under my sandals. Just when I started getting the hang of it, the music had stopped and I had to hide my disappointment. At least until Zach kissed me—the only thing better than dancing with him.

But if I'm being honest, the idea of taking Zach to the wedding is starting to feel more like a far-fetched fantasy than a plausible reality. Zach is nowhere to be found. I've searched restaurants, Instagram hashtags, TikTok videos. No one recognizes his picture. If I didn't have these snaps of us, I'd be wondering if he's just a figment of my imagination.

"I don't know," I say with a shrug.

"What about taking Ben?" She notices my frown, but pushes past it. "If you don't find Zach, of course. You and Ben could go as friends. People do that."

"What about *your* date? Are you going to bring David, or is that a secret, too?"

While I've been busting my butt at work, Luz was out with her friend one night and met a guy. They texted a lot for a few days and then finally went on a date two weeks ago. David works evenings—in a bar—so their schedules don't match so well, but they're on date number three now. Luz still won't show me a picture, and says she doesn't have any, but I know the real reason: she doesn't want to rub it in my face that she met a guy when I'm so desperate to be with Zach.

"I've decided not to do it," she says.

A waiter brings our plates and sets them down on the table.

"Why not?" I take in the roasted potatoes that came with my omelet. They glisten with olive oil, making my mouth water in anticipation.

"My whole family's going to be there. I feel like I should wait to see if it's going to be serious between us. He's so driven, so passionate, and he's had a pretty tough life. He doesn't know his mom, and his dad has barely been around. He was raised by his grandmother, but it wasn't a stable situation. Anyway, we're taking it slow."

"Well, you seem to really like him," I say, feeling a twinge of jealousy. Maybe she's right to protect me. I'm not sure I can handle Luz being madly in love when I'm just madly *sans* Zach. Still, if I could have him by my side at the wedding, I wouldn't hesitate for a moment. "And if you do, wouldn't it be really romantic to have him there? You'll be thinking about that for years."

Luz tucks into her avocado toast. "We're not all like you, Margot. You spend one night with a guy, and you just *know* he's the love of your life."

I swallow hard. Not wanting to look her in the eyes, I tear up a piece of bread and slather it with a thick layer of butter.

"I'm not judging you!" she adds. "I just don't get it."

"Yes, you are!" I put my fork down and it clatters against the plate, startling both of us. Luz and I have never fought before, about anything. "My whole life I've felt that I was missing out on something. I was born here, but we left before I could remember anything of New York. My dad would tell me all about my other culture, and I always thought I'd come here to experience it for myself. I'm French, but I'm American, too. And then I met Zach . . . who lives in New York. A cook. The signs were everywhere. And maybe I was only with him for one night, but you can bet your baguette that if I find him before the wedding, he's going to be my date. It's meant to be. It doesn't have to make sense. It just is."

Luz nods. There's a calmness on her face, like she knows this has gone too far. "I'm not inviting David. It's too soon for us, and if things don't work out, I don't want to spend every family dinner from now on talking about what went wrong with that cute guy from Miguel's wedding."

"Okay," I say, feeling the annoyance melting. "You do you and I'll do me."

"Deal," Luz says.

We finish our meals, and when the waiter asks us if we want any dessert, I'm the one who declines. More important than dates, we have dresses to find.

We make our way across Broadway, toward Nolita. After a few stops—during which Luz finds a polka-dot skirt with a high slit, and I splurge on a cozy sweater—we arrive at Sézane, the Frenchiest store in all of the land. The windows are framed with white flowers and potted plants, and topped by awnings striped in white and gray. Inside, the herringbone pattern of the floorboards makes me feel like we're in a Parisian apartment, especially when we reach a tiled mat spelling out *Bonjour New York.*

Luz beams. "I have a good feeling about this. Your people know a thing or two about fashion."

"And food!" I add. "Especially food."

"Fine, you're better at everything. Happy now?"

"Oui!"

I was never this proud of my country until I left it.

We split up. I make a beeline for the back of the store, where a navy maxidress calls my name, at least until I cast my eyes on a lavender number gathered at the waist and with lots of little buttons down the front.

Suddenly, Luz rushes behind me. "Margot, Margot, Margot!"

I turn around to see that she's holding an asymmetrical hot pink minidress with frills on the bottom and across the chest. A metallic thread goes through the fabric. While it's not my usual style, I have to admit that, even on the hanger, it feels sexy.

"It's gorgeous," I say.

Luz's face lights up. "To the changing rooms!" She says, her index finger raised high.

As soon as I slip on the pink dress, I feel different, in a good way. It skims my hips and shows off my shoulders. The color brightens my face. I love it.

I step out of the room in synch with Luz. We stare at each

other from top to bottom, and then our eyes pop wide open. This is it.

"You look hot, *hermana*," I say.

"Right back at you, *ma sœur*."

We're still swirling in front of the floor-length mirrors when my phone beeps from inside my cross-body bag. I check it. It's a text message from Ben, a picture of a baguette. The color is perfect, honey-like, and I can feel the crustiness through the screen.

Pour le goûter, he wrote. Also got strawberry confiture.

Goûter is French for snack time, more specifically, afternoon snack time. It's what we eat after coming home from school, to tide us over until dinner. Though grownups are allowed *goûters*, too.

I respond with three smiling emojis and So French of you.

Another text message comes through.

What are you up to?

I glance at myself in the mirror: it's a much better look than when I'm sweating over the steaming-hot water of the dishwasher. Without thinking too much, I make a scrunchy face, snap a picture of my reflection, and send it to Ben.

Bridesmaid dress shopping

Luz shoots me an inquisitive glance.

"I'm texting Ben," I say.

She puts both hands on her hips. "Are you sure you don't want to invite him as your date to the wedding?"

I shrug. I guess it could be fun? And if Luz thinks it's okay to bring him as a friend . . . I don't know.

Nice! Ben responds. I'm thinking we go to Katz's Deli next. Maybe tomorrow, before work?

I smile. Yep! Ur the best

Do you mean I'm le meilleur?

Oui

"Margot?" Luz says.

She's standing there, staring at me.

"Sorry." I chuck my phone on top of my clothes, then come back out to study myself in the mirror. "These dresses are perfect. Does that mean we're done here?"

Luz nods. "I say yes to the dress!"

With one lingering gaze at the mirror, I imagine Ben in a suit leading me to the dance floor.

It *would* be fun.

But only if I can't find Zach first.

Chapter Fourteen

Chef's in a mood.

That's the warning I get from Raven before I've even entered the restaurant. She's drinking coffee from a to-go cup outside, not far from the front door, something we're always told not to do. We're the background people. The invisibles. Our breaks—when we dare take them—are supposed to happen in the back alley, hidden from view. I leave her to her phone—she looks like she was texting with someone—wondering who that might be. After Chef, Raven seems to be the hardest-working person in this place. She's always here when I arrive, when I leave, when I have a question, even if she doesn't always seem happy to answer it.

The thing is, Chef's *always* in a mood, so I just assume that Raven is particularly tired today. I begin to change my mind as soon as I arrive in the locker room. Two of the prep cooks are having a lively conversation in Spanish—which includes lots of hand gestures, but I only catch a word here and there.

"Everything okay?" I ask.

I don't think they even hear me. My job doesn't intersect much with prep work, plus I'm one of the youngsters. We don't mingle with the veterans. That's just one of the downsides of my role: I come in after much of the team has been working all afternoon, which means I miss out on the day's drama.

In the kitchen, Ben looks tense and focused. We had so much fun at Katz's Deli—even though we obviously didn't find Zach, *again*—but today he barely even nods in my direction. Some of the other cooks roam around silently, carrying trays and arranging the mise en place on their stations: sea salt flakes, black pepper—hand ground, obviously—slices of lemon, a bottle of virgin olive oil, various vinegars, cups of sauces, and a slab of butter. They also each have a stack of white cloths, to clean the edges of each plate before passing it on to the next station.

I don't see Chef until we're sitting for family meal. His face is stony, harsher than usual.

"All right everyone, listen up."

Usually he starts with some kind of greeting. This is our team-bonding moment, the time when we're really together. Chef will praise us on how we got through three-hundred covers last night with close to no refires. He'll read a review from *Eater* aloud, or mention there was a glowing post from an Instagram influencer. Chef knows the importance of good morale, but today, he has no time for that.

"We're going down a slippery slope," he starts, standing at the top of the table. "I came in this morning and the fridge looked like it'd been ransacked. I couldn't believe the mess! That's one. Now, about service last night."

He goes on with a long list of grievances. Complaints from guests that the roasted beets were sour, the Caesar salad lackluster, light on croutons, the green pea tartine too bland. I can't help but notice that all the dishes Chef mentions are on the cold station. It's not only that it's Ari's turf, but Chef is openly staring at him now, so we all get his gist. The whole table has gone silent, and I sneak a glance at the cook. I can't imagine he loves being dressed down in front of the entire staff.

"And your station!" Chef says, now raising his voice, his gaze drilling through Ari. "It's a pigsty, getting worse and worse every day."

"I told you why!" Ari says.

Tension radiates across the room. No one is enjoying this.

"We're short on staff," Ari continues, his tone going down just a notch. "We need more bodies in the kitchen, and until we have that—"

"Until we have that, what?" Chef cuts in. "You don't get to give me an ultimatum. I'm running a business."

Ari glances at Raven, looking for support. She ignores him and turns to Chef, the equivalent of a slap in the face. There's no point trying with Bertrand; he never gets involved in conflicts. Watching him during a shift, you'd think only Chef exists—that's how much attention he pays to the rest of us. As the other next-in-command, Raven has a certain amount of sway with the boss. She softens blows, advocates for causes—like better food for family meal, or hiring extra staff—and listens to complaints on both sides. But today, it seems pretty clear she's not on Ari's.

"Then *you're* the problem," Ari says to Chef. His jaw is

clenched, his eyes shooting daggers. This is not going to end well. "I cut my finger twice yesterday; Angela tripped and hurt her ankle. Ben's asking for more shifts, but you won't give him any because it's all about 'saving money' here. We're doing the best we can with what we have."

"Then the best you can is not good enough," Chef says.

Ari gets up. The two men have a silent standoff.

"Does anyone else have a problem doing their job?" Chef says, casting his eyes around the table. His question is met with silence and a few shaking heads.

"Really?" Ari says, kicking his chair back. It scrapes against the floor angrily. "No one has the courage to speak up? I'm sick of this. I've given everything to this restaurant. *Everything!*"

"And yet your endives are still watery."

Ouch.

Ari's face goes red. Then, he steps back from the table and takes a deep breath. I hold mine, not daring to look at anyone.

"I'm out of here," Ari says.

"Fine," Chef says coolly.

The air stops circulating. After what feels like a long time but is probably just a few seconds, Ari lets out a grunt and storms off to the locker room. Chef shakes his head and goes back to the kitchen. It's another minute or so before anyone starts filling their plates. Soon, you can only hear the sound of chewing.

"Should we all worry for our jobs?" I ask Ben as we're clearing the table after the meal.

"Nah, these things happen."

But I can tell he's still bothered by the whole thing. "Really?"

"You don't know the whole story. Ari asked for a raise, and Chef blew him off. But Ari has been talking with the sous-chef at an Italian restaurant in Tribeca, so I think he was tempted to leave anyway."

"So Ari's definitely gone, then?"

"Who knows? People come and go all the time."

An idea forms in my head. "Do you think—I mean, who's going to take over for Ari tonight?"

Ben cocks an eyebrow. He knows exactly where I'm going with this. "Raven might find someone last minute. Sometimes we all pitch in to make it work until the next shift." He pauses, faces me. "I guess you could ask."

But last time I tried, it didn't go so well. And Chef wasn't in the same kind of mood.

Ben reads the hesitation on my face. "I know you. You'll regret it if you don't."

My fingers tingle, but whether it's with fear or excitement, I'm not sure. "If I get in trouble . . . ," I say. But I don't finish my sentence because I know Ben is right. I have to keep asking.

I find Chef in the walk-in fridge, deep in conversation with Raven and Bertrand. He's checking items against a list, rummaging through jars and containers as they speak.

"Hi," I say tentatively, slowly moving closer to them. "Since you're down one line cook—"

Raven turns to me first, pondering. Then, she looks at Chef. "Leo might be free tonight." Leo is one of the part-time dishwashers, on shift when I'm not.

Chef and Raven exchange a look. Something passes between them. They've worked together for years, so I'm guessing they're used to dealing with these situations. Bertrand keeps going through the jars, taking stock. I don't think he has any idea who I am.

Chef turns to me. "Fine."

I'm stunned. How can it be this easy?

"You wanted your shot," Chef says, noticing the surprise on my face. "You told me you're a great cook. Now's your chance to prove it."

"Merci," I say, but I know before the word has fully left my lips that it's the wrong sentiment, so I spin quickly. "I can do it," I add. "It's going to work out."

Chef nods as he slips the list in his coat pocket, and rubs his eyes. He looks tired. I've seen the stresses running a restaurant put on Maman, and it almost never has to do with the actual cooking. The grocer's delivery is late, or there was an error in the order and your stock of lettuce is probably going to run out halfway through the service. Your cook burns herself on the stove and you have to step in while she tends to her wound. Cooking is a glorious, transcendental experience, but running a restaurant brings a lot of headaches.

"And, Margot," Chef says as I'm already walking away, "you really need to step up tonight. If you want to do this."

I'm tempted to ask if he means doing this forever, but then Luz's voice rings in my ears. *Nothing is forever in New York, Bella. Everything is for right now.*

"I'm on it."

Okay, so I don't *fully* believe it. Deep down I'm terrified of having to jump into the deep end, but I don't have time to worry, I have a job to do. *My* job. I find a cook's uniform in the locker room. The jacket is freshly ironed, and the cotton feels crisp as I put it on, like it means business. It's a little big on me, so I roll up the sleeves. Then I'm as ready as I'll ever be.

I'm not going to lie. The shift is arduous. Ivan, who's on the cold station with me, grumbles about having to teach me the recipes. I'm yet another one of the young crew given a sought-after position, and I feel all eyes on me throughout, expecting me to trip. But I won't. This is where I belong. This little dance, this perfect cadence, it's mine.

It goes like this:

Chef calls out every order that comes through, and we all stop to listen. We have to be aware of everything that's going on so we can work with each other in perfect rhythm. If the hot station has a backlog of dishes—like the popular roasted cauliflower with its pistachios, pickled red onions, and turmeric sauce—then I need to slow down on my end so plates from the same order can be synchronized.

"*Oui,* Chef!" we all respond after he finishes reading the ticket.

Once we've gathered all the ingredients—the roasted walnuts, the gobs of goat cheese fresh from a farm in upstate New York, the vinaigrette, made by one of the prep cooks—it's time to slice, chop, snip, scoop up, squeeze out. Things get loud: a mix of popping, squeaking, yelling, clattering. It's deafening.

The next step is to carefully plate it up and send it down the line, where Raven or Bertrand, and then Chef, put on the finishing touches.

There's very little time to marvel at my creation before moving on to the next. Every move counts, every false step could get me behind. I have to measure it all up. When do I need to pull out that container? How much space can I take on the counter to chop these herbs? Cooking is all of the things: emotions, chemistry, culture, taste, and even math. It all needs to fit together in our endless race against the clock.

Lucky for me, Ben is right behind me on the hot station, and it's like he knows what I need before I can even ask. He slips the right knife on the counter, points at the lowboy where I'll find the ingredient I'm looking for. Every restaurant's dance is a little different, and I still need to learn these particular steps. And while I'm grateful for Ben's help, a sense of dread courses through me as the service inches toward the end. This cannot be my one night, my one shot. It's so incredibly hard, but it feels *right*. I'm working as a cook. At a fancy restaurant. In the heart of Manhattan. Pinch me.

Chef has made no comments about my performance tonight, and I can't decide whether that's a good or a bad thing. I know I'm not the only one he has to worry about, but until he offers me the job, it's not really happening.

"Great work, partner," Ben tells me at the end of the service, as we're wiping down our respective stations, the job of the younger cook. The others walk away without another glance.

"Thanks," I say. The adrenaline has left my body now. All that remains is doubt and exhaustion. "I really want this," I mumble, so no one else can hear us.

"You *have* this."

I know he's trying to be supportive, but I can't get my hopes up. Back in the locker room, we take off our jackets and put them in the dirty laundry basket.

"But until Chef tells me—"

Ben flicks his locker open, then points behind me.

I swivel around to find Raven standing there.

"Margot, I'm putting you on the schedule for tomorrow, okay?"

Ben is shaking his head, telling me not to ask, but I have to. I need to be sure. "On the line?"

Raven nods. "Yeah. Be here at two, okay?"

My heart knocks against my chest. "Permanently?"

She lets out a deep, frustrated sigh, which I know is not really directed at me. "Sure. As permanent as anything ever is."

And just like that, I have a new job.

I wait until Raven is out of earshot to jump up and down. "I got the job, I got the job, I got the job!"

Ben smiles as he watches me.

"What? Is this when you say I told you so?" I'm smiling so hard my cheeks hurt.

"No, this is when I say bravo, you deserve it."

He wraps me in a hug. I lean into it. This is what happiness feels like.

See, New York? You can't keep me away from my dream life. And I know there's so much more to come.

Chapter Fifteen

This isn't a date, but it *is* the first time Ben and I have hung out just because. We're not working tonight, and we're not looking for Zach. We're just . . . eating together, at his apartment. It's what I tell myself as I select an outfit, and it's what I repeat over and over to Luz, who will not give it up.

"Right," Luz says, watching me wrap a black patent leather belt around my waist. "You're putting on a cute romper to go have dinner at his place, just the two of you—"

"His roommates might be there!"

Luz rolls her eyes so hard that I half expect them to pop out of their sockets. "Just the two of you," she continues. "And if we're being honest here, you haven't mentioned Zach in a few days now."

She came over to hang as I got ready for this definitely-not-a-date, and I'm starting to regret it. I love Luz but I say *non merci* to this kind of pressure.

I look down at myself. "It's just an outfit." I'm wearing it with my black suede sandals, the highest heels I own, which make my legs look way more toned than they actually are. Still, it's *just* an outfit.

"Margot, it's okay if you like the guy. Even if you work with him, even if you also like him as a friend, even if . . ." She trails off, knowing that I don't want to hear it.

It's not that I've stopped looking for Zach, exactly. It's just that I'm running out of places to search. And maybe, just maybe, I've started to wonder about my memories of that night. I wasn't in *love* with him. I just felt . . . fireworks, like every fuse in my heart was lit up. But what about now? Do I still feel like this or am I just hanging on to how I felt that night? I don't have the answer yet and I can't let go so easily. I can't ignore the fact that Zach is still out there, that we could still be together.

"Ben's a friend, Luz. And I'm just going to taste his onion soup."

Luz makes a sexy face. "I bet it's *real* good."

I grab my bag, shaking my head, but I agree with her. I'm not admitting that out loud, though. "Let's just go."

We leave Papa and Miguel in the depths of wedding planning—the DJ asked for their playlist—and walk together to the subway station. Luz is meeting David at a famous vegan Mexican place on the Lower East Side, and by the way she smooths her dress every few seconds, I can tell she's nervous. I still haven't met the guy, but she promised she'd introduce us soon, whenever we can all be free at the same time. Between my schedule and his—based on what Luz tells me—this will be a challenge.

"Enjoy your date," I say when we're about to part ways. "Text me with a full report afterward."

"And I want to know all about your date, too."

The swooshing sound of a train incoming on the platform drowns my protests, and then she's running down the platform, slipping between the doors just as they're closing.

I'm going in the opposite direction, to Williamsburg, across the river. Apparently, the Brooklyn neighborhood used to be grungier—populated with artists and trendsetters—but now luxury high-rises have mushroomed along the waterfront and young professionals moved there in droves to enjoy the up-and-coming restaurants, cocktail bars, and vintage stores.

The smell of caramelized onions hits me as I climb the stairs to Ben's apartment, a fragrant reminder of why I'm here. One of his roommates—a guy named Karim, stocky with a thick mane of black hair—opens the door. Karim is Ben's best friend from high school, and he's currently finishing his first year of college while interning at a tech start-up.

"Bonjour," Karim says, before turning toward the inside of the apartment. "Ben, she's here." Then back to me. "Come on in. Sorry, that's about all the French I got."

"That's okay," I say, taking in the place. There's a long row of sneakers along the wall, a bench covered in unopened mail, and a bike cluttering the hallway. The furniture is mismatched, but the brown couch looks cozy enough. It's thrilling to see my first real New York City apartment. Papa and Miguel's place doesn't count—it's manicured and sophisticated, so adult. This one is gritty and homespun, with all the makings of dreams waiting to happen. It's the kind of place I want for myself, but less boyish. Ben pops his head out of the kitchen, wiping his hands on an apron just as Karim disappears behind a door.

"Bienvenue," Ben says, motioning for me to follow him into the kitchen. It's small, with barely any counter space. A large stockpot simmers on the stove—almost full to the brim and bursting with the aromas of onions and salty stock.

For a moment, I'm at Chez l'ami Janou, Maman's restaurant. I resist the urge to open the cutlery drawer—I wouldn't know which one it is anyway—and dip a spoon in the pot.

"I thought you were making onion soup for *me*?" I say jokingly. "Who's going to eat all this?"

"I always make food for an army. That's what it's about for me. Bringing people together, sharing one of the most primal experiences we can have as human beings." He lets out a laugh and then adds, "That, and the fact that my roommates suck at cooking. They'll starve if I don't feed them."

"Respect, my friend. That's very noble of you."

I take a seat at the kitchen counter. Ben goes on to explain his long history with batch cooking while stirring the soup. Growing up, most of his family lived nearby: grandparents, aunts, uncles, cousins. There was an unspoken open-door policy; anyone could drop by at any moment. When dinnertime came, they never asked people if they wanted to stay, just pulled out extra plates and served whatever they had on hand. They'd never have missed an opportunity to share a meal with loved ones.

"I'm also going to need more info on that onion soup." I sneak glances at the pot; the smell is so intoxicating it makes my mouth water.

"*Évidemment.* Of course, you need good baguette to soak up the juice," he says, scooping a piece from the pot to prove his point. "But I think the real trick is taking the time to caramelize the onions to perfection."

"Do you also make your own stock?" It's not like I'm trying to quiz him, but I need to know how serious he is about this. It's onion soup we're talking about. Real French business.

He scoffs in mock outrage as he brings a spoonful to his face to smell the mixture. "Of course, you can't make anything worthwhile quickly." Then, he pulls two bowls from the cupboard and turns to me. "I'm cooking the most classic French dish for a French girl. Do you really think I'm taking shortcuts here? The pressure is real."

He's joking, but there's a tightness to his voice. I don't know how to react to that. We're colleagues. We're friends. We're co-founders of Operation Find Zach. We're just . . . hanging out. Aren't we?

Traditional onion soup is *gratinée,* meaning it goes under the broiler so that the thick layer of cheese on top gets this beautiful glow. Soon, the scent of onion mixes with a new one: melted, broiled Gruyère. A few minutes later, Ben scoots next to me at the counter. We're ready to eat.

To be honest, September is too early in the year for onion soup. It's a comforting dish, something you whip up in the dead of winter, when you need to wrap yourself in warmth and gooeyness. But this isn't just a soup, it's the embodiment of French cuisine, a celebration of rustic pleasures, the elevation of basics—onions, stock, bread, and cheese—into something iconic yet unpretentious. And it's obvious it was made with love. Friendship, I mean. It was made with *friendship*.

I grab my spoon, the anticipation simmering inside me. I grin at Ben and he smiles back. It's like we're having a moment . . . with the soup.

"I'm going for it," I say, taking my eyes off him.

The cheesy layer on top is thick, uninterrupted, and it takes some wiggling to break through. When I do, I twirl around the bowl, assessing the surroundings. Finally I scoop out my spoon, which is filled with onions, broth, and a small piece of perfectly soggy bread. Ben doesn't say a word. In fact I'm pretty sure he's holding his breath as I take my first bite.

The flavors burst in my mouth, the taste of home hitting front on. Ben stares at me sideways, and I feel like a food critic whose verdict has the potential to make or break his future. I take another spoonful while he clenches his jaw, the veneer over his smiling face cracking just a bit. Is it mean that I kind of enjoy that?

Finally, I admit it. "Oh my god, you really are the best."

I'm not sure if this is what I actually meant to say, or if my tongue just twisted. A flash goes through the air as our eyes lock and we exchange a look that is . . . hard to describe. I clear my throat and put my spoon down. "It's really hot, though. I might need a minute."

Ben chuckles awkwardly. "Sure. For now can I just enjoy the fact that my onion soup impressed a French cook?"

"*Oui, Chef.* Any French restaurant would definitely take you as an apprentice."

His smile drops instantly. "That would be amazing but it's not part of the plan."

"Plans *should* be amazing."

"My dad's already getting on my back about finding a better-paying job. He doesn't understand that I'm working toward something bigger. I can't imagine the look on his face if I told him I was suddenly moving to France."

"But you're a line cook at Nutrio! Give me his phone number; I'll tell him what a huge deal that is."

Ben doesn't laugh at my joke, just sighs loudly. "I asked to borrow some money and that did not go well. Raven keeps saying she's going to give me more shifts, but it's still not happening."

"It will! Remember what you told me, you gotta ask. And ask again."

"Sure, but in the meantime, my dad is using that against me. My plans aren't happening fast enough."

"I'm sorry. That sounds painful. Honestly, my mom doesn't believe in me, either. For years she thought I was joking about moving to New York. Now that I'm here, all I get is comments about how hard life is here. How the restaurant business is so tough in the city, and that I look so tired. She keeps asking if they are treating me okay and reminds me constantly that I could just come home if it doesn't work out. It sounds supportive from the outside but I know what she means by it. Little Bambi can't handle the big city."

It feels good to get that off my chest with someone who understands.

Ben shakes his head, like he's as worked up about this as I am. "Can't they see how hard we work for what we want?"

I shrug. "I think my mom cares more about what she wants for me. Which is exactly the opposite of what she did."

"What's that?"

I tell him about how she moved to New York at around my age to be a chef, met Franklin Boyd, then my dad, worked hard and had so much fun, until I came along.

Ben's eyes open wide. "I didn't know you were born here!"

I nod. "But I don't remember anything. We moved back to France when I was two. My mom found a job at a restaurant near where she grew up, and then she took over the business when the owners retired. She doesn't say it explicitly, but I know she wants me to be next in line, when it's time."

Ben raises an eyebrow. "Wouldn't that be great, though?"

"No offense, but I don't think you understand small-town life. Like, on Sundays, birds chirping in the garden is the hot gossip . . . because there's no one else around."

"You have a garden? That's the ultimate luxury."

"Right, but it's also a lot of work. Maman grows her own vegetables, all organic, so she can serve the freshest food. I used to spend my mornings going around with my watering can before school."

Ben smirks. "Organic vegetables on your doorstep? Yeah, I'm definitely not going to feel sorry for you there."

"Okay, well, you're used to working in one of the most beautifully designed restaurants in the city. Look at this."

I whip out my phone to show him pictures of Maman's restaurant: the square tables covered in gingham tablecloths which have been washed a million times, the dark red leather booths, the tarnished antique mirror on which the *menu du jour* is handwritten in cursive lettering, and the mismatched chandeliers dangling from the ceiling. It's all so old-fashioned. Just old, actually. Not to mention the fact that it's about one-tenth of Nutrio's size.

But when I look up, Ben is glowing. "It's cozy."

"It's dark."

"It's charming."

"Some would say stuffy."

"And it's only an hour and a half from Paris?"

"It's closer to two hours!" I counter, a little too loudly.

Ben lets out a laugh. Even I heard how ridiculous that sounded.

"Come on, Margot. It all seems pretty dreamy." He points at my screen. "And look at all these glowing reviews! You have a restaurant waiting for you. When it's yours, you can do whatever you want with it, even get different tablecloths. Imagine that!"

I don't tell him that I kind of love the tablecloths. They're so soft now. I also don't mention that Chez l'ami Janou received a Bib Gourmand symbol, because Maman's food is truly outstanding. And while that's not a Michelin star, it's still pretty great.

"But it's not New York," I say, to close out the topic. "New York is like nothing else in the entire world."

"Cheers to that," Ben says, raising his almost empty bowl of soup.

We refill our bowls and keep talking for what feels like hours.

Ben has many family stories from their time in France—his grandfather, a history buff, was so emotional when he first visited the D-day beaches in Normandy, and his grandmother still talks about the *grands magasins* where she shopped in Paris.

There's plenty to gossip about Nutrio, too. Bertrand is being courted by another restaurant uptown, and Chef would be devastated if he left. Erica has started dating one of the other waitresses, and there's a rumor that Chef and Raven had an affair while she was with her ex-boyfriend. Ben says that last one like I should find this scandalous, but isn't he the one who told me emotions run high in a kitchen?

"I'll walk you back to the subway," Ben says when I'm ready to go.

I think about protesting but I still feel like a New York newbie, and everything looks different in the dark. Deep down I'm a country girl, and from a different country, at that. I'm used to riding my bike through sunflower fields, not taking underground trains in the middle of the night.

Outside, you'd never be able to tell that it's late on a Monday. Crowds spill out of restaurants and bars, a cheerful buzz in the crisp air. Sometimes I wonder why New York even bothers with days of the week. There's no slowing down, no rhythm to this city. The vibe is different on this side of the river, young and chill, but it's still just people and parties and effervescence everywhere. I can't believe that I get to be a part of this. This is the kind of night I always thought I'd have with Zach: eating great food, walking around this magical place, and talking for hours. Still, tonight has been wonderful, and it's all thanks to Ben.

He has an unlimited MetroCard, so he offers to walk me onto the subway platform. Once again, I don't protest: twice last week I found myself on the wrong train, including when I accidentally took the express one and couldn't get off until I was halfway up Central Park.

Downstairs, the screen tells me that the L is coming in three minutes.

"I had a great time," I say, feeling the clock ticking.

"*Moi aussi.* We—" Ben pauses, takes a breath. "We should do it again."

"*Oui!*" My mouth suddenly feels dry. "Maybe next time I can cook you something from my repertoire."

"I would love that."

These four simple words send sparks up and down my body. Ben steps toward me, and my mind starts to scramble. The way he looks at me, the way *I feel* when he looks at me . . . I'm just not sure how we're supposed to leave it there. How do you say goodbye to a friend-slash-colleague-slash-not-a-date? Because this wasn't a date. Still isn't a date. But also . . . Is this a date?

And just when I think I can't be more confused, Ben comes even closer.

"So, um," he says, "I wanted to tell you that Olivia and I, well, we're . . ."

On the other side of the platform, a train swooshes in, drowning out the rest of Ben's sentence. A few seconds later, it departs again, clearing the view to the other side, where a few people have stepped off. That's when I see him. His blond hair is slightly longer. His blue backpack is the same. His jaw is just as square. This time, I know it's him. I feel it in my heart, in my bones.

"ZACH!" I call out at the top of my lungs. He's so close. *So close.* "ZACH!"

I only have a split second to act.

Running off and up the stairs, I scan the entire station. My heart knocks against my chest, my temples pulsing. There's a flow of people coming from the other side of the platform and I have no idea if Zach might be among them, or he's already left.

"ZACH! ZACH! ZACH!" I'm screaming and panting and hopeful and scared at the same time. It was him. He's here. This isn't like at the airport.

But no one moves. I spin around, feeling the seconds slip away from me. Then I make another mad dash up the stairs, to the outside. He *has* to be here.

I call his name again and again. People brush past me, ignoring me, none of them Zach.

I lost him. Again. I know I did, and yet I can't accept it.

The universe can't be doing this to me. *New York* can't be doing this to me.

And yet, Zach is gone.

Chapter Sixteen

When I make my way back down to the Manhattan side, Ben, too, has vanished. It's not that I expected him to wait for me, exactly, but I don't want to be alone right now. I feel like the sky has fallen on my head: one moment I was having the best night, and the next I'm reminded of how much I'm missing out, how my dream adventure with Zach just fizzled and disappeared. I look for Ben everywhere, my stomach queasy. He was going to tell me something about Olivia. The whole evening is ending on a bad note, and I feel like it's my fault.

Sorry about that! I text him. I can't believe I missed him again. The soup was amazing. Merci!

I stare at my phone as I wait for the train, during the whole journey, and as I walk home on the other side.

Ben's response doesn't come until I'm in front of our building, fishing inside my bag for my keys.

No worries

That's it? Two little words? This isn't Ben. He's always said he wanted to help me find Zach, even before we really knew each other. I mean, it was *his* idea. I'm not sure I would ever have let myself hope that this could happen if Ben hadn't encouraged me. And look, we did find Zach! Ben should be happy for me. I want to text him again, but I'm not sure what to say.

I still don't know by the time our next shift together rolls around, on Friday. We haven't texted since Monday, even though I thought about it many times. I was itching to suggest another Zach adventure, but Ben's icy response stopped me every time I opened our message thread.

Ben is in the locker room when I come in, but so are some of the waiters and two of the prep girls. I'm not sure if I'm relieved or disappointed.

"Hey," I say to all of them, my eyes firmly on Ben.

"Hey," the others respond. Ben just nods with a half-smile.

Could it be worse than I thought?

"Bambi! Are you taking a coffee break between each dish or what?"

Ari may be gone, but Chef is most definitely here: watching my every move, breathing down my neck, waiting for me to fail. At least that's how it feels. He's never called me Bambi before—I figured that was beneath him—but tonight is different. Weekends are relentless: the first patrons arrive around six p.m., and we don't get to breathe until the last orders have gone out around eleven, sometimes even later. There's so much more pressure on the line.

"Coming right up!" I yell across the room, when I've barely even started on a dish.

"Just a second!"

"I'm on it!"

"Chef, oui, Chef!"

I don't know if I'm fooling anyone, but I'm definitely not fooling myself. I thought dishwashing was grueling, but I didn't know the meaning of the word. All throughout the night, my timing is off. I start on something too early and it has to sit there, getting in the way of other dishes, or I miscalculate and finish up too late, delaying everyone else: the hot station, the sous-chef, Chef, and even the waiters. I'll be lucky if one person in this kitchen still tolerates me by the end of the night.

"If you keep this up, I'm putting you back on dishwashing!" Chef grunts at some point.

No one comes to my rescue—Raven is understanding, but she doesn't stand up to Chef unless she absolutely has to—and Ben is too busy keeping up to even look in my direction.

I manage to make it through the shift, but the night is a total blur of yelling and feeling like I'm messing up. Before I know it, we're all putting containers away and wiping down our stations. I can barely stand on my own two feet as I make my way to Chef.

"I'll do better tomorrow, I swear. I won't let you down."

He snarls in response.

On the bright side, it takes me so long to change back into my street clothes—every part of my body hurts—that when I'm done, it's just Ben and me in the locker room.

"Hi," I say, tentatively. We haven't spoken all night, and it feels weird. *Too* weird.

"Hey. Tonight was a lot, huh?"

"Yeah . . . I probably shouldn't admit that out loud, but I don't know what hit me."

Ben slams his locker shut and comes closer. "You're gonna have to hang on, Margot. Chef does that with the younger crew. We have to prove ourselves over and over if we want to make our mark. There's no choice. Nothing's going to be handed to us on a silver platter."

I hear his own frustration behind this, and maybe some fear that my subpar performance might reflect poorly on him. Every chef has their own trusted circle, their preferred staff. If we want to break in, we have to work twice as hard while keeping our heads all the way down. It'll be months—years even!—before Chef considers me one of his own. But am I going to be able to keep up like this? I'm not sure.

For now, I just want to change the subject. "I'm sorry about the other night," I say as we make our way through the mostly dark and empty restaurant.

Outside the air is biting, a stark contrast from the humid heat of the kitchen. I button up the flimsy cardigan I'm wearing. Luz and I will need to plan a winter shopping session stat. Ben shrugs in response. We're both going in the same direction—him to the Union Square subway station to catch the L, and me farther southwest to the West Village.

"I want to keep looking for him," I add. Between work, wedding stuff, and catching up with my friends and family back home, it's almost impossible to fit in Operation Find Zach. Even when I have time, it's hard not to be discouraged when all of my leads turn out to be dead ends. But after seeing him the other night, I know it's a sign. I *have* to keep looking. "I'm thinking of going to Bushwick on Monday," I add.

Zach had mentioned a famous pizza place in Brooklyn near a few blocks covered in funky murals, and Ben had immediately thought of Roberta's.

"Cool," Ben says, not really looking at me.

My throat tightens. Something is obviously off, but I keep pushing through. "I know I'm probably not going to find him there, but we started this thing and . . ." Maybe it's the arduous shift or the roller coaster of emotions I've been going through since coming so close to Zach, but I feel beaten-down, not like myself. And Ben, who is always so warm, so kind, so *available,* is giving me nothing. "Do you want to go together?"

My voice sounds small. I feel like I'm begging.

"Monday, huh? I'm busy then. Family things going on."

"Oh," I try hard to hide my disappointment. "Everything all right?"

Deep down my mind is spinning. Is that an excuse?

"Yeah, don't worry about it."

"Okay, I guess it doesn't have to be Monday. We could . . ."

I trail off. After last Monday night, I feel like I need to double down on finding Zach, that it needs to happen *now* or else it never will. But I don't want to do it without Ben. This is our thing. And we're friends. Aren't we?

"You should go as soon as you can, Margot. You're the kind of girl who goes after her dreams, and finding Zach is all that matters to you, right?"

"Well, it's not all—" I grip my handbag's strap, uneasy.

Ben shrugs again. I stop talking.

"I'm sorry, I can't," he says.

My mind goes to Olivia, the girl he's dating, and my insides twist. I want to ask more about her, about what he was going to say the night of the onion soup, but it's clear he's not in a talking mood. Besides, it feels like that conversation was a million years ago now.

We stop in front of the subway steps.

Ben looks down, ready to leave. "I hope you find him. I really wish that for you."

"Ben, I—"

"And if you do, *when* you do, I hope it was all worth it."

Then he's gone, and I don't think I've felt more alone since I arrived in this city.

Chapter Seventeen

Monday morning, Luz and I are sprawled on a bench in Washington Square Park. I'm not working until the afternoon, and she only had a couple of early classes. We have coffees in hand and sunbeams on our faces, and someone in the park is playing a piano. It's a beautiful October day in New York City.

"You still haven't told me about your date with David," I say, after taking a sip.

"Do you really want to hear about it?"

Of course we've already debriefed via text message, but we haven't had a chance to properly talk until now.

"Why wouldn't I?"

She grimaces.

"Oh, you think because my love life is such an absolute disaster, I don't want to hear about yours? No, *guapa*. I still love love. I'll never *not* want to hear about a romantic night between you and your mystery man. Lay it on me."

Luz seems to give it a thought, but then caves in. "I like him.

He's really sweet, and kept asking if I enjoyed the food or if I wanted anything else. He seemed to care if I was having a good time, a lot. And I was."

"So you said." I keep sipping on my coffee, waiting for the rest.

"He's kind of shy," Luz continues. "Or maybe he's not shy but just . . . uncomfortable? When I ask a question, he'll answer with one quick thing, and then I have to probe him to get more. You know I'm a talker"—I chuckle in agreement—"and it feels so awkward when there's a lull in the conversation. Like, I can't fill the blank space *all* the time."

"I'm sure you could," I say jokingly, "but I understand that it'd be nice if you didn't talk by yourself all night."

Luz shoots me a look. "You're making fun of me."

"Lo siento."

We sip our drinks in silence for a moment, before Luz adds, "He's a very good kisser. Like, my god, the *best.*"

I let out a long, envious sigh. Zach was, *is,* a great kisser, too. Definitely *my* best. I still remember every single one of our kisses, that's how incredible they were.

"That certainly enters into consideration," I say.

I'm trying to sound lighthearted, but maybe I did lie to Luz earlier. Hearing about this hurts a little. It reminds me of what I don't have, of what I can't seem to make happen. I should be happy. I'm in New York, working my dream job, living my best life. Well, when I have a minute anyway. Zach was going to be a gorgeous cherry on top of the world's most delicious cake. And I love the cake but can I really live without the cherry? I came so close. How am I supposed to let it go? And why would I want to?

Luz interrupts my chain of thought. "So, what are we doing today?"

I didn't tell her until now, because part of me was hoping that Ben would change his mind and that we would do this together. We both worked over the weekend, but we haven't spoken since he disappeared down to the subway on Friday. I shake the thought away and explain the plan to Luz: pizza and street art in Bushwick, with maybe, *just maybe,* a Zach sighting along the way. It's an easy sell.

We get up and start walking toward the subway station.

"I know you and I have different views on love, but is this really what you want?" Luz says.

"Pizza?"

She raises an eyebrow. "Margot!" I'm acting all innocent, so she continues. "I don't want you to get hurt. What if you never find Zach?"

"I did find him. I looked for him everywhere around the city, and there he was, when I least expected it."

"But—" Luz stops herself. We both know what she's going to say. What if it wasn't him? What if I wanted to see him so much that I made it up in my mind? And then, when I told her all about what happened, she made me recite every detail of my night with Ben, down to his tone when he said he wasn't available today.

We go down the stairs.

"Margot, I'm not telling you to give up—"

"That's exactly what you're doing. I'm not proud of how things went down with Ben. We had a great night and then . . . I just ran off. I know he's mad at me, and I hate that. But now I feel like I have to find Zach even more. It has to have all been for something."

"Okay," Luz says. "I'll stop."

The trip to Bushwick takes about forty-five minutes, and I look for Zach all the way, just like I've done every time I've roamed around the city. I've searched for him on packed trains and busy sidewalks. I've scanned every store and coffee shop I entered. I've straight-up stared at guys who even remotely looked like him, doing comical double takes, my head whipping sideways, my heart skipping a beat. I hold my breath, narrow my eyes. I hope. I allow myself to hope. Luz watches me. Sometimes her eyes seem to say, *Is that him? Is it happening?* And others, I notice a twinge of irritation on her face.

"You know," Luz says as we get out on the street, "I'm not mad about this part of Operation Find Zach. I've been meaning to come here forever."

Bushwick is a far cry from Manhattan, but like everywhere else in this city, this neck of the woods has its own vibe. Every other building looks rusty, with corrugated walls covered in graffiti, and interrupted by large fenced-in parking garages, where trucks are lined up. Electric poles create stripes against the blue sky, only adding to the industrial feel of the neighborhood. Among this, Roberta's and its bright red entrance are easy to spot. It's all very, *very* cool.

"See, my plans aren't all bad." I force a smile, but the truth is that I wish I were here with Ben. And not just so we could have a passionate debate about our ranking of various Italian cheeses. I tend to think that Gorgonzola is underrated, when mozzarella unfairly gets so much of the spotlight. The fact is, Ben's the one who figured out the clue.

Because it's a weekday, we don't have to wait for a table. Roberta's is quite full, though, with about half of the wooden tables covered in round metal trays, the smell of pepper and basil floating in the air. Young, tattooed, vintage-clad people sip on beers and juices, nibbling on bread and marinated olives as they wait for the main attraction.

Luz and I decide on grilled sweet corn to start with, and the white and greens pizza with mozzarella, mustard greens, lemon, and Parmigiano. With that out of the way, I repeat the same song and dance I've performed all over town: showing Zach's picture to anyone willing to look. Shrugs ensue. Heads are shaken. *Don't know him. A lot of people come through here.* I smile and thank them all. I don't want them to notice how tired I am of hearing this. Zach is nowhere. I get it. This is hopeless.

The pizza is out of this world. You can find pizza anywhere, probably within a few minutes of where you happen to be. It might even be the one food that needs no translation. Pizza just is, in all its splendid simplicity. Flour, water, and salt, topped with a few carefully chosen ingredients that go perfectly together. Tomato sauce and basil. Ricotta, garlic, and olive oil. Sausage, mushrooms, and red onion. The possibilities are endless.

New Yorkers, I've noticed, are more than a little proud of their pizza. I've read my fair share of "Best Pizza in the City" lists, and none of them seem to agree. My opinion on the topic? There's no such thing as best, because that means different things to different people. Me, I like my dough chewy, rather than crisp. A little charred, but never burned. This one was perfect down to the last bite.

Bushwick is not just famous for Roberta's, but for the many streets featuring entire walls of street art. We're not talking about graffiti, but intricate paintings stretching for meters and meters, wrapping around buildings, in every style imaginable. A leopard walking against a bright blue background here, pretty pink peonies covering up the entrance to a parking garage there. It's almost like an amusement park.

"I'm sorry this didn't work," Luz says as we pass a gang of smiling skulls. "What're you going to do now?"

I let out a deep sigh. "It was never going to happen anyway, right?" I have *nothing* to go off except for this list and some pictures taken in the dark Paris night.

"Margot, it's okay if you want to give up. Think about the big picture. You wanted an adventure, and isn't that exactly what you're getting? Sometimes things just don't pan out, and that's okay."

"I wanted an adventure *and* an epic love story. Why do I have to choose? And what if I'm about to find him? What if all it takes is one more try?"

Luz answers with a contrite look. When it comes to Zach, there are no answers, only questions.

I'm checking the map on my phone, figuring out where we should walk next, when something catches my eye. "Williamsburg is not far from here," I say, zooming out.

A spark lights in Luz's eyes. "That's where you saw Zach, right?" I nod. "Come on," she says, grabbing my hand. "I have an idea."

She won't tell me what it is until we're back in the subway, getting off at Bedford Avenue, near where Ben lives. My heart pinches when I recognize the small bodega on the corner, overflowing with buckets of flowers at the front.

"Here's my question," Luz says as we stand near the subway entrance that Zach must have used that night. "Maybe he was just passing through. He was visiting a friend, or going out for drinks." My mind pauses on that "friend" and who she might be, but I shake the thought away. "Or," Luz continues, "that's his usual commute. He could be living or working around here."

I start to spin around slowly, studying everything, buzzing with possibility.

"You're not going to find him like this," Luz says, walking toward a lamppost. A few flyers and stickers are taped around it. One says "VOTE" and another is offering guitar lessons. There's a phone number repeated over and over, so people can tear off the piece of paper and keep it.

"I've always wanted to learn to play the guitar," I say. Luz opens her eyes wide, like I'm very much missing the point. "We should make a poster for Zach!" I add, the lightbulb finally going on.

"Mais oui!"

We find a stoop to sit on, and hunch over my phone to write it up.

Looking for Zach, I type.

"No, wait. You need to make it interesting or no one will read it," Luz says.

I nod. "New Yorkers have no time for anything, right?"

"You're learning," Luz says with a chuckle.

We both think on it some more, and then she offers, "LOST, cute guy answering to the name of ZACH."

"Ooh, yes. *Very* cute guy."

"We're going to need more of a description." Luz taps on my shoulder like it's going to make me go faster.

Blond, tall, I add.

"Last seen—" Luz says, nudging me on.

Last seen under the Eiffel Tower

"What about when you saw him on the subway?" Luz says.

I shrug. "'Last seen on the platform of the Bedford Avenue stop' doesn't have the same ring to it. And how many Zachs do you think pass by here every day? Whereas how many Zachs pass by here *and* have been to the Tour Eiffel?"

"Good point."

We debate each word choice for a while longer, and finally come up with this:

LOST

Very cute guy answering to ZACH.
Blond. Tall. Dreamy (objectively).
Last seen under the twinkling lights of the Eiffel
Tower after a magical night last summer.
The universe is calling, Zach. Answer by texting
347-330-1994.
Bisous, Margot (remember me?)

Then, Luz and I run to the closest copy shop and ask them to print twenty copies.

"Or should I get even more?" I say, turning to Luz. "If we're going to do this, we need to paper the town. This is my last shot."

"There's no such thing as a last shot, but sure," Luz says.

The pages feel warm straight out of the printer, or maybe it's just that my palms are sweaty. Before we leave, I buy a roll of tape and a pair of scissors. Then, Luz, my hopes, and I take to the streets of Williamsburg. We go about it methodically, post after post after post. A few people stop to read our sign as soon as it's taped up, filling me with glee. I lean over trash cans, avoid dog leashes, and almost get knocked over by delivery men on their electric bikes. Soon, my plea is all over the neighborhood.

After putting up the last sign, we step back to admire our work.

"Do you feel like we helped the universe enough?" Luz says with a smile.

"Yes," I say, delighted.

But I see it on her face: this is funny to her, just an idle way to spend the afternoon. Zach and I had a lovely night a year ago, and our big plan of meeting in Times Square simply fell through. I'm not sure she ever believed that it could happen, that it *would*. But she wasn't there that night. I don't think I ever opened up to someone the way I did with Zach. I told him about my biggest fears: how I worried I'd never be as good a cook as my mother, or that I wouldn't be able to forge my own path. I shared with him how I craved coming to New York for my entire childhood, always disappointed when my dad made the trip to visit us instead. I talked about my friends, whom I adore, but who never fully understood why I needed to get out of our small town so badly. All the while,

Zach listened. He wrapped me tighter in his arms, and made me feel more understood than I ever had. I need that feeling again.

I can't just keep on going, thinking like he didn't really mean it, that he lied about wanting to be with me again. Did he just forget about me? Did he never plan to meet me in Times Square? No, I can't even go there, it would be too sad.

Still, I feel like I'm rapidly exhausting my chances. Or maybe I already have. If this doesn't work, if Zach doesn't come to me after I've tried so hard to go after him, then at least I've gone down swinging.

Chapter Eighteen

With only three weeks go to before the wedding, I'm a little nervous to hear Raven say that Chef's going to need all hands on deck for the foreseeable future.

"We're starting to ramp up for the holidays," she explains to me at the end of the night as we're taking a quick break in the back alley. I've stopped looking for rats, though I still jump a little when the wind blows a lone black plastic bag. "Between now and January, it's a looooong stretch. Be warned."

I didn't realize the grueling hours I've been working could get any longer, but I have noticed the change in the air. Luz is in the swing of things at school, the wedding plans are pretty much sorted, pumpkins are everywhere, and Halloween decorations have taken over the streets. It's like I've gone through five different versions of New York already, and I've been here just over two months.

"Chef's finalizing the holiday menu and his investors are coming by soon."

"To do what?" I say, curious. Maman definitely doesn't have investors for Chez l'ami Janou, no one to answer to. She just makes good food and people like it enough to come back. The end.

Raven shrugs. It seems like everything rolls off her back, which might be the best way to survive when you work so closely with Chef Boyd. "They like to check that the place is in order, that their money is well spent. It's about their investment, of course, but many of them want to back a restaurant that has a certain cachet, too. They couldn't trim an asparagus to save their lives, but they want to be able to say that they have a hand in Nutrio's success, that our artichoke purée wouldn't exist without them."

"They sound like no fun." I'm teasing, but Raven just nods.

"We don't need them to be fun, just to keep giving us money. And that is where you come in."

"Me?" No doubt I look surprised. Money is not exactly my forte. I've been able to save since moving here, but only because I'm getting free room and board, which is clearly the ultimate privilege in New York. All in all, my savings don't amount to much. I understand why Ben's dad gets on his case about that.

"You and all the other cooks," Raven says, an eyebrow raised. "Chef's doing tryouts of the new menu during the day, before the dinner service." My eyes light up, and Raven smiles. "I thought you'd like that. So can I count on you tomorrow, around twelve?"

I was supposed to be off then, but I can't miss an opportunity to cook with Chef.

When I come in the next day, I learn that he's planned to work with two cooks at a time to perfect the menu until it's ready. I'm both terrified and delighted to discover that I'm paired with Ben for the afternoon.

It's been a couple of weeks since the night of the onion soup, and we don't really talk anymore. I've wanted to suggest we hang out once or twice, but then I overheard Ben tell another cook about a franchise that is opening a few more outposts in the city soon. I know that's part of his plans, the next item on his list. I've also seen him buried in a celebrity chef's memoir at every break, so it's obvious that he's focusing on his career right now, the logical next steps. It makes me sad, honestly. I can't believe Ben really wants to work at a restaurant like that.

"All right," Chef says when the three of us gather in one corner of the kitchen, while the others prepare for the dinner service at their respective stations. "Here are the two items we're working on." He turns to Ben. "A green pasta with peas, kale, lemon, and ricotta," and then, to me, "and a beautiful crispy ratatouille."

Now I understand why he wanted the French girl on the job. Ratatouille is one of Maman's specialties—but unfortunately, I can't just text her for tips. Chef has a policy that we're not allowed to bring our phones inside the kitchen: not only are they covered in germs, but people get so easily distracted trying to sneak a glance at their screens.

He puts down the list of ingredients in front of us, written in an indecipherable scrawl, but I don't need to read it to know what goes into a ratatouille. Ben and I waste no time heading to the walk-in to retrieve what we need.

Him: fresh rigatoni, handmade on site by one of the prep

cooks; green peas; long leaves of kale, still on the stem; a few lemons; and a container of fresh ricotta.

Me: lots and lots of vegetables, including tomatoes, eggplants, zucchinis, red peppers, and yellow squash; a jug of olive oil; and a handful of garlic cloves.

We prep things in silence next to each other, while Chef goes to talk with Bertrand. It never ceases to amaze me how little cooking he actually does day to day. Maman is not just the chef at Chez l'ami Janou, she's the main cook, the person behind every dish, start to finish.

But in a big restaurant like this, chefs spend much of their time doing, well, pretty much anything else. Meeting with suppliers, checking stock, refining the menu, interviewing staff, schmoozing investors. And while every dish does pass his hands before it's served up, often that might just mean that Chef is the one brushing on the *sauce au vin,* or checking that the onion confit has the right amount of sweetness to it.

While Ben snaps off the kale stems and puts water to boil on the stove, I get on with the business of chopping all the vegetables in neat little cubes.

I came to New York for something new and different, but there's only one way to make ratatouille: Maman's. I can practically hear her coach me, like she used to. *In ratatouille, the most important ingredient is patience,* she'd always say. I'd roll my eyes, but she was right. You could try cooking the vegetables all together, saving yourself gobs of time in the process. But then you'd end up with mushy zucchini or underdone eggplant. Each of these need their own special attention, and a precise cooking time. That, and an ungodly amount of olive oil.

Once my first batch of vegetables is sautéing on the stove, I head back to the walk-in to rummage through the herbs we have in stock: fresh oregano calls to me first, though I'm always partial to basil. And then there are *herbes de Provence,* which enhance pretty much any dish. I bring back a few jars and stems, then lay them out onto the counter.

"I need an opinion," I say to Ben. His corner is covered in squeezed lemon halves, the acidic smell filling the air between us. Next to him, the blender—packed with cooked kale and toasted garlic—is going full force. "*Herbes de Provence* is the right move here, *oui ou non?*"

Chef simply wrote *herbs* on his list, and I wonder if he was being vague on purpose, to test me.

"*Absolument,*" Ben says. He lowers his voice, like he's about to tell me a secret. "But if I were you, I'd add some red pepper flakes for a little kick."

I nod, considering it. Ratatouille can be subtle in taste, once the tomato sauce is mixed in. A little something extra can't hurt. In fact, it might be just the thing to make it sing.

The blender stops, and Ben removes the lid. "Will you taste this for me?" He hands me a spoon. "How much lemon is too much lemon?"

I dip my spoon in and put the sauce on the top of my tongue so my taste buds can decide. "I think you could add just a touch more."

Chef checks in on us a few times. He asks several questions, but his expression remains neutral as we answer. Now I'm worried. Was it too risky to make this dish the old-fashioned way? It's not really Nutrio's style. I feel like I'm on one of those cooking shows. I won't know if I've succeeded until it's too late to change the course of action.

Finally, Ben and I are ready. His pasta and my vegetables are cooked. Our respective sauces are smooth and done. We don't need to worry about presentation; that will be Chef's job, once the dish has been perfected.

Chef grabs a fork and digs into my creation first. After bringing it to his mouth, he chews for a few seconds, his eyes narrowing as he focuses on the flavors.

The wait is excruciating, but finally the verdict comes. "Your onions aren't soft enough. I think they could have used a few more minutes."

"Got it," I say, cursing myself. Undercooked onions? Rookie mistake.

He takes a few more bites, during which I hold my breath. Ben, too, is very still next to me. I don't know if he's worried about me or himself, but the pressure is on.

Finally Chef nods as he puts his fork back down, his lips pinched. "Okay, Margot. Now I know why I put you on the line."

I take a deep breath, trying to keep my cool. This is clearly the best compliment I'll ever get. I consider giving him a hug, but that would be so very not French of me, not to mention unprofessional. Still, I can't help it, I turn to Ben, my face frozen in a silly grin. He smiles brightly, the look of a friend who's genuinely happy for me. His tan skin glows against the white of his jacket, the light stubble on his chin giving him a bit of an edge. For a moment, it feels like everything is good between us again.

Chef makes a few comments about his dish too—even more lemon, is his verdict, but slightly less ricotta so the dish doesn't feel too heavy—and then Ben and I are off the hook.

"I'm happy for you!" Ben says as soon as Chef leaves us.

Everyone else is gone, too; it's family mealtime. We can hear them talking in the background, but here, in the kitchen, we're on our own.

I want to celebrate, I really do, but there's something more pressing. This is the only alone time I've had with Ben for a while, and I have to tell him what's on my mind. "I'm sad that we don't hang out anymore. I miss you."

My throat catches at the end, my confession coming out raspy and weird.

Ben avoids my gaze as he grabs onto discarded kale stems before throwing them in the compost pile. "I've been busy."

I let out a sigh, which comes out louder than I intended. The truth is, I know he's been busy. I don't blame him for not having time to indulge my fantasies of finding Zach. But Ben was my friend, and then he wasn't and that just . . . doesn't work for me.

Ben studies me, pursing his lips. A few seconds pass before he speaks. "I missed you, too."

"I really didn't mean to leave you there that night. It was shitty of me."

"It's not that." His voice is soft, measured. "You thought you saw Zach. . . . I don't blame you for running after him."

But there's hurt in his eyes and it makes my heart twist. "Ben . . ."

I wonder if he's seen the posters around his neighborhood, if he thinks I've gone too far.

"No, wait. Let me just say this." He wipes his hands on his apron and turns to me. "I think you're great, Margot, and I really admire you for going after your dreams. I wish I were as brave as you."

"You *are* brave," I say. "You're working so hard and helping everyone around you. Plus, I know your dad's putting pressure on you and—"

Ben grunts, and I drop it. Silence hangs in the air between us.

"Hey," I finally say. "I want to ask . . ." I trail off, gathering the courage to continue. It's weird how nervous I am. Ben is the first friend I made in New York. I want him in my life. "Can we hang out again? Just for fun." I'm not sure how to say, *not for Zach.* "I know you have a lot going on, and my dad's wedding is coming up, but maybe we could find some time? If you want to, I mean."

Ben nods slowly. For one excruciating moment I think he might say no, and I'm not sure how I'll be able to keep a straight face. "I want to."

I smile in response. No, I beam. I don't think I've felt this happy since I saw Zach on the other side of the platform.

"Let's have a classic New York night," he adds.

"That sounds absolutely *parfait.*"

I may not know what a classic New York night entails, but I can't wait to find out.

Chapter Nineteen

The next few days are endless stretches of work—amazing and incredibly tiring—and I wake up on Sunday morning to find Papa sitting at the dining table, hunched over a notepad.

"Wedding vows," he explains when I ask what he's doing.

The paper is blank, only covered by a shiny black pen.

"How long have you been working on this?"

He leans back in the chair. "Words aren't really my thing, but Miguel's going to be hurt if I don't find something extra special to say. Isn't it weird to have to declare your feelings to someone you've already loved for years, in front of everyone you know?"

"I think that's called a wedding," I say, taking the seat next to him.

I'm still in my pajamas, my hair wild, my eyes puffy with sleep. I know this is what I wanted, but being on the line brings me to a level of exhaustion I'd never imagined before, both mentally and physically. Who knew dreams could be so draining?

Papa picks up his pen and stares at the piece of paper.

"Can't you just say that you're so excited to spend the rest of your life with him?"

"I think I'm supposed to go a bit deeper than that. Knowing Miguel, he'll have written five pages, and I'll be in tears before he's halfway through."

I kick my legs up on the chair next to me. They feel so sore, like they'd be happy if they never had to carry me again. "Why does love have to be so complicated? I wish you could fall in love with someone and be with them. Just be together and that's that."

Papa gives me a strange look. "Um, you *can* do that. It happens all the time. But I have a feeling we're not talking about my wedding vows anymore."

"Sorry."

I rub my eyes, trying to wake up.

"Are you okay, *ma chérie*?"

"Yeah—" This sounds fake, and we both know it.

"Talk to me. I feel like I've barely seen you since you got here. How's New York treating you?"

The truth is I'm not sure. So much has gone on since I got here and I haven't had a chance to process half of it. "You know how New York looks in the movies? The glamour, bright lights, the constant hustle and bustle, the city that never sleeps?" He nods. "Well . . . it's really like that. Which is great, but also freaking hard." I gesture widely. "All of this is a LOT."

Papa chuckles. "Yep. This city is fabulous, but it makes you work for it. The ride is bumpy but I think it's worth hanging on. There's no place like it."

"So bumpy! But yeah, I see what you mean. I've been here

three months, and sometimes it feels like I've never been anywhere else, like this is the only place in the world. New York or nothing."

"That's the spirit!" He scans the room to make sure we're alone, even though Miguel is out running errands. "But don't say that in front of Miguel. He keeps talking about living a quieter life in the sun, closer to his family."

This isn't a total surprise. Miguel dropped several hints that he wished they'd had the wedding in late summer, but their venue wasn't available then. They both agreed they didn't want to wait until next year, so they booked the first availability, in early November. Still, Miguel has been complaining about the fact that it might be too cold on their day.

"And what do you think about that?" I say.

Papa doesn't need to think about it. "Like you said. New York or nothing. And you do get used to everything. You'll see."

I've already stopped being startled every time I see the orange cones in the middle of the streets, the ones covering manholes, with sewage-y smoke rising from the top. I haven't jumped on the wrong train in weeks, and I never stop in the middle of the sidewalk anymore. Luz is so proud of me. But there are still so many things to learn, to explore. In the same day I can feel like I'm a total New Yorker *and* that I'll never understand all the unspoken rules it has.

"I will," I say, getting up.

My stomach is grumbling, asking for breakfast, though it's probably lunchtime by now. I go over to the kitchen and pull out the carton of milk. The fridge has been much better stocked since I've been here.

"And you should stop thinking so much and follow your heart. The words will come," I add, pointing my chin at his notepad.

Papa smiles. "Look at you, all grown up, giving me relationship advice."

"Don't blame me if it doesn't work out. I'm still figuring it out myself."

After breakfast, I leave Papa to his big, bold declarations—he wrote and crossed out four lines while I ate my granola—and get ready for the day.

Ben and I are hanging out later. I take a long shower, put some product in my hair so it goes wavy, and choose a dress Luz and I bought together. It's black with a floral print, fitted and a little short. It's not really "me," but I like what I see in the mirror. I know girls are not supposed to say that. We're meant to point out our crooked nose, round hips, or uneven teeth and never mention that we have a killer smile or lovely legs. I wonder who decided it should be that way.

But I don't care. And I bet New York doesn't, either.

Ben's jaw dropped when I told him I'd never had dim sum, and he insisted we correct this gap in my knowledge immediately. He had a hard time picking a place, he said, but finally settled on one of the oldest restaurants in Chinatown. Nom Wah Tea Parlor looks like it's straight out of a Wes Anderson movie. The name is inscribed in a whimsical yellow font against faded red-painted boards and—I assume—repeated in Cantonese. It's on Doyers Street, a winding little alley that's home to a few other restaurants and a speakeasy cocktail bar, but clearly *this* is the place to be.

Inside, it looks like a Chinese restaurant and an American diner had a baby: patterned tiles, numerous portraits hanging on the wall, metal stools at the counter, and red vinyl booths along the edges. There's a quaintness to it that makes me feel like we've stepped out of time, and away from the city.

"You look very pretty tonight," Ben says as we're led to our table.

I'm stumped; Ben has never commented on my outfits before. I'm glad he's not facing me, that he doesn't see me blush. I'm not a big blusher, usually, but sometimes I feel like New York is bringing out a different Margot. I'm still getting to know her.

"So do you," I reply.

Ben's wearing a black shirt and jeans. We're actually matching. His short hair is shiny and perfectly in place, his face closely shaven. He smells like mint and fresh air.

"*I'm* pretty?" There's an amused look on his face as we take our seats.

"Why not? It's a word, and more importantly, it's a compliment. Just take it."

Our eyes lock as a smile forms on his lips. There's something about the way Ben looks at me. It's like a visual hug, the reassurance that while I'm with him, everything will be okay. And not just because he's become my unofficial tour guide of the city.

"I gladly accept it." He shoots me an even bigger smile, and grabs one of the sheets of paper that are held together by two napkin dispensers, along with the pencil that's on the table. "This is how it works: you tick the box next to every dish you want to try, and then just hand it to the waiter."

I look over it. Everything is spelled out in Chinese next to the English translation. "You choose," I say, pushing the piece of paper back to him. "I trust you."

Frown lines appear between his eyebrows as he studies the menu. Then he starts ticking boxes. Shrimp dumplings. Scallion pancakes. Sticky rice. I quickly lose track and just accept that if Ben likes it, then chances are I will, too.

Soon our teas arrive, followed by pork buns. The dough is so white and smooth, it almost looks like toy food. But then I bite into it. It's chewy and fatty—just right.

"How's Luz doing?" Ben says as he licks his fingers.

He only met her once during that first group night out, so I'm a little surprised that he's asking. But I guess I talk about her a lot. "She's busy with school, so I don't see her as much. And she's dating that guy, David. I think I told you about him?"

Ben clears his throat. "Um, I guess?"

"Sounds like it's going really well. They can't see each other that much but they text a lot."

"You sound dubious," Ben says with a smile.

The waiter brings out a covered straw basket. Steam rises as soon as we lift the top. Six piping-hot dumplings greet us on the inside. They're more elongated than the momos in Queens, which were nice and round.

"I think she likes him. But they're taking it slow and steady."

"And that's not how you operate."

My mind automatically goes to my night with Zach in Paris. The butterflies in my belly for hours, the adrenaline with every passing moment, knowing the end was coming. How every second seemed to burst with new and wonderful feelings. It was incredible. At least I *think* it was. The feeling is starting to fade away.

Ben continues. "You want love at first sight, undying passion, and signs from the universe that you're made for each other." There's a bite to his tone but he also sounds too serious, not like himself.

"Is that a bad thing?"

"No. It's just how you are."

His tone makes me feel queasy.

"And *you* think you want a ten-year plan even if that means giving up on exciting possibilities, like going to France and forging your own path along the way. Have you ever thought that you might be letting your dad's idea of success determine your whole life?"

He stares at me for a while before speaking again. "Maybe that's just who *I* am."

I nod. He's right, we're different people, and that's okay. So why doesn't it feel like it?

We polish off our food, and when we're done, the night is just getting started. Ben has an idea of where to go, but he doesn't tell me what it is.

"A touristy thing" is all he says as we take the subway to the southernmost point in Manhattan. "You still have so much to see."

At the other end of our subway ride, the fall air whips my hair as we find the entrance to the Staten Island Ferry.

"What's in Staten Island?" I say.

Ben smiles. "I'll give you a hint: this isn't about the destination."

That doesn't actually clue me in, so I guess I'll just have to wait.

By the time we board the ferry, the sky has turned five different shades of black. It looks unreal with the clouds, like a painting. A fresh breeze blows on our faces as the boat departs. Back at the shoreline, the city sparkles in the night sky. It's magical. Thousands of twinkling lights dot the skyline like stars. Each of them represents a person in this big wild place. One of them has to be Zach.

There are lots of people on the deck, and we have to lean close to each other to get a spot overlooking the water. I don't know if it's being out in the open, or feeling Ben's body pressed against the side of mine, but I'm the most relaxed I've been since I got to New York.

And just when I think the night can't get any better, a tall green statue comes into view. Alone in the middle of the harbor, looking over all of us. I've seen the Statue of Liberty many times in pictures, but nothing compares to the real thing. I squeal as we get closer, joining the crowd of people leaning over the railing, just as excited as I am to see her up close.

"It never gets old," Ben says.

"Did you know she's French?" I can't contain my glee.

Ben glances at me sideways. "That's just one reason we all love her so much."

The warmth of his smile courses through me, and for a moment I don't hear anything else, just the swoosh of the waves. A thought pops up in my head.

"Do you want to come to my dad's wedding?"

Ben jerks back in surprise, and to be honest, I feel the same way. I hadn't planned on saying that; the words escaped my mouth before I could really consider them.

He raises an eyebrow. "Are you sure?"

I don't need to think about that too hard. "Yes. He keeps asking me if I want to bring anyone, and they need to finalize the guest list. The wedding's in a couple of weeks now."

"Right, but I figured you'd want to bring Zach."

Of course I want to bring Zach. That's one of the first things that came to mind when Papa and Miguel announced they were getting engaged, and then that they would get married this autumn. Zach and I would be together. We'd make *such* a cute couple and it would be soooooo romantic to have that night together after finally meeting again. It was all so very meant to be.

"Except that I have no idea where he is."

I can admit it to myself now: the posters Luz and I put up really were just for fun. It was a silly thing to do, to make me feel better. Ben never even saw them—or I'm sure he would have mentioned it—which means they've probably been ripped off by now.

"You might still find him," he says.

My heart swells at the idea, but it's okay, really. The possibility has been on my mind since that moment in Times Square. We missed each other. There's no point in denying it. And deep down, I've known this for the last year, haven't I? There was always a risk that our plan wouldn't work. It was thrilling, and it kept me dreaming every night when I couldn't wait to finish school and start my life. But in my dreams we always did meet in Times

Square. It was *always* the beginning of an epic love story. Maybe that's all it ever was. A dream.

"And I might not," I reply.

"You're seriously inviting me?" Ben says, an eyebrow raised.

"Of course I am! It'll be so much fun."

"Okay. Then I'd love to come."

Ben stares into my eyes and I get this feeling again that something . . . but then the ferry rises suddenly, throwing me off to the side. Another, bigger boat is going by, creating a ripple of waves that sends us all moving around, unbalanced. The lady behind me catches my hand, stopping me from toppling over. Ben grabs onto the railing, laughing as I try to steady myself.

We stare at each other and laugh some more. Whatever that feeling was, it's gone.

Chapter Twenty

The first thing I notice about Papa and Miguel's friends' "cottage" in the Hamptons is that it's not actually a cottage. Not even a house. It's a mansion, a palace, a modern-day castle, maybe. I started to suspect something was off when we took a right turn down a tree-lined lane that would never end. The gravel was so white it looked like it had been hand-bleached, and the vast expanse of space made our rented Audi look tiny.

And then there's the . . . building. I count ten windows on the front, which are so tall and wide that I can actually see right through to the ocean. The ocean! Now I understand why Miguel chuckled when I asked if we needed to bring blow-up mattresses. That's what we do when we go visit Maman's cousins in La Rochelle; there aren't enough beds for us kids.

"And this is just their beach house," Luz whispers to me as we pull our duffel bags out of the trunk. "Can you imagine what their Park Avenue penthouse looks like?"

Papa and Miguel told us about their friends on the drive over: Dev, a hedge-fund manager, and Leonard, the heir to a software development company, who met at Stanford. They hired Miguel to design their first Tribeca loft, and hit it off right away. None of these words meant anything to me when I heard them, and it's only as I stand in Dev and Leonard's double-height foyer—drenched in sunlight and half the size of our West Village apartment—that I understand that it was all just code for *unfathomably rich*.

The theme of the next day's party is fall extravaganza: perfectly shaped pumpkins of all sizes are spread around the house and the patio, and candles are lit everywhere, including on the mantel of the working fireplace. There are large straw baskets filled with blankets and heat lamps turned on so no one gets cold. A huge spread of cheeses and canapés has been laid out on a long table by the floor-to-ceiling windows overlooking the estate.

The professional DJ has been setting up his equipment on the terrace while the catering company has taken over the kitchen, with waiters dressed in plaid vests and crisp navy chinos. An inflatable witch and skeleton float around in the pool. Halloween is next week, in case anyone had forgotten it. The hosts originally thought about making this a costume party, but Miguel put that idea to bed pretty quickly. Their bachelor fiesta wasn't to be confused with everyone's favorite spooky night.

Luz and I are sharing a bedroom with a king-sized bed—and

a view of the ocean (what?!)—where we spend the morning getting ready. Last night we stayed up and talked for hours, and my hope for a good sleep quickly evaporated. It was worth it, though. A Spotify playlist chimes through my phone as we evaluate our outfit choices. Luz chose this amazing maxi burgundy skirt and I'm wearing a navy lace dress with white trim. Then, we fight for mirror space as we each put on our makeup. We have our own bathroom, and it's not like we're cramped, but Luz brought enough products to cover every surface.

"Is this too much?" I say, pointing at the thick gold bangle on my arm, the three layered pendants around my neck, and my black suede strappy sandals.

Luz doesn't even need to look at me to answer. "It's the Hamptons, *bébé*. Make it shine!"

I got a sample of a fancy floral perfume at Sephora, which I spray in front of me before walking through the fragrant cloud.

And then we're ready to party.

When guests arrive—wearing high heels and designer dresses, bow ties and blazers—they're greeted with trays of drinks featuring rainbow umbrellas. Everyone looks glossy and shiny and a little too bright, like an influencer's photoshopped Instagram feed. The house smells like lime and cilantro, marinated tuna and melting cheese. Outside it's just sea air and sunshine—and not even that cold. A perfect day.

Soon everyone is swarming around the grooms—in matching light blue outfits and fedoras—so Luz and I observe them from afar, outside by the pool.

"They look so happy," Luz says, beaming. "I'm really glad my uncle met your dad, and not just because that means I got you." She wraps me in a bear hug and I coo in a silly voice. We may have snuck in a cocktail. Luz insisted it was our bachelor party, too! And we'll have to be on our best behavior at the wedding. I'm starting to feel a little buzz, that jolt of glee that comes from loosening up.

Luz grabs two miniburgers from a passing tray, and hands me one.

"So," she says after taking a bite, "I know we agreed on no boy talk last night, but I actually have something to tell you."

That was my idea. When I told Luz that I'd taken her suggestion and invited Ben to the wedding, she wouldn't shut up about it. I needed a break from that conversation, and she agreed to drop the topic, for this weekend at least.

She pouts, looks away, and then says quickly, "David is my boyfriend now. We talked about it the other night. He asked if he could call me his girlfriend and I said yes."

"That's cute," I say, feeling a surge of envy. "Does that mean I get to meet him now?"

"He's a good guy, Margot."

"Um, okay? I never said he wasn't."

She lets out a sigh. "I think I might actually invite him to the wedding now, so yes, you'll definitely have to meet him before."

"Yay!" I say, clutching my fist in victory. "The famous David! You know I've built him up in my head now? Like, he's this handsome, kind, smart, ultra-perfect guy."

Luz finishes her burger and wipes her oily fingers before going to put her plate down on a nearby table. A few other guests are enjoying the fresh air like us, but they're too busy chatting to pay us much attention.

When Luz looks at me again, her face is stern. "I've been hiding something. I'm sorry, Margot. So much has been going on and you've been really stressed at work, but I hate keeping secrets from you."

I ball up my napkin. Luz is being weird. "Then don't?"

"Right, but first you have to promise you won't get mad at me. I had reasons."

"I promise!" It's an easy thing to say when you have no idea what you're talking about. I just want Luz to get on with it. We have some dancing to do.

She takes a deep breath, and something changes on her face. I can't put my finger on it, but for a moment it seems like she's changed her mind.

And then it comes out. "Miguel got a job offer in Miami, at an amazing interior design firm."

I wait for more, because as far as secrets go, this one feels a little tame. "He's already working at an amazing interior design firm in New York."

"Yes, but it's not Miami. Do you know how cold it gets in winter here?"

Obviously I don't, but I've seen pictures of Papa and Miguel in humongous down parkas. And Luz wouldn't shut up about it last year, her first winter in the city. "*They* know how cold it gets here, and they're happy in New York."

She looks around, making sure no one is listening. "Your dad doesn't know yet."

I lean closer, tension rising within me. "Are you saying Miguel wants to take the job?"

"He's been missing the family. I don't think he ever meant to stay in New York long-term and then he met your dad. . . ."

Fragments of past conversations come to me: Miguel's complaints about the weather and Papa's insistence that, as far as he's concerned, it's New York or nothing.

"When is Miguel going to tell him?"

Luz shrugs. "They've been so focused on the wedding . . . Miguel told my mom and then she couldn't resist telling me. Please don't say anything."

"So neither of you could keep a secret, but now I have to?"

"Sorry!" she says. "But really, Margot"—she mimes zipping her lips—"it's none of our business."

Except it kind of is, though, at least for me. I'm living with them. I always planned to move out and find my own place, but I haven't saved enough money yet. Besides, New York is everything to Papa: it's where he grew up and where he's lived his whole life. Maybe it's me being selfish, but I can't imagine him ever agreeing to leave. Why hasn't Miguel told him already? It doesn't seem fair to leave it so close to the wedding. Oh god, what if Miguel doesn't tell him until *after* they're married? Someone has to look out for my dad. I know Maman would never keep that from him if she knew.

Now I can see why Luz made me promise not to say anything. And right now, I know better than anyone how it feels to watch your happiness slip away because of things outside your control. Plus, there's not enough room in this family for both Papa and me to have a broken heart.

Oh god.

I have to do something about this. Don't I?

Chapter Twenty-One

I try to shake these thoughts away as the party moves on. Luz and I mingle with the guests, introducing ourselves as the bridesmaids and reveling in the gleeful reactions. We enjoy the great music, the gorgeous view, and the even better food. All afternoon long, we nibble on guacamole and chips, watermelon-feta salad, tomato bruschetta, and tempura shrimps. I've got to admit: I'm pretty into this Hamptons style.

As the sun goes down and everyone seems merry, Papa and Miguel tap on their glasses with a knife, asking for attention. Then, they search for Luz and me in the crowd and motion for us to come over. We do.

Miguel's speech is innocent enough. He thanks Dev and Leonard for this amazing party, talks about how happy he is to see all their friends gathered on this beautiful day, and how lucky that the weather cooperated enough that we spent some of the afternoon outside.

Papa speaks after him. He goes on about how excited he is to marry the love of his life, as long as they don't kill each other first. They've been trying to learn the steps to their first dance for days now, but the results aren't promising so far. And then he wraps his arm around my neck and pulls me close. "And I'm particularly happy that my daughter, Margot, is with us. It's been tough being far from my family, and I'm so glad she decided to move to New York."

A few people let out emotional *awww*s. Papa's eyes get shiny as he looks at me, while my own brim with tears.

Then he turns to me, his cheeks flush. "I'm so proud of you, and I can't wait to see everything you accomplish in this wonderful city of ours."

People clap as he hugs me. I can't take this anymore: tears roll down my cheeks, and there's nothing I can do to stop them.

"Papa, I need to talk to you."

I quickly pull him to the side, while he smiles awkwardly at Miguel and all their guests. Luz shoots daggers at me. I have to be fast.

"Miguel got a job in Miami," I whisper. "He wants you to move there together and he's been keeping it from you. I'm sorry but you deserve to know."

Miguel catches on and comes closer. "What are you two talking about?"

"You got a job in Miami?" Papa says, his jaw clenched.

Everyone is watching us now.

"Let's talk in private." Miguel grabs his hand and they walk past everyone into the kitchen.

"MARGOT!" Luz says, once they're out of sight.

"I had to tell him, okay? He has a right to know."

But as the grooms' voices start to trickle from the kitchen, I'm starting to rethink that decision.

"Were you just going to take the job without telling me?"

"Of course not!"

The guests have gone completely silent; you could hear a pin drop. My stomach ties in a knot. We shouldn't all be listening to their argument, but it's hard not to. We're here celebrating their upcoming wedding, so it's kind of a big deal that they stormed off and started fighting.

"This is all your fault, Margot," Luz says a little too loudly. "If they call off the wedding—"

I gasp. "They won't!"

Deep down, I can't say I'm certain about that, especially after I scan the faces around us. A few people have heard Luz, and are starting to whisper about the wedding. *If* it's still on. More of the conversation filters through. I hold my breath as we all listen in:

"We've been so busy with the planning. I wanted to take the time to really talk about it. That's why I made this dinner reservation on Tuesday."

"You told me we were going to a work thing!"

"I invented that. I wanted to explain what this means to me. I never planned to live in New York forever."

"Well, I do. And what's worse is that you told your family and not me."

Luz lets out an exasperated sigh at me. "Great timing, Margot."

She has some nerve. "Hey, it was *your* secret to keep!"

But still, guilt twists in my gut.

"Yeah, but I never thought you'd spill the beans to your dad during his party."

I grunt, trying to think of a comeback, but then a door slams shut.

A moment later, Miguel reappears. His face is red, and he's trying to fake a smile. "Sorry, everyone. Please have another drink. The festivities continue."

I stare toward the hallway, where Papa just stormed off to.

"Don't," Luz says, guessing exactly what I'm thinking. "We need to stay way out of this."

I look around at the crowd—people are just starting to get back to the task of pretending to enjoy themselves—but I know the night is over for me. Did I just ruin this important weekend? If they cancel the wedding, I'll never forgive myself.

The mattress dips, making me lean toward the edge as someone sits next to me. Light filters through the curtains, but I'm still too woozy with sleep to get my bearings.

"Margot," Papa whispers to me, gently nudging my arm. "I'm going for a walk on the beach. Do you want to come?"

Last night I went to bed with tears streaming down my face and shame rising inside me. By the time Luz came in, I was under the duvet, pretending to sleep.

"Oui," I say, my voice still croaky.

Fifteen minutes later, we're walking down the beach, our toes digging into the still-wet sand, the sun rising over the horizon. Papa got us big to-go mugs filled with coffee, which is still an anomaly to me. In France, half the point of drinking coffee—or anything else, for that matter—is to take a break and enjoy it. To sit on a terrace and watch the world go by, to catch up with a friend, or to just breathe for a moment. Americans grab their giant coffee and just go go go. Not a minute to waste.

"I'm sorry about last night," I say, taking a sip. I'm not sure how many hours I slept, but it's only eight a.m. now, and I'm still not quite awake. "I ruined your party."

"You didn't."

"Is Miguel mad at me?"

"Of course not. Or, if he is, he's mad at his sister and at Luz first, so you're third on the list."

I chuckle awkwardly. "And how do you feel about the whole thing?"

"Honestly? Still working it out. I don't like that he kept it from me, but I can sort of see why he did. Still—"

"You feel betrayed."

He takes another sip of his coffee, pondering. "Something like that. This idea of getting married . . . it's kind of strange in a way. It's not supposed to change anything—you're just with the person you want to be with—but then somehow it does. Our lives will be connected forever, and if Miguel doesn't see his in New York, then I have to think about what that means for me."

We pass by a group of young people spread out on a few beach towels and wrapped in blankets. One of the girls has eye makeup down to her cheekbones, while a guy's shirt is stained with what must have been red wine. They look like they came straight from a party to the beach, with no sleep in between. I feel even worse for ruining all the fun we were supposed to have.

"I'm sorry I made it all so much more difficult."

"You didn't." I wince, and he chuckles. "Okay, you did a little, but you had my best interest at heart. And I'm glad we're getting a moment to hang out. I've barely seen you lately."

I open my mouth to say sorry again, but Papa raises his free hand to stop me. "No, wait. I want to tell you this. I'm so impressed with you. You're working incredibly hard and it's paying off. Your mom had her doubts but I was really crossing my fingers that it would all work out."

"That's what you taught me. We have to hustle hard for the things that matter to us. Isn't that the same way with relationships?"

"You're right, it is. I know we'll figure it out. Preferably before the wedding."

He lets out a laugh and we both stop walking to stare into the ocean.

"Not to make this all about me," I say, against the crashing sound of the waves, "but you know I can manage in New York without you, right?"

"Margot, I haven't—"

"Listen to me. You and Maman made a lot of sacrifices for me. She works so hard and I know one reason you've been staying at your job all this time is because it meant you could travel to France to see us. I spent my whole childhood looking at my friends' families and thinking, *how did I get so lucky?* Their parents were either fighting or divorcing, or they had all sorts of drama with their siblings. I could tell I had the best: two parents who added up to more than one set. I'm not telling you what you should do, but if Miguel really feels like he needs to be near his family . . ."

He nods for a long time. "And Miami *is* pretty nice."

I motion for us to keep walking. The salty air is doing me good, clearing my head.

"Besides, I'm eighteen. I'm supposed to act like an adult, *apparently.*"

Papa lets out a laugh. "Don't get too serious on me. This time in your life: it's for mistakes." I make a funny face at him, halfway through another sip of my coffee, but he insists. "It's easy to get scared by your own dreams but that's exactly how it should be at your age. This is the moment to leave room for . . . life. The unknown, unplanned, and unexpected."

I tap my coffee cup against his. "To the unexpected! There's been a lot of that already."

"Anything you want to talk to me about?"

The look on his face tells me this isn't just a random question. "What did Luz say to you?"

He laughs. "Luz is the absolute worst person to keep a secret. Let it be known."

I shake my head in exasperation. "I think we're going to need more coffee. I don't understand how relationships are supposed to work. At all."

"No one knows, Margot. I don't think there's a single person on earth who does."

Maybe he's just saying that to make me feel better, but it works. Zach and I were always going to be messy. We took a chance and, well, we all saw how that turned out.

Chapter Twenty-Two

Yesterday Ben came to work with sparks in his eyes. His dad had gotten four tickets to a Yankees game through work, and, since he couldn't go, he gave them to his son. I know less than nothing about baseball—is that even the sport the Yankees play?—but Ben seemed so excited that it quickly became contagious. Then, he suggested we go with Luz and her boyfriend, and I suddenly got way more interested in ball games.

Yankee Stadium is in the Bronx, and while it's a long trip there, the subway ride itself is part of the fun: we're surrounded by fans dressed in the team jersey or cap, all extra cheerful and eager to get there. Luz texted me to suggest I wear a striped tee—it's more French than Yankee-related, but no one has to know—and I'm glad I followed her advice. By the time Ben and I get off the subway, the crowd's excitement is coursing through me, too.

Though in my case, it's less about seeing baseball than about meeting David. Finally. Luz and he were doing something today, and Ben wanted to get to the game as early as possible, so they're meeting us in a bit. I've been literally begging to meet the guy for weeks now, so if I have to watch men throw balls around and pretend to understand the rules for the next few hours, then so be it.

Ben's jaw drops when we get to our seats. I have no point of reference, but even I can tell that they're pretty sweet. We're in a company box, with a nice amount of space around us and a great view of the field. Looking around the stadium, it's dizzying to see so many people—most of them dots, really—in this iconic space. The music is loud, the air abuzz with amped-up energy, and Ben has a trick to get me invested in the experience.

"They sell the best pretzels in the city!"

I've smelled them all over New York, mostly from the carts on the street, the salty yeasty scent recognizable everywhere, but I still haven't tried one.

"Ooh," I say. "I love that you're making sure that everything is a culinary experience, even a sports game."

Ben looks me straight in the eyes. "It's not just a sports game, Margot. The Yankees are playing."

There's a solemnness to his tone that warms my heart. He's clearly so happy to be here, and he invited me. How nice is that? I'm sure he has other friends he could have brought.

My phone chimes with a text from Luz. Going through the gate now!

Woohoo! I text back.

A minute later, another text comes through. Remember that you love me, okay?

I frown. "Luz is weird sometimes." I show my screen to Ben by way of explanation.

He looks at me funny. "But she's right. You love her, and everything will be fine."

"Okay now *you're* weird."

He shrugs in response, then looks behind me with a concerned glance.

I turn around and see Luz a few meters away, trying to carve herself a path through the crowd, an exaggerated smile plastered on her face.

"Where's David?" I ask as she comes closer.

I don't see a guy with her. I mean, there are lots of guys around, but . . . wait. Before she can answer, I spot someone I know. Ari, the former cook at Nutrio. The one who was such a jerk to me.

"Did you invite Ari?" I ask Ben, confused.

He shakes his head, not looking me in the eyes. "I didn't."

"*I* did," Luz says. Then, speaking really quickly, "I'm so sorry I lied to you, Margot. I made up a different name because I knew you didn't like him—" She cuts herself off as Ari approaches. He interlaces his fingers through hers.

Luz and Ari are holding hands.

WHAT?

I glance from one to the other, then turn to Ben, who avoids my gaze.

"Hey," Luz says sheepishly. "So, um . . . this is my boyfriend."

That . . . No. Nope, nope, nope. It doesn't make any sense.

"Hey, Margot, nice to see you again," Ari says, like he's ever spoken my actual name before instead of calling me Bambi.

An announcement comes through the speakers, introducing the teams and the players, but the game is the last thing on my mind now.

"I'll get us drinks," Ari says to Luz.

"And I'll buy the pretzels," Ben adds, quickly following him out of the box and up the stairs.

Luz watches Ari walk away, and I feel my whole body tense. I've bared my soul to her so many times and she's been secretly seeing this asshole behind my back.

As soon as the guys are out of earshot, she turns to me, looking contrite. "I know you don't like him—"

I cut her off. "I don't. And you know how he treated me when I started at Nutrio."

"He feels so bad about that."

I don't care how Ari feels. This isn't about him. "You lied to me!"

I'm not trying to be dramatic; I'm upset. Luz means everything to me. When I call her my sister, it's not just as a joke. She's mine. We're each other's.

"I— Yes, you're right. That was a horribly shitty move on my part. When I met him that night we went out in the East Village, he didn't tell me his name until we'd been chatting for a while and I already kind of liked him. You were on the other side with Ben and I thought, this can't be the guy Margot hates. I was going to tell you at the bachelor party, but it was so obvious that you would hate me for it. So I spilled the beans about Miguel's secret instead."

I cannot believe this. "And then you blamed *me* for telling my dad."

"I panicked, okay?" Luz looks like she's on the brink of tears.

I think back to all our conversations about fake David. How much she liked him and insisted that he was a nice guy who'd had a tough life. I thought maybe she wasn't sure about her feelings for him. Turns out she wasn't sure about *my* feelings.

"But he's so—" I don't know what to choose between *arrogant* and *snobbish*. "He's such an asshole!" I'm not trying to hurt her, just stating some truths.

"But he's really not!"

I roll my eyes and look around us. The crowd is getting rowdy, and the game should start any moment. Ben and Fake-David-slash-Ari are on their way back down—one carrying plastic cups, the other striped paper bags. I can see the pretzels sticking out, but I'm not hungry anymore.

Luz notices the guys approaching and leans over me. "Margot, listen. It's all a big misunderstanding. He worked so hard to get to where he is and you came in, a cute and proper French girl who bragged about her connections and tried to elbow her way onto the line. He thought you were pretentious and entitled and reacted to that. He was wrong about you; he knows that now. You two just got off on the wrong foot."

The guys are back to us and Ari hands me a cup. "Hey, Margot—" I take the drink, my nostrils flared. I'm mad, y'all. "I'm sorry for the way I treated you." I raise an eyebrow. "Seriously.

I didn't know you and I shouldn't have acted that way." I grunt. "And I'm happy for you that you got put on the line. You deserve it."

Okay, um, it's becoming a little hard to hate him. Especially when he glances at Luz and they both have hearts in their eyes, like they're so into each other already.

"Well, okay, thank you."

I'm still annoyed at him, at both of them, but we came here to have fun and the game is starting. I can always be mad again later.

The four of us sit down. The players wear striped uniforms—which look a lot like pajamas, to be honest—and stand around in a diamond-shaped field while one of them is thrown a ball he has to hit with a bat. And then, for some reason, that same guy has to hope no one catches it so he can run around for the purpose of coming back to where he started. Confusing much? Still, this is sort of entertaining. We cheer, we scream, we get on our feet, we clap and jump up in the air. Also, the pretzels are as good as Ben said they would be. Of course he was right.

An hour in I've forgotten that Luz is a total liar and that I don't like her boyfriend. I pull the four of us closer so we can take a selfie.

She beams. "Say 'wedding crew'!"

Ben has the longest arm, and he manages to get us all in as we make funny faces. Afterward, we hunch over his shoulder to see. It's a cute picture.

Then Ari wraps his arms around Luz and kisses her. It's going to take me a while to get used to that.

"I can't wait for the wedding," Ben whispers to me. "It's going to be so great."

The countdown is on, just a week away now.

"I borrowed a suit from my roommate," he adds. "It's a little long in the legs."

He pulls out his phone to show me a picture.

Seeing him all dressed up and looking proudly into the mirror makes my heart flutter. This is a very good look on him. "It's perfect," I say.

"And I found this for my pocket square." He flicks to a different picture, showing a piece of hot pink fabric. "Will it match your dress?"

Color me impressed. It does match my dress, almost exactly. I know I sent him that picture of when I tried it on but still, that attention to detail is . . . attractive. I nod. "You're going to look extremely cute."

He blushes as a chuckle escapes his throat. "That is the goal. I have to up my game if I'm going to stand next to you."

My tongue twists. I don't say anything back. The truth is, I agree with him: we'll look pretty amazing together. But I can't say that out loud. We're friends. Not like those two over there, sucking on each other's faces. Totally gross but also kind of enviable. Not that I'd want to be kissing Ari, but . . . you know what I mean. Love is pretty great, and I'm happy for Luz. I just hope I can have that, too.

The game starts again. It's the last round, also known as the last inning. Ben has taught me all sorts of things along the way, and I have to admit I'm getting into it. It's the bottom of the ninth, and it's the Yankees' turn to bat. The scores are tied, almost every person in the stadium is holding their breath, or at least that's how it seems. The player—someone famous whose name I forgot as soon as Ben said it—steps up to the plate. He whacks his bat against the ball flying at him, sending it up and away, into the stands. Next to me, Ben lets out an excited growl, coming from deep inside. The famous player trots around the diamond, and as soon as he gets back to the plate, the crowd erupts in cheers so loud that my whole body vibrates.

"Home run!" Ben and Ari scream at the same time. It's easy to get caught up in the excitement. I've never felt more alive, or more *American*.

"I'm guessing this means the Yankees won?"

Ben laughs, gesturing widely at the delirious crowd. "Um, yes, Margot. The Yankees won." Then he points in the air, smiling. "And now, this."

Before I can ask what he's talking about, Frank Sinatra's "New York, New York" comes onto the speakerphones.

"Start spreading the news. I'm leaving today. I want to be a part of it, New York, New York. . . ."

Tens of thousands of people sing in unison, the emotion and joy palpable all around us. I scan the stadium in such awe that, even though I know the lyrics, the words don't come. Does anyone ever get used to this? The feeling that you're at the center of the universe, that nothing more exciting happens than happens here? This is what I've been dreaming of for so long, but reality is so much brighter. And I get to experience it all with great friends.

Will I still marvel at all of this in six months, two years, five years from now? Is this really going to be my life? Not just for now, but forever? Ben wraps his arms around my neck, taking me into a little dance. Suddenly I'm a little dizzy, and I all can think is *I hope this feeling never goes away.*

Chapter Twenty-Three

Two days later, Luz still feels bad about lying to me—as she should!—and invites me to eat at Jack's Wife Freda, a Mediterranean restaurant in Chelsea. Ari is also off tonight, and she wanted to hang out just the two of us. I'm sure I'll get used to her dating him eventually, but I'm not going to like him overnight. Besides, this is my last break before the wedding, and I'm glad we're getting some girl time in.

"The game was really cool," Luz says as we sit down at our table. "I'm pretty sure you actually enjoyed yourself."

I raise a dubious eyebrow. "You mean, after I discovered that you betrayed me, your quasi-sister who adores you?"

Luz makes puppy eyes, and I shake my head. I'm still sour about that, but it's hard not to be happy for her.

She starts browsing the menu and lets out a sigh. "I'm so relieved that you finally know. It was one of these things where, once I'd started, I couldn't find a way out. He and I swapped numbers and started texting. I couldn't bring myself to tell you, to give you something else to stress about. You've been going through a lot."

I shrug, like it's really not that much.

"Margot, come on. It's true. You deserve all the credit for what you accomplished. You moved to a new country, got into an amazing restaurant, and you're already climbing the ranks. The New York dream is happening for you! I wanted to tell you about Ari so much, but I hated the idea of hurting your feelings."

"Well, you were right. My feelings *are* hurt." I pause, take a deep breath.

A waitress comes by and we order fried zucchini chips, the vegetable curry bowl, and a side of grilled Halloumi, all to share. My stomach flips with anticipation.

"But the four of us had a great time, right?" Luz says afterward.

I can't hide my smile. We really did. One of my best memories of New York so far. On the subway ride home, we cheered and laughed with the hundreds of fans around us, and happy tears pooled at the corners of my eyes.

"And it'll be even better at the wedding," Luz adds.

Just a few days ago she wasn't sure if she wanted to invite Ari, but now it's like it was never a question. "Have you told your mom yet?"

She takes a sip of her water and beams. "Yep. We're going to go to lunch the day before, the three of us."

"Oooh," I say. "Introducing the boyfriend . . . You guys really are serious."

She chuckles. "I can't tell who's more nervous about it, Ari or me. My mom is the kind of person who will break your legs if you ever hurt her daughter."

"I think she'll just look at your face and know what's going on."

They seemed so into each other at the game, and even after. The moment Luz shivered a tiny bit, Ari gave her his scarf and asked if she wanted his sweater, and as soon as his cup was empty, she was offering to get new drinks.

"I hope you're right," Luz says, a twinge of anxiety on her face. "But, speaking of boys—" She waits for me to jump in, but I don't. She's going to have to come digging. "How are things with you and Ben?"

"Things are fine?" I say it like she should know this already. It doesn't need to be a topic of conversation.

"Come on, Margot. If you don't want me to have secrets from you, then don't have any from me."

"I don't have secrets." She stares at me, like she doesn't buy it. "Okay, well, Ben is great. He's the nicest guy. He's obsessed with all things France, which I thought would get annoying but is actually kind of nice. The way he talks about it—the food, the culture, and all—it's giving me a new appreciation for everything I took for granted growing up. And he's just so fun and easy to be around. He's a really good friend."

Luz smirks. "Yeah, a friend."

"That's what I said. We're friends and colleagues, and—"

"And he's also your date to your dad's wedding."

"That was *your* idea! You're the one who said it was perfectly normal to bring a friend to a wedding."

"Sure," Luz shrugs. "I mean, yes, some people do that. But, Margot, can't you see that you two—"

I cut in. "Don't." My stomach ties in a knot. "Zach is somewhere in this city."

She lets out a deep, unnerved sigh as our plates arrive. For the first few days after we put up the posters, Luz would frequently text me to ask if I'd heard anything yet. She'd often add a laughing emoji, because this was all a joke, right? Just a thing we did on a fun day together. She stopped asking after a while, and I didn't tell her that I'd jump every time my phone beeped or rang. It was Ben showing me what he was cooking for his roommates, or it was my friend Julien from home, sending me pictures of a party he was coming back from. Or it was Maman calling to make sure I was "being treated okay" at the restaurant. But it was never Zach. Of course I knew the posters wouldn't work. I just didn't know for *sure*.

"You're still—" She pauses as I start digging into the dishes.

It's easy for her to judge. She's in love and happy. For some of us, things are a little more complicated.

"Yes, Luz." The exasperated tone in my voice must be obvious. "I'm still hoping to find him. I don't care if that's unrealistic, if that makes no sense to anyone but me, I can't shake that feeling that if I hadn't been late to Times Square, if, if, if—"

The words catch in my throat. There it is: I'm not over it. Over him.

She places a hand on mine. "I just don't want you to miss out on someone great like Ben, just because you're holding out for something that's not . . . there."

I take a deep breath. It doesn't matter how much I explain it to her, or to anyone. It's just a feeling I carry deep inside me. Even Ben has stopped mentioning Operation Find Zach, and I don't feel like dragging him into this anymore. This is my thing; only I truly get it. Or do I? Maybe I'm just hanging on to something that only existed a year ago, for a few hours. And I'm out of clues. I've looked everywhere. I've run out of options. But hope? I still have a smidge of that, even if I can't explain why.

We talk about everything else as we finish dinner, then Luz heads off to meet with Ari. Like me, he's working every night until the wedding after tonight so he can have Saturday off. They have tickets to a comedy show in the East Village, another hot date for these two lovebirds. Okay, fine, I'm jealous.

As for me, I'm not sure what to do. It's not even nine p.m. yet. Ben is at Nutrio. My dad and Miguel are working long hours, wrapping things up before they go on their honeymoon. Without thinking, I start walking west, and soon notice people wandering the Highline. I haven't been on it since that day with Luz, when everything seemed up in the air, which felt full of so many possibilities.

It's pitch black now and quite chilly, so I pull my coat tighter around me as I get up the steps. It's so cool up here, watching the city from above. I take my sweet time walking down the path, lost in my thoughts. New York is so shiny and marvelous, but I've never worked this hard in my life. I haven't even been here that long and I feel bruised and battered. Exhausted all the time. Maman always brings it up when we FaceTime. *You're not yourself,* she said to me last time. *You sound worn out. This is exactly what*

I was worried about. And your dad might not say it, but he agrees with me.

I don't love it when my parents talk behind my back, but I guess Papa did warn me, too. New York is tough. Some people get chewed up by the hustle and bustle, by the breakneck speed of life, the sheer volume of people and the tininess of everyone's living space. But I've wanted to do this for so long. So what if it's challenging and not quite how I expected it to be? This is life, right?

I'm gazing out at the Hudson River, the Statue of Liberty in the distance, when my phone rings. A few times, Raven has called me on my day off in the middle of service, asking if I could come in right away after something happened: a cook got in an argument with Chef and quit, started feeling unwell, or sliced their finger open. Of course, I raced there as fast as I could, even once when I was out having dinner with Papa.

But on the screen, it's an unknown number. It could be someone else at the restaurant, I guess, if Raven is too busy to call herself. People come and go all the time—I still don't know everyone, and I'm not sure I ever will.

"Hello?" I say, picking up.

"Margot?" It's a guy's voice on the phone. I don't recognize it, but it makes my stomach twist.

"Yes, this is Margot."

"It's really you?"

My legs feel shaky. There's a bench near me and I go sit down.

"Who is this?" I say, barely able to breathe.

"It's the guy you met under the twinkling lights of the Eiffel Tower."

My heart drops. I don't know how to think or speak anymore. Because this . . . can't be, right? Not after I've wanted it so badly.

"Margot? Are you there?"

I nod feverishly for a few seconds, until my brain grasps the fact that he can't see me. "YES."

No other words come.

"So you did move to New York? You're here? Right now?" The guy—Zach?—sounds puzzled, like he can't quite believe he's talking to me, even though he punched in my number and called *me*.

But what if this is a prank? Some dude saw my poster and is having a little fun.

My hands shake. I need to be sure. "Tell me where we met exactly."

His answer is immediate. "On a bench in Champ de Mars."

I hold my breath, wondering if I wanted to hear this so much that I'm dreaming.

"Margot, it's Zach. It's really me. You found me."

"I found you." My voice feels like it belongs to someone else.

A million questions knock around in my brain, but my train of thought is interrupted by a fire truck wailing by. The siren is so loud that it drowns out everything around me, making it impossible to speak. Only a few seconds pass, but they're actual torture. I've been waiting for so long already. I can't anymore. Just when I think I'm about to lose my mind, the truck moves on.

"I need to see you," Zach says, breathlessly. "What are you doing right now?"

But I can't respond, because *another* fire truck drives past, blaring its impossible soundtrack.

Hold up.

There is no second fire truck.

The shrieking sound is coming from my phone.

Zach comes to this realization at the same time. "Wait, are you here?"

Um, now is not the time to point out that I have no idea what he means by "here." I'm definitely *here,* but that's not going to help us, is it?

"I'm on the Highline," I say. I try to sound calm, but I'm freaking out on the inside.

"Where?" His breath becomes ragged, like he's running.

I look around me, suddenly dizzy. "Near the Chelsea Market, facing the Statue of Liberty, at the—" I try to think of the street number, but my mind goes blank.

"Don't move!"

I hear footsteps clunking on metal, like he's climbing up the stairs. I'm beyond frozen. People walk past me on their late-night stroll, completely unaware that my universe has just shifted on its axis. I clutch my phone.

My heartbeat is on a rollercoaster. "Zach?"

"Margot!"

I hear my name, not through the phone, but somewhere in the crowd.

And then he's here, running toward me. Just as tall and blond and devastatingly beautiful as I remember him. He's here, in front of me, and I can't move. I've wanted this so much, dreamed it so hard. I have no words. My heart jumbles like in a pinball game. I'm not even sure if I'm alive anymore, or maybe I'm too alive, because Zach is here, and the happily ever after I pictured in my mind for over a year is starting right now.

"Margot!" Zach calls out when he sees me.

This is really happening.

I rush over to meet him, and a moment later, I'm throwing myself in his arms, wrapping them around him. He smells like the night, musky and a little damp. I bury my head in his neck. Suddenly we're under the twinkling lights of the Tour Eiffel again. It's not just a dream. Dreams cannot feel this good. It's chemistry. It's destiny's work. An epic love story.

"Hi," I say, out of breath.

"Bonjour," he says back. "You're here."

I look up. *"You're* here." And now, finally, I can ask the question that's burned inside me all these weeks. "Were you there in Times Square? August 1 at midnight, bleachers, bottom right?"

There's a funny smile on his face. "Of course I was."

I thought I'd have more questions for him, that I'd want to know everything that happened in his life since that night in Paris. But none of that matters anymore. I raise my head up to his—he's even taller than I remember—and kiss him. A kiss one year in the making, coursing through my body from top to bottom and back up. People brush past us, bump against us, but there are only his lips, his strong arms holding me, and the warmth of his body. New York falls away.

We're together again. Finally.

Chapter Twenty-Four

And just like that, we're back in Paris. Except, you know, we're in New York.

"You saw my flyer," I say.

Our foreheads touch, skin against skin, like we're inseparable.

"Technically I didn't," he says. "I was on my way home from work, scrolling through Instagram, and I saw a picture of your poster. Someone shared it with a caption like, *Oh, this is romantic.* I only half read what it said and flicked past it. But something must have caught my eye, because a few seconds later, I was like, 'Wait, what did that say again?' By the way, I agree, it *is* romantic."

I laugh but it comes out like a quiet shriek. We *almost* missed each other, again. I know it was always the risk in a city of eight million people—and when you don't have the other's phone number—but phew, I'm never making that mistake again. On that note . . .

"Can I have your phone?" I say, pulling from our embrace for a very good reason.

He raises an eyebrow but does as he's asked after unlocking it.

"I'm saving myself as a contact," I explain.

"I'm not going anywhere!" Zach says with a laugh as I type in my details. "But you're right, it was kind of dumb of us."

I look at him, my heart knocking against my chest. All this time I've been wondering and there it is, the truth. "Yeah, it was supposed to be this grand gesture but—"

Zach shakes his head as he cuts in. "I didn't even know your last name, or the region you're from."

"It's Lambert, and Touraine."

"Mine is Miller. And anyway, I knew why we did what we did, but—"

"It made no sense in the light of day," I finish for him.

I never admitted this to myself, but it's true. We got swept up by the magic of the night, by what was happening to us. It was too beautiful, too pure, to look at through a screen for months to come.

"Well, we're together now." He kisses me again.

My lips remember his like no time has passed at all. *This* is what I was holding out for. This is what was always supposed to be.

He takes back his phone and says, "And now you have my number, too. But I really hope you won't have to use it for a while."

"What do you mean?"

"I've got all night."

I smile. "Me too. I don't have to be at work until tomorrow afternoon."

"Work, huh? We have a lot to catch up on." He kisses me again, softly. "Do you feel like going for a walk?"

"Um, yeah. This is what we do: walk around cities all night." And kiss. Especially the kissing.

We walk to the south end of the Highline, exiting by the Whitney Museum, Luz's favorite in the city. Then we head south, away from the busyness of the Meatpacking District and down the cobblestoned streets of the West Village, with their boutiques and little restaurants, still packed at this hour.

I tell him about my first few months in New York, skimming over my early days as a dishwasher, and happily bragging about being put on the line just a few weeks in. Zach seems thoroughly impressed.

"You know, I actually applied to Nutrio," he says as we cross over to the waterfront. "But I hear the chef's pretty intense."

"I would say that rumor is one hundred percent correct. But isn't that everyone in New York?"

"Wow," Zach says with a laugh. "You're even talking like a New Yorker now. Does that mean you're staying here for good?"

It turns out that his contact at Le Bernardin—where he was supposed to work after coming back from his worldwide trip—had left before he got back. Zach never even stepped foot there. For the last few months, he's been job-hopping, from the restaurant at a swanky hotel in SoHo to a retro burger joint in Harlem, and a few other places in between. He's been struggling to find his place, where he's meant to be, but he likes the diversity, too. I smile at this because I get it. This is our time for adventure and fun and figuring things out—and that's why I'm in New York, too.

"What about your travels? I need all the stories! And the pictures. Please, I've been waiting for a year."

He chuckles. "I'll tell you about them, but we have time. There's no need to rush."

He's right; I just want to be with him. No thoughts, just feelings. "I can't believe you were right here, tonight, a few minutes away from me. What were the chances?"

"That we randomly meet in two different cities, across an ocean, over a year apart?" He smiles, looking exactly like I pictured him in my dreams.

"I guess we beat the odds."

"And I'm so happy we did." He stops us in the middle of the street and kisses me.

There will never be enough kisses.

We keep walking down to Washington Square Park, and without consulting each other, we plop down on a bench. I don't feel like talking anymore, and by the look in Zach's eyes, we're on the same wavelength.

Suddenly, his hands are inside my coat on my lower back, mine in his thick short hair. We're kissing and kissing and kissing until it feels like we're going to run out. Of what, I'm not sure. I guess, technically the temperature is low right now—it's almost midnight—but I don't feel cold at all. Instead, I'm wrapped in his body, engulfed in his warmth, entranced by being in his presence again. I'm vaguely aware that the back rest is digging into me, and that people are playing chess at one of these stone tables nearby, but the world doesn't matter anymore.

"You taste so good," Zach whispers in my ear.

Electricity courses through me. It's like no time has passed at all. I guess, in our hearts, it hasn't. "This was definitely worth waiting for."

Zach smirks—gosh he's so sexy—his stare drilling through me. "Oh yeah?"

"Yeah."

A year I waited for him, but my heart was marked with Zach's touch. We were meant to be together; no one else could compare.

Eventually, we decide to head toward the Hudson River, holding on to each other tightly as we walk.

"Are you going to tell me about the poster now?" Zach says, when we reach the water.

I feel myself cringe on the inside. I forced destiny's hand so hard. Should I really be surprised that it worked? Or maybe the tightness in my chest is not surprise, but disappointment that it took so long.

"After we missed each other in Times Square, I felt like I had to do something. I thought that maybe I could find you."

He raises an eyebrow. I think back to the missions Ben and I went on together, all the fun we had and the hope I felt. I'm not going to mention another guy now, though. Zach doesn't need to know everything just yet. Or maybe ever?

"And then I saw you," I continue. "Across the subway platform, at Bedford Avenue. I called after you, I ran—it was you, right? A Monday night around eleven p.m., at the end of September?"

Zach searches his mind for a moment. "Yeah, my friend lives around there, and we often hang out on Monday nights, when I'm off."

The confirmation hits me harder than I thought it would. It wasn't for nothing that I ran away into the night and made things all messy with Ben.

"Anyway, you were gone," I say. "I'd come so close and—" I stop again. None of it matters now.

I let the silence settle for a while, but my mind is bubbling up. "Did you ever think we should have done things differently?"

Zach takes a deep breath. "Yes. No. I went over it in my head a lot."

He tells me about the train to Berlin, the next destination on his backpacking trip, and how he thought about me the whole way.

"Did you ever think to look for me after we missed each other in Times Square?" My voice is a whisper. He *was* there. He *said* he was there. Was he really there? I'm glad it's dark around us. Night always helps bring bravery out of me; I'm not so daring in the daylight.

Zach shrugs, averts his eyes. "How?"

"I don't know," I say, even though I totally do.

I called the restaurant he was supposed to work at. I searched Instagram and TikTok back to front. I enlisted a friend—we came up with a list, and let it take us all over the city. If I did all these things, Zach could have as well. He could have called every restaurant in a two-hour radius around Paris. He could have contacted Le Tablier and asked about one of their students. And there are probably other ways I'm not thinking of. But that wasn't our deal. It wasn't the *plan*.

It's getting pretty cold now, especially by the water, but this night cannot end. We cross over to the other side of Manhattan, exploring the quiet streets of Chinatown, with all its colorful signs and pieces of street art painted on the sides of buildings. Slowly, we make our way up Bowery, Zach wrapping his arm around me to keep me warm, and soon find ourselves on the Lower East Side. There are enough bars and clubs in this area that we see people on almost every block. Still, the city feels like ours to explore. Every corner of New York turns out to be a perfect spot to kiss Zach.

"When can I see you again?" Zach says as we enter a twenty-four-hour diner. The booths are made of black vinyl and squeak as we snuggle up on the same side.

I smile. "Today? Tomorrow, every day?"

Yes, there's work. But I can't picture doing anything other than being with Zach.

I order blueberry pancakes with maple syrup and Zach gets fries and mac and cheese. Of course, as soon as our meals arrive, I want his and he ogles mine, so we end up splitting everything. It's weird and delicious and comforting. Heaven.

"What?" he says, when I've been staring at him too long.

"I can't believe we're together again."

He laughs and kisses me, his lips sticky with maple syrup.

"My family is arriving in town for my dad's wedding on Saturday. Do you want to come?"

I'm trying to sound casual, even though this very question has been on my mind for the last hour. I know it's fast. Luz would not approve. But Zach is part of my life; he has been for a whole year.

"Of course I do. Should I wear a suit?"

I nod. "With a tie and your absolute best dancing shoes. It's going to be so wonderful!"

"I can't wait."

My heart fills with glee. This is what life should be all about, *non?* You make plans and you work hard and you allow yourself to dream. Then, when you least expect it, everything falls into place, exactly how you imagined it would.

Chapter Twenty-Five

Chef's investors are coming for a big dinner in a few days, and he's cranked up the pressure to one thousand. Outside of the regular services, the cooks have taken turns spending every moment refining the holiday menu to make it extra special. We're constantly playing around with the ingredients Chef and Bertrand are getting from the suppliers, with various degrees of success.

Yesterday, I burned an entire batch of Brussels sprouts—a reviled vegetable in France, most used as a threat for badly behaved children, but one that is inexplicably popular over here. On the upside, I was pretty proud of the endive cups I made, with pomegranate seeds and crumbly blue cheese. Chef felt like my vinaigrette was too heavy on balsamic vinegar, but you can never fully please him anyway.

Today, I'm paired again with Ben; the first time I've seen him since the Yankees game. We've texted back and forth and I thought about sharing my big news, but this felt like a face-to-face conversation. That, plus: nerves. I'm not even sure why.

"I have something to tell you," I say as soon as Bertrand and Chef step out to discuss something. The rest of the team is here, too, prepping for dinner, but the two of us are at the very back, near the pantry, away from everyone else.

Ben looks up from chopping a large bunch of scallions. "What's up? You're literally glowing."

My mouth goes dry. "I'm so happy right now."

Ben puts his knife down and smiles. "Me too. That other night was so fun and I've been thinking a lot about the wedding—"

I can't hold it any longer. "I found Zach."

"You . . . what?"

I nod fast as Ben's eyes grow wide. "We did it! I found him!"

I jump up and down, not really caring that Chef will come back in any second.

"But how?"

I get why Ben would be confused; he doesn't know the full story. So I give him the highlights: Luz's idea of putting up posters near where I saw Zach on the subway, which turned out to be a stroke of genius. And then the phone call I got out of the blue. I skim over the night that followed, because it feels weird to kiss and tell.

"And you and Luz did that weeks ago?" Ben says.

I guess he really didn't see them. "Yeah, sorry. Maybe I should have told you, but it felt a little ridiculous, you know?"

The onion smell hangs in the air, and I'm getting a weird feeling in the pit of my stomach. I've had a few hours to get used to the idea that, in an ever-buzzing city of eight million people, I managed to find my one true love when I was least expecting it.

Ben frowns. "I'm happy for you, Margot."

A weight lifts off my chest. "You are?"

"Of course! This is what you wanted. Finding Zach and being with him. You made it happen." He smiles. "Look at you! Nothing can ever stop you."

I chuckle. "Yeah, I guess that's true. Watch out, New York! I'm getting my own. But it's all thanks to you. It was your idea to try to find Zach. I couldn't have done it alone."

"Yep, what can I say, I'm full of great ideas. This is exactly what was meant to happen."

I lean in for a hug, excitedly, but it's quick and lukewarm. We're at work, and we have so much left to do. There are rumblings from outside, Chef shouting about something or other.

"And now we're all going to the wedding together!" I say, while it's still just the two of us.

Ben steps back, startled. "We are?"

"Yes, I invited Zach, too, and my dad is so happy for me. He said the more the merrier. And we're all ready to partyyyyyyy."

I do a little dance. I think I'm delirious. Zach and I spent most of the night out and I only caught three hours of sleep.

Ben picks up his knife and resumes his chopping duties. "Right, but, um—" he starts, not looking at me.

"But what?"

For a minute or so he just focuses on his work, as if I've suddenly disappeared. And then, "I'm not sure I can go to the wedding anymore."

At first I think he's kidding, but he definitely doesn't look like it. "Why?"

"I finally convinced Raven to give me more shifts and she said there might be an opening on Saturday."

He brushes his hand across his chopping board to gather up all the spring onion and chucks it into a bowl.

"You're serious?"

How long has he known about this?

"Yeah, actually, I'm relieved that Zach is coming with you now."

"But you borrowed a suit and everything."

I can't believe this. It's like the air around us has turned to ice. Ben won't even look me in the eyes.

"I have to take it, Margot. The second the holiday rush is over I'll be back to begging for shifts."

"Okay," I say, feeling defeated. "But I'd still love to have you there. I'll talk to Raven if you want. You deserve a night off."

He gets back to chopping again, but I put my hand on his arm to stop him. "I've just got to follow my plan," he says. "Not everyone can afford to dream and have fun."

Ouch. This talk is going from bad to worse. "Imagine if I'd given up on finding Zach? Think about what I would have missed out on!"

Ben takes my hand and gently pushes it away so he can get back to work. I should, too, but I can't focus now.

He lets out a deep, pained sigh. "Okay, you know what? Forget what I said. I'll come to the wedding. I don't want to mess up the seating chart."

Then he turns his back on me, literally, and the conversation is over.

I got what I wanted; Ben agreed to come, and I can't wait for us all to be together.

But as I head to my station and pull my supplies out of the lowboy, I can't shake the thought that this isn't a victory at all. Quite the opposite, actually. It feels like I lost. Or maybe like I broke something. I'm just not sure what it is.

Chapter Twenty-Six

It's a whole family affair. Papa's parents are here from Normandy, and staying for a few weeks to see friends from when they lived here. Their other son—my uncle—is flying from Chicago with his wife and three children. Maman's mom was invited, but she just had eye surgery and wasn't feeling up to flying. Miguel's relatives have started to trickle in as well, though we won't see most of them until the wedding.

Maman and her boyfriend, Jacques, are staying at an Airbnb a few blocks away so we can get ready together for the big day. She brought an extra suitcase with all of the stuff I asked her for—coats, boots, cookbooks, and other things I didn't think about when I left but that I need now that it's almost winter. She didn't even complain about bringing all of that; I think she's starting to accept that New York and me are for real. It wasn't such a bad idea for me to move here after all.

I miss out on the first family dinner because I'm working, but when I exit the restaurant after midnight, I find both of my parents and their partners waiting for me outside.

"We had a late meal at ABC Kitchen," Papa explains. The restaurant is just a few minutes away, one of his favorites in the city.

"And we're jet lagged," Maman adds, meaning she and Jacques. "I can't go to sleep yet."

Papa is fidgeting with his keys, and Maman's eyes are puffy from the flight, so I have a feeling there's another reason why my parents are picking me up like I'm at school and don't know the way home.

We fall into step as we head down Broadway, me between Papa and Maman, Jacques and Miguel behind us. Maman makes me tell her all about my night, what dish was most popular—the baked Camembert, which Chef is particularly proud of—and what time was the busiest—between 6:30 and 9:00. We see a lot of businesspeople during the week, wining and dining their clients. No one in France would ever dream of eating at 6:30, especially if they're trying to close a deal.

"There's something I wanted to tell you," Papa finally says as we cross over to Fifth Avenue. "Miguel and I have been talking about the job. It's a really great opportunity for him."

"It sounds like it," Maman says, eyeing me sideways.

Papa hasn't brought it up since that weekend in the Hamptons, but Maman and I have been talking about it nonstop. We couldn't pretend it wouldn't affect us all as a family. We've almost always been apart in some way, but never this scattered.

"I've been in touch with a few companies there—" He stops, but neither of us jumps in.

Instead, we let the sounds of the city—people speaking loudly on their phones, stereos playing ahead in Washington Square Park, a car honking—fill the silence between us.

"I always thought it'd be nice to have a house and a car," Papa adds.

Maman gives me a look, guessing my reaction to that.

"I know it must sound boring to you," Papa says, turning to me. "But these are the kinds of things you think about at our age. New York is great, but it doesn't have everything."

"And . . . *les palmiers*," Maman says. "I'd like to live at the beach, too, one day."

"So you're going to cheat on us with some palm trees?" I say to Papa. I'm kidding, but really, I just want him to get it over with. It's hard to pretend that I haven't been dreading this moment.

"Right," Papa says, a little tense. "I'm going to do it. We're moving to Miami."

Maman wraps an arm around my shoulder. "And we're happy for you, aren't we, Margot?"

"Yeah, of course." My voice catches, and it comes out like a croaked whisper.

"Margot," Papa says.

"I am, really." But I know I don't sound like it.

Sure, I knew that I couldn't live with Papa and Miguel forever—I didn't want to, anyway—but I expected things would happen on my own terms. I'd come here, I'd be with Zach again, I'd find a job, and then I'd figure out where to live. One of the bussers gave me a website on which to search for roommates, and I've been casually browsing it, but the order of things is throwing me off. I'm just getting my footing at work—always having to be on my toes depending on Chef's mood du jour—and I only just found Zach. But this is what I wanted, and everything will work out in the end. I have to believe that.

We're almost home when I speak again. "When are you going?"

"Miguel won't start until January, and I have to look for work. We won't be moving out of the apartment until the end of winter, at the earliest. And even then, we could keep it a little longer," Papa says.

"You don't need to do that for me. I'm really happy for you and Miguel. I'll be fine. I'm going to be *so* fine."

"We'll make sure of it," Papa says, turning to Miguel, who has caught up with us.

"I'm sorry I'm stealing your dad," Miguel says. "But think of all the fabulous beach trips you're going to take. We'll pay for your flight, whenever you feel like it."

Huh, I hadn't thought of it like that.

"Trust me, Margot," he continues. "When it's the middle of February, the sun goes down at four, and the ice won't melt from the snow that fell three weeks before, you're going to want to move to Miami, too."

"But before that happens," Papa says, "there's something I want to ask you."

Our little group is gathered on the sidewalk in front of the building, and I look sideways to make sure we're not blocking anyone from walking by. Luz would be proud of me. I've learned so much since I got here, including this: never get in a New Yorker's way.

"What?"

"Will you walk me down the aisle?"

I was not expecting that. "Me? What about Grandma?"

"I talked to her. She wants you to do the honors."

"But I'm a bridesmaid!" I turn to Miguel, who knows exactly what I'm thinking. This is not the proper way; Luz will not stand for it.

"I spoke with Luz," Miguel says. "Your dad wants you by his side, every step of the way, and she's going to walk me down, too. It's what would make us happy."

"So?" Papa says.

I nod but the words won't come out. A moment later we're wrapped in a bear hug. It feels like the safest place in the world.

I pull back. "I really have to break in my new shoes. I can't afford to fall flat on my face."

Maman and I have a whole routine planned out on the morning of the wedding. Luz is getting ready with her family, the grooms left for the Wythe Hotel in Brooklyn—where they stayed last night and are getting married today—and Jacques is more than happy to sleep in.

We start our morning with coffees and a mani-pedi at a local nail salon, then have appointments at Drybar—a blowout for

Maman and a messy updo for me. How so very New York of us. In France, we'd be doing everything ourselves.

We've sent each other pictures of our dresses, but Maman still coos as I put on the pink beauty that's been patiently waiting in my closet. The silk feels cool against my skin, and sleek across my hips. It's not that it's sexy, exactly, but it's definitely a different version of me—more polished and shinier. Maman looks me up and down for a few long seconds before she says anything.

"Ma fille," she says, her voice raspy. *"Tu as changé depuis que tu es ici."* My girl. You've changed since you got here.

My mouth is ready to protest, but my brain stops it. Because if I think about it, I *have* changed. I moved to a different country. I have a busy job. And I have a boyfriend, a real one, not just a guy I dreamed about for a year. Thinking about that makes my stomach flip.

"Qu'est-ce que tu en penses?" I say, doing a little spin. *What do you think?*

Maman attempts a smile. *"Tu es magnifique."* I really do look good in this dress.

"Bon, ce garçon alors?" So, about that boy?

My brain freezes.

I don't know if it's because she notices the confusion on my face, but Maman clarifies. *"Comment il s'appelle déjà, celui que tu as invité au mariage?"* What's his name, again? The one you invited to the wedding?

"Ben et, uh, Zach," I say with a grimace.

She frowns. I'd told her all about Ben, and our wedding crew with Luz and Ari. It was all going to be so much fun! Of course Maman already knows how I met Zach, but, like everyone else, she'd assumed it wouldn't go further than one romantic evening in Paris. Honestly, I'm still quite proud of myself for proving them all wrong. But, with my long work hours and Maman preparing her trip over here, we haven't gone over all the details of what went down over the last few days, like the fact that I have *two* dates to the wedding now, both of whom are supposed to meet me here. It's not as weird as it sounds: I want them to get to know each other before the ceremony. After my awkward conversation with Ben, I'd prefer to clear the air sooner rather than later. I'm sure they'll be friends. Gosh, I *hope* they'll be friends.

I explain the two-date thing, then tell Maman about Zach as we do our makeup. How finding him again was better than in my dream, and that it's been worth all the heartache I put myself through since I got here. We've been texting every chance we get, which isn't as much as we'd like considering we're both working a lot. But I know it'll all be fine in the end, because we're meant to be. We have been since that night in Paris.

"Il a l'air parfait," Maman says with a funny smile when I've finished. *He seems perfect.*

And he has perfect timing, too. I'm strapping on my sandals when a text chimes on my phone. It's Zach.

I'm downstairs

Come on up, I reply, buzzing him in.

I check myself in the mirror before I open the door. I showed him a picture of the dress already, but this is the full look. Hair, makeup, perfume, high heels—I'm the most put-together I've ever been.

My heart flips inside my chest as I open the door.

On the other side, Zach is standing in a dark gray suit—fitted just so—with a matching silk tie, a crisp white shirt, and shiny black shoes. I've always found Zach jaw-droppingly gorgeous, but this is a whole other level of hotness. Like, *bonjour,* scoop me up, spin me around, and kiss me already.

"*Um, hi,*" he says, his voice totally sexy. "You look . . . *absolument resplendissante.*" *Absolutely ravishing.*

And he learned some French, too! Ticking all the boxes, are we?

"*Merci.* And you look hot. If my mom wasn't right back there . . ."

I point toward the other end of the apartment, but he doesn't let me finish my sentence and just wraps me in his arms as he kisses me. He smells like soap and shaving cream. He really is perfect. What did I do to deserve him?

Chapter Twenty-Seven

Tears start to blur my vision before we're even taking our first step down the aisle. Too many emotions battle inside me. There's seeing my dad so happy and being surrounded by much of my family. There's finally meeting Luz's mom, Amelia, who has heard as much about me as I've heard about her. There's the stunning view from the hotel's rooftop, overlooking Manhattan, where the ceremony is taking place. The decor is superb, all twinkling garlands and bold flowers.

My hands shake as I hook my arm on Papa's, and not because it's chilly for an outdoor ceremony. That view makes it all worth it, but he's looking a little jittery himself. For months he's been saying that the wedding doesn't mean that much to him, that he just wants to be with Miguel. The bells and whistles are fun, but that's not what marriage is really about. But seeing the day come together like this, and watching his heart rise and fall underneath his fancy custom suit, I bet he's rethinking his stance.

I try to catch Zach's attention as we go past him, but he's

staring deep into his phone. I hope everything's okay. He's sitting behind Ari and Ben, and I can't tell if they've met already. After Zach arrived at the apartment, Ben texted that he was running late and would meet us at the venue. I've been taken up by bridesmaid duties ever since we got here, so I didn't get the chance to introduce them.

Miguel's vows are incredibly moving. He talks about the first time they met, how quickly he felt deep in his heart that he was in the presence of someone truly special, not just "the one" but "my one," as he calls it, and how hard he tried to manage his expectations after previous disappointments. He describes how he pictures their future together—living the sunshine dream in Florida, taking trips to France so his new husband can remain connected to his roots—growing old and deeper in love at the same time.

The grooms have hired a translator for the occasion, so that the French guests don't miss a thing, and there isn't a dry eye in the assembly when Miguel hands the mic over to Papa. His own vows are lighthearted and funny. He describes ducking into a store ten minutes before his first date with the uber-stylish Miguel, self-conscious about his outfit and feeling the need to step it up a notch. There are jabs about Miguel's repeated attempts at learning French—something he swears he wants to do, but on which he gives up after speaking two or three sentences.

It's all incredibly *fantastique* and I've never been more in love with love. This is what I want—not a wedding, I'm way too young for that—but just pure, gorgeous, unfiltered feelings. *L'amour, l'amour, l'amour.* And I'm on my way.

We take a lot of family photos with the Manhattan skyline behind us, and then on the streets of Brooklyn, before leaving the grooms to their wedding portraits. Maman and I walk back to the venue, where waiters have started circulating with trays of drinks and canapés. Maman scoops up two champagne flutes with a wink at me. She knows about the age limit for drinking in the States, but I'm three-quarters French and this is my dad's wedding. She slips me one of the flutes as soon as the waiter has his back turned.

"Best day ever!" I say as we clink.

"*Un mariage vraiment magnifique!*" Maman replies, bringing the glass to her lips.

"See?" I say in French, "Everything worked out perfectly."

"Yes, they planned everything really well," Maman replies, also in French, while gazing at the floral arrangements surrounding us. "I love the music, too."

I agree with her, but that's not what I'm talking about. "I mean me being here in New York. You've been so worried about it, but I made it all work in the end. And yes, things got messy more than once, but I'm so happy I did it."

Maman nods slowly, like she's pondering, not what to say next, but *how* to say it.

I put my glass down on a nearby table. "What?"

"*Comment il te traite, Franklin?*" How's Franklin treating you?

We were all smiles just a few minutes ago, but now her fingers are gripping her satin clutch.

I let out a sigh. Are we really having this conversation right now? "Well, I don't call him Franklin, for a start. It's *'Chef, oui, Chef'* all day long. And yeah, he's tough, but . . ." I trail off with a shrug.

I'm not in the mood to describe exactly how hard it is to work under Chef Boyd. The man changes moods faster than I can poach an egg.

"Is he nice, at least?" Maman says in French.

My hackles rise. "I'm not a kid anymore. I don't need anybody to go easy on me."

"Hmm," Maman replies, her jaw clenched.

For a moment, neither of us says anything. I'm tempted to go off and find my friends but there's a funny feeling in the pit of my stomach, and I realize there's something I need to say to her.

"You had this life, Maman. You did the whole moving to New York thing, with lots of jet-setting and climbing the ranks in the restaurant industry. And when it didn't suit you anymore, you chose for us to go home. That was *your* choice and clearly you're happy you did that. But I'm an adult now and I get to make my own decisions about where I live and how much I work."

"I don't want you to make the same mistakes I did," Maman says, lowering her voice.

"Who says I'm making a mistake?" She looks away, which only frustrates me more. "Why do you think I won't survive here?"

"It's not about that. I've just been down that road. It never gets easier."

"I don't need it to!" This, I realize as I say it, is a lie. I don't know how much longer I can keep going like this. It *has* to get easier, at some point. Once the investors have come and gone, once I've proved myself on the line for a while, in the new year, maybe . . .

Maman glances over my shoulder, and I turn around to see my grandparents—Papa's parents—coming our way with bright smiles and their own half-empty flutes in hand.

"On ne devrait pas parler de ça aujourd'hui," Maman says quickly. *We shouldn't be talking about this today.*

She switches the topic just in time, but I can't move on so easily. She doesn't get it and I'm going to have to accept that she might never. She doesn't want me to be here. She doesn't think I can go the distance. Even after I've done all of this. After I've come this far. I can't believe that after all I've done, Maman still looks down on my life choices, waiting for me to trip so she can gloat and say "I told you so."

Chapter Twenty-Eight

At dinner, a fabulous feast awaits us.

"Do you ever feel like working in a kitchen spoiled fine dining for you?" I say, leaning over to Zach, after the appetizer. Luz, Ari, and Ben are also at our table, along with a few of Luz's cousins. Ari glances sideways at Ben. I guess this is a question for both of them, too.

"Not really," Zach says. "That tuna tartare was to die for. This is all so awesome. Thanks for inviting me." His warm smile has been replaced by a grin I can only describe as wildly kissable. Which is exactly what he leans over to do. *Swoon.*

"What's for main?" he says, checking out the printed menu on the table. "Miso glazed sea bass? Score!"

I chuckle. "Almost sounds like you came for the food."

Zach takes in the room, the mood lighting, the DJ station, and the dessert bar set up at the back.

"And the party afterward!" he says, missing my joke. "Lucky we bumped into each other just in time."

"Right, so you could eat wedding cake?"

Zach shrugs. "I'm more of a savory kind of guy."

There's an awkward silence around the table, but I keep on smiling. Attending my dad's wedding together when we just reconnected might be a little much. It'll be easier when it's just the two of us. Right? Then we'll get to really know each other.

"Well, it's not too often we get to eat food we *didn't* cook," Ari says. "But some of us are pretty good at picking our way around different plates." He shoots a weird glance at Zach, who ignores him.

"What's Ari's deal?" I whisper to Luz. "This is a wedding. It's supposed to be fun. Why is he acting like his old grumpy self?"

This has been going on since we sat down for dinner. After the ceremony and during the cocktail hour, Luz, Ari, and Ben mostly hung out with Luz's family. I found Zach again after my conversation with Maman—he was chatting with a girl near the bar, a guest on Miguel's side. But ever since we got to our table, Ari has been making snide comments toward Zach, who focused on me instead. I know I promised Luz I'd cut Ari some slack, but I am not into his attitude. Not today.

"I don't know," she whispers back. "He and Ben keep mumbling about Zach, but when I asked them earlier, they just said it was nothing."

She grimaces. I expected her to tell me to be nice to her boyfriend, and her response gives me a strange feeling.

Zach grabs a piece of bread and tears it up. "Well, I think it's nice to enjoy the good life while we can."

"Yeah, we believe you," Ari says right back.

I glance at Ben, who's sitting tight with his jaw clenched. *You okay?* I mouth.

Are you? he mouths back. The look on his face is of pure concern.

Something feels off. I want to talk to Ben some more, but he starts up a conversation with Luz's cousin next to him, and I don't feel like trying to catch his attention across the table.

"Let's go mingle," I say, grabbing Zach's hand.

He's looking at his phone, and it takes him a moment to tear his eyes away from it and follow me. I can't wait until the grooms have their first dance and the floor opens up to everyone. The DJ is playing my kind of pop music and any minute spent in Zach's arms is my favorite kind of minute. But for now we go check out my masterpiece, which has been set up in a corner of the room: the dessert bar. It looks as perfect and delicious as I was envisioning it: the traditional *pièce montée* with puff pastries, the strawberry and vanilla naked cake topped with fresh flowers, the multitude of cupcakes in various flavors and colors, the tower of macarons in rose petal, pistachio, and passion fruit . . . It makes my mouth water. But we have a few more courses to get through before this.

"You did a great job," Zach says, taking a snap of me in front of the colorful display.

Then he grabs me in his arms and kisses me. A few selfies ensue, more memories of our first official date together. I don't know how we're going to top it on our next one, but I'm sure we'll manage somehow. Every time we've spent together has been more exciting than the last.

The thrill starts to die down when we get back to our table. Ari and Ben won't look in our direction, and Luz seems stuck in the middle, shooting me apologetic smiles. I try to focus only on Zach as we finish off our mains, and then while the cheese course is being served. Papa insisted upon this French tradition, which required a bit of convincing with the catering company. But here they are: a full wheel of Camembert, a slice of Roquefort, another one of Ossau-Iraty—a medium-firm cheese made from sheep's milk—and a Reblochon, along with chutney, honey, and grapes. Not to mention the baguettes, obviously. Never forget the baguettes.

But by the time I tear off a piece, Ari has moved on to giving us full-on death stares. I know Luz loves him, but this guy is a lot to deal with.

"Having fun?" Ari says to Zach, his tone all snarky.

"I am, actually," Zach says, turning to me and giving me a peck on the lips.

"Of course you are. Lots and lots of fun," Ari quips back.

"Ari," Luz says. A warning.

"What's going on?" I say.

Luz is a little too quick to respond. "Nothing!" She sounds too chipper.

"But—" I start. Luz smiles at me strangely and I stop. Weird. Silence falls on our table as we fill our plates.

"I can't wait to start dancing," Zach says, turning to me in a way that obscures Ari and Ben.

But he's not quiet enough. "Yep, you can't wait for anything!" Ari says loudly.

This is too much. "Do you two know each other?" I say.

I glance at Luz, who's acting all innocent. Meanwhile, Ben is staring at his plate.

"Yes," Ari responds at the same time as Zach says, "No."

Um, okay?

"It's really nothing," Luz says. "We shouldn't worry about it tonight. We're here for this beautiful wedding and to have fun, right?" She tugs on Ari's sleeve, but he's fuming now.

"I'm sorry, I can't do this," Ben suddenly says.

"Let's not ruin the night," Luz says softly.

"Is anyone going to explain what the hell is going on?" It feels like everyone knows except for me.

Instead, Ben gets up, his chair scraping against the floor as he does. He shoots me one last look, and walks away.

I follow him. I'm practically running, as much as I can in my heels. I feel like I might sprain an ankle by the time I make it out onto the terrace after him. The view of Manhattan all lit up is splendid, a fairytale backdrop for a dreamy night. Though I have a feeling it's about to take a different turn.

"I knew this was a mistake," Ben says, wrapping his arms around his body. He left his jacket inside. "I shouldn't have come to your dad's wedding."

There's no one else on the terrace with us, it's too cold for that.

"Is this about the shifts Raven promised you?"

"I like you, Margot. I can't believe I have to say it out loud. I felt like we were . . . I figured it was . . . Anyway. When you invited me to the wedding, I thought it meant something. We were getting closer and yes, maybe I should have told you sooner, but I felt like it was mutual, even if you needed some time to get there."

"We were looking for Zach!"

Even before Ben's face drops, I know this isn't really what I wanted to say. But what? Ben likes me. It's a total shock and completely obvious at the same time. I'd never stopped to think about it, because . . . Zach. Ben knew from the start that my heart belonged to someone else.

"I know, Margot. I can't control my feelings."

"I'm not asking you to. It's just that . . . I wasn't expecting that."

"Really?"

I don't know what to say. We're at my dad's wedding. I'm finally with Zach. I've had the best time with Ben these last few months. This is all way too much to think about for one night.

"I'm sorry, Ben. I can't—"

"I get it," he says, cutting me off. He's never sounded so curt before. "I hope you're happy together. But I have to go home now."

"Please don't! I'm sorry we didn't spend much time together tonight. I've been a bad friend."

I step toward him but he shakes his head. "I can't sit there and watch you with him. Please, Margot. You have to understand. If you're my friend, let me go."

My throat is so tight, I can't speak. I nod instead.

"Bye, Margot."

"Bye, Ben."

But by the time the words come out, he's already gone.

Feeling deflated like a three-day-old balloon, I get back to our table. Ben has already grabbed his jacket and left. Zach isn't here either.

Luz guesses what I'm thinking. "He got a text message and I think he went off somewhere."

I start to look around the room for him, but Luz gets my attention. "We need to tell you something." We being she and Ari. Luz glances at her boyfriend and waits.

"You do it," he says. "Margot already hates me."

"She doesn't hate you." Luz looks at me for confirmation, but I'm feeling too raw to deal with whatever is going on here.

"I'm going to hate you both if you keep this up."

Finally, Luz takes a deep breath and lets it out all. "Ari and Zach know each other. They have a mutual friend, and they've hung out before."

"Okay?"

"When you found Zach again, I was so excited for you that I told Ari your whole story. How you met in Paris when he was just starting his trip around the world, your pact . . . and how you missed each other in Times Square but managed to get together again. He thought it was really cute. But then you guys arrived this afternoon and he put two and two together: your Zach was the Zach he knew."

Zach didn't say anything about knowing Ari, but I guess we've been kind of busy today.

Luz swallows hard before continuing. "They've only hung out a few times, but Zach is good friends with Ari's buddy, which is how he knows that Zach—"

"Zach what?"

"I hate being the one to tell you this. And on this night, too. But when you and Zach walked away earlier, I had to ask Ari what was wrong. I didn't want dinner to get any worse, so I made Ari spill the whole thing. I didn't know until today, Margot. I promise! Otherwise, I would have told you."

She grimaces.

"Told me what?" My heart is beating a million miles an hour and my toes feel crushed inside my sandals. I need this to end. Now.

Ari cuts in. "First off, his trip around the world lasted all of four weeks. He ran out of money and came back here to start working again."

That would explain why Zach was vague when I asked him about his travels. He showed me some pictures of Berlin, but that's it.

I guess he didn't lie, exactly. "We've only just found each other again. He hasn't had a chance to tell me."

But Luz has more to say. "Zach hasn't been waiting for you like you've been waiting for him. Ari says he's seen him with a different girl at every party they've been to. He's not who you think he is."

I turn to Ari, hoping that he has an explanation for this. Maybe it's all just a big misunderstanding.

"I'm really sorry, Margot. I know you might not believe me, but I didn't want you to get hurt, which is why I tried to keep my mouth shut tonight. This guy's a total player. You deserve better than that."

Mostly, for now, I feel like I deserve a do-over on this entire day.

Chapter Twenty-Nine

Luz comes in for a hug, but I don't have time to feel sorry for myself too long. Zach gets back to his chair next to me just as Miguel's dad stands up for his speech. As he clinks a knife against his champagne flute, I sit there reeling, pretending Zach isn't there. He's acting like everything's fine, when I'm pretty sure my face is on fire.

For the next fifteen minutes I have to endure listening to multiple stories on great love, as the speeches move on to the grooms, and then to my grandma, Papa's mom. Everyone gushes about what a wonderful moment this is for all of us, while I begin to question everything I believed about love. To bide my time, I pick at crumbs of bread with my index finger, my mind spinning faster and faster.

When Mamie—my grandma—is done talking, we all raise a glass to the happy couple. I hold back tears that I so wish were of joy. Zach had girlfriends? Plural? We agreed that night in Paris that we were made for each other. If this is all true, then Zach stole not just this night from me, but the last year of my life.

"Can I talk to you?" I say, taking a tiny sip before placing my flute down. I'm in no mood for celebration, but it's bad luck to put your glass back down without drinking.

Moments later, I'm back on the terrace, with Zach this time. The view is just as glorious, mocking me.

"What's going on?" Zach says, looking nonplussed.

How can he not see the hurt on my face?

"Did you come to Times Square that day, like we agreed in Paris?"

"You already asked me that."

"I'm asking again. Did you?"

"Margot, c'mon."

He steps toward me, opening up his arms, ready to wrap me in them. How I wish I could just nestle on his shoulder and breathe him in.

"I need to know."

He sighs. "Did *you*?"

I can't believe we haven't really discussed this before. When we found each other that night on the Highline, everything felt incredibly perfect. It happened, right? I didn't dream that? The spark in his eyes as he saw me across the crowd? The way we fell into each other's arms? How could this not have been real?

"Of course I did!" I say. "August 1 at midnight in the Times Square bleachers, bottom right. That was our plan. We were going to be together."

"I know what we said that night." Zach sounds weary, almost pissed off. He starts pacing between me and the edge of the terrace. "But didn't it seem wild to you in the light of day? We weren't going to see each other for a whole year!"

"You didn't even travel around the world. What else did you lie about?"

"Who told you that?"

I shake my head. Does it matter how I know?

"We didn't exchange phone numbers—" Zach continues.

"That's what you wanted!" I scream. "We both decided it was the best way, the *romantic* way."

A memory flashes before my eyes, from that first night out with Ben and the others from the restaurant. When I told him about the pact Zach and I had made, Ben had laughed. It wasn't mean; it just didn't make sense to him. Who wouldn't want to be able to contact someone for whom they've fallen so deeply? Why did we need such an elaborate plan if we were made for each other? Ben was right. He saw immediately what I couldn't understand, because I was too smitten with Zach. Or with the Zach I thought I knew.

"It was romantic that night," Zach continues. "And I felt just like you did. But then, after I left you and over the next few days . . . it didn't make sense anymore. So many things could go wrong. You could change your mind about New York, you could meet someone else. You could just . . . not make it to Times Square."

This last one stings even more than the rest. I was so panicked that day, completely frazzled from being hit with so many things at the same time: my first two days in New York, a brand-new job, navigating this wild city. I tried so hard for us, and what did Zach do? *Nothing.*

"So you were never going to come meet me?"

Zach sighs as he leans against the balustrade, facing me. I can't bear this distance between us, but then again, I don't feel like being close to him, either.

"If you must know," Zach says, crossing his arms, "I still had the date in the calendar on my phone. I thought about it sometimes. I never really decided one way or another. That night in Paris felt like a dream. Sometimes I even wondered if it actually happened."

"It did happen!"

I hate that I feel the need to say it out loud, but it's true. He can't take that away from me, from us. We made those plans, we agreed. And we did all of that because we felt something, deep inside. I didn't invent that.

"I know. That's not what I'm trying to say. Just that it was a night unlike any other. Reality felt so different. Anyway, I was in between jobs that week in August, and when I looked at my calendar, seeing your name put a huge smile on my face. It brought back all the memories from our hours of walking around Paris and I wondered . . . but then a buddy called me about a job, and I pushed it out of my head on purpose. I figured there was no way you'd actually be—"

"I was there," I cut in, my voice a whisper. "I was twenty minutes late, but I was there. And I looked for you everywhere. I went nuts going through everyone in the crowd, certain it was all my fault, that I was the reason we missed each other."

Tears roll down my cheeks. I'm a complete and total fool, an embarrassment.

Zach pushes himself off the balustrade to rush to me. "Hey, Margot, come on, no."

I hold my arm out, warning him not to come closer as more tears make their way down. How could I have been so naive?

"We found each other again!" Zach adds, following my lead and keeping a reasonable distance. "We're together now."

"No, we're not," I say without thinking. "You've had girlfriends, you've been living your life—"

"So have you!" Zach says. "Okay, maybe you haven't dated other guys, but what does it matter? I wasn't cheating on you. I just didn't think I would see you again."

I swallow hard. This right here is the problem, no? This whole year, we became completely different people. I was so sure that the universe had put Zach in my way because he fit so perfectly within my dream future. I remained focused, dedicated, in love. With a ghost, a guy who lived his life like I didn't exist, like he expected to never see me again.

"Then we shouldn't. See each other, I mean." I'm surprised by the words coming out of my mouth, but not enough to take them back.

This is all wrong.

"Margot, please! You were right, we found each other. Isn't this great?" He gestures from me to him.

But this was only great when I didn't know he'd lied to me. That everything between us was fake, this big romance that played up in my mind, and mine only. I can't even look at Zach anymore. He's a stranger.

And Maman was right. I *have* changed since I got here. I thought everything would happen so quickly, so perfectly, so smoothly. But it hasn't been like that at all. Instead, it was the slow and steady process of showing up, and putting my best foot forward every day at work that got me the job on the line. And here's another thing I'm realizing: it's the relationships you build day after day that really matter, not the ones you dream up in your head. Take me and Luz. Before it felt so rosy and fun, when all we'd do is chat on WhatsApp from across the ocean. But now it's deep and wonderful. We have our ups and downs, and we've become closer as a result.

And then there's Ben. He's the reason New York has been so good to me. I've been lying to myself, too. We're not just friends. And we might be more than friends if I hadn't spent so much of my energy chasing a phantom.

"I'm sorry, Zach, this isn't for me. Not anymore." To my surprise, I feel nothing as I say these words. It's like Zach snapped his fingers and I finally saw him for who he is. And for who he isn't.

"Are you serious?" He looks pained, but I don't care anymore. "Why can't we be together now and forget about everything else? I want you, Margot."

I don't feel like crying anymore. The wheels click into place in my mind, in my heart. I know what I want. Who I want. And it's not Zach.

"You're right that a lot can change in a year. Because all this time, while I was looking for you, I started falling for someone else."

Zach opens big, wide eyes. "What?"

"I'm sorry. Actually, no. I'm not sorry. You're not the one I want to be with."

I'm not trying to hurt him. This isn't payback. The truth is out, and I can't smuggle it back inside. I need to tell Ben how I feel. Now.

Chapter Thirty

It's over. Not the wedding: people are dancing, the drinks are flowing, and the cupcakes have quickly disappeared from the dessert table. Luz saved me a plate, but I'm not hungry. Zach left. He kept trying to plead with me out on the terrace, but I couldn't unknow what I knew, couldn't ignore what I felt.

For the next few hours, I hardly let go of my phone. I text Ben. I call him. I leave him voice messages, telling him that I'm sorry, that I need to speak to him. That Zach and I were never meant to be—I got it all wrong. I beg him to respond, not caring how pathetic I sound. I want—no I *need*—to get this off my chest tonight. There's only silence in return.

When Maman asked, I told her that both Ben and Zach weren't feeling well and went home. Worst lie ever, but I wasn't ready to explain. Only Luz and Ari know the truth. Even though my night is ruined, I'm kind of thankful for Ari. If he hadn't spoken up, I would have kept believing in Zach. And for how long? How long would it have taken me to discover the true Zach?

"We could go stand outside his building until he comes out. It's not that far," Luz suggests when she comes back from the dance floor and sees me hunched over my phone. "And he'd have to talk to you then."

I entertain the idea for a second or two. "That feels really stalkerish."

"Maybe he'll think it's romantic. I have faith in you two."

It hits me then. "You always knew there was something there, even when I didn't want to admit it to myself."

She nods. "And can I tell you now that I always thought Zach wasn't good enough for you?"

"You just did."

Luz smiles, trying to lighten the mood. "The guy left Paris without taking your number! What a fool. I'm glad he's gone."

"Me too," I say sadly.

It's like a weight has been lifted off my shoulders. A whole year of anticipation, of wishing and hoping and dreaming. Of missing real life. And then, of hurting the guy right in front of me.

"You have to fix this, Margot."

"Geez, you're so annoying when you're in love."

"Annoying and right." She grabs my hand, forcing me up. Then she takes my phone and puts it down. "But maybe let things cool down for right now and try to enjoy yourself a little. You've had a night. Come on, I love this song. Let's go dance."

I know Ben will have to talk to me at some point, because we're both working the next day's dinner shift. I've been off for just two days, but it feels like it's been much longer when I walk in. There are two new people on the team—a dishwasher and a pastry cook—and Raven is nowhere to be found, even as we approach family meal. Ben is there, but he won't look in my direction. I shouldn't be surprised, and yet his indifference cuts deep. The shift hasn't even started and I have to accept the fact: There's no way I can get through this. I can't pretend Ben is a stranger. I can't ignore everything that went down between us. I have to make him talk to me. Now.

I find a window of opportunity when everyone comes out for family meal. Ben was in charge of cooking for the staff today, which means that he's still in the kitchen as others set up the table. It only takes me a few seconds to work up the courage to go find him there, but I'm still a puddle of nerves and a sweaty mess when I push through the door.

"Hi," I say.

Ben is wiping down his station and getting his *mise en place* ready for service, but I don't think that's why he doesn't look up.

"Ben," I try again.

Any minute now, someone will barge into the kitchen and I'll have to wait all night until I can talk to him again.

"Hey," he says, finally. His voice is dry, unaffected.

"I can't tell you how sorry I am," I start, stepping forward. He stiffens as I do, a subtle gesture that slices through me. "I've been lying to myself these last few months. I really felt like I *had* to find

259

Zach. That's the only thing that made sense to me for the longest time. I thought we were meant to be and that's why I couldn't see . . . you."

Ben chortles. He clasps on the lids of plastic containers, the clicking sound resonating through the room.

"It's true! Deep down, I knew I was starting to have feelings for you. I was ready to give up on him, but then he called that night, and I had to—"

Ben looks up, his mouth a thin line. He's pissed. "You didn't even think twice about inviting him to the wedding."

"I messed up, okay? I was caught up in a fairy tale that was all in my head."

"A few days ago, I would have done anything to hear this, but it's over, Margot. I don't want your excuses."

"Let me explain. I want to be with you. If you'll have me."

"You only want me now because you discovered who that guy really is."

"I'm sorry!" My voice rises in spite of me. I need Ben to understand. I know what I did but I can fix this. It will all work out if only he would listen to me. "I had to try with Zach. How could I not when we'd been looking so hard for him?"

"I don't know, Margot! That's not my problem, is it?" Ben says, loud enough that his voice echoes against all the stainless steel. I've never seen him like this. "Look, I get that this whole thing was my idea. I thought you were fun and you sounded so sad about not being able to find him. I liked you and I wanted to help. But then . . . my feelings changed. I didn't want to play that game anymore, and I figured maybe you'd come around. You'd realize that something was going on between us."

"You were right!"

"I don't think so. It feels like you just want a boyfriend because it was all part of your dream: move to New York, fall in love, have a great adventure . . ."

He trails off and makes a face like he's expecting me to react, but I don't. I can't. Because there's some truth to it. Ben is the one person who sees right through me, always, but I can't force him to be with me if he doesn't want to. All my silence does is infuriate him more.

"When you invited me to your dad's wedding, it really meant something to me."

"I wanted to be with you," I start. His eyebrows shoot up, his head already shaking. "I was lying to myself, thinking we were just friends."

I liked Ben from the moment he got up to shake my hand, when I'd just made a fool of myself in front of the entire staff. I'm pretty sure I started falling for him right there and then. I just wasn't prepared to accept it.

"We were friends and now you've ruined that. I'm not just a bit of fun you can have."

He turns his back to me, continuing to set containers and jars about. I don't know what else to say, just that this cannot be it. I have to try harder. Ben squirms past me to pick up tongs and a frying pan. I notice how he leans sideways, making sure not to brush against me. Outside of Luz, he's been my best friend the last few months. Now the thought of touching me makes him recoil. I did this. This is all on me.

"At least I let myself dream," I say. I don't know what comes over me, but since we're letting it all out . . . "Unlike you."

His nostrils flare, giving me a silent warning.

But I'm not done. I'm far from perfect, but I have things to get off my chest, too. "Why are you so afraid of dreaming? You have these big plans of ticking off boxes on your restaurant checklist because you feel like you have to, but do you ever let yourself think about what you truly want? You've been telling me how much you'd like to learn cooking the French way, but you're still sticking with your idea of going to some soulless American franchise. Don't you think it will make you *miserable*?"

While I'm talking, he pulls out a few saucepans from the shelves and stacks them up on the stove. The top one wobbles for a second before settling in.

"Says the girl who dreamed about a guy she barely knew for a whole year. How'd that work out for you?"

Then he gets on his toes to pick up a colander, and adds it to the pile. It immediately starts to sway. I step forward to help, but Ben holds his hand up.

"Don't!" he says, his voice booming across the room.

I point at the too tall stack. "This is going to—"

And then it does. Every pot crashes to the ground in a tumble so loud, so screeching, that I flinch and jerk back, knocking over a jug of olive oil. The cap wasn't screwed on all the way, and the gold liquid drips on the floor, next to Ben.

I rush over to grab a towel, but Ben just stares me down. "I don't need you, okay?"

He kicks one of the pots.

And then he just blows up. "Tell me this, and be honest. If you hadn't found out that Zach wasn't who you thought he was, would you have come back to me? Or would you have picked him? The guy you've wanted from the start? Huh?"

I don't respond. Somebody else beats me to it.

"What the *hell* do you two think you're doing?"

Ben and I both whip to the side at the same time, in the direction of the entrance, where the voice is coming from. Chef stands there, his arms crossed in front of his chest. He's flanked by three people in suits, two men and a woman. His investors. The ones he'd been planning to impress. I don't think I even knew the dinner was tonight. The date kept changing, and then I was so busy with the wedding that I didn't pay attention.

I'll admit, the scene does not look good. There are pans all over, olive oil dripping from the counter, sliding across the floor, and on my pants. Ben's face is bright red after screaming at me, and I'm on the verge of tears. Okay, maybe not just on the verge.

"It's all my fault," I stammer. "I can explain."

"I don't care whose fault it is!" Chef spits. I sneak a quick glance at Ben, whose eyes have popped wide open with fear. "No one behaves like this in my kitchen. What kind of place do you think this is? No one fights in here. Ever. Get out. NOW."

He turns to his guests. "I'm sorry about this. This is *not* the kind of restaurant I run."

I have no idea what to do, but since Ben seems frozen in space, I decide to follow his lead. Then I take a deep breath. I *have* to fix this. Today cannot get worse than it already is.

"We're going to clean everything up right away," I say as calmly as I can. "Service is about to start—"

"Not for you it isn't. Get out. Both of you!" Chef yells. "You're fired."

Chapter Thirty-One

I wander around the streets of New York for a while. Sniffly, stunned. Unsure of what I'm most upset about: my fairytale idea of Zach turning to dust, Ben rejecting me so fiercely, or getting fired from the first real job I've ever had. Screamed out of the place like a pariah. The greenmarket is on in Union Square today, the many farm stands bustling with colorful vegetables, baked goods, jars of artisanal jams, and organic eggs. People are going about their business. New York moves on. Always forward, never looking back. I thought coming here was going to be the start of a great adventure, but it's been tougher and tougher every day. I'm not sure I'm brave enough for this place.

Heading toward Washington Square Park, I realize I'm close to Parsons, Luz's school. I keep going for a few more blocks and pull out my phone as I walk under the arch.

Hey, are you around? I text.

I need her to shake me by the shoulders and tell me that this didn't just happen, that I didn't blow up the life I've been dreaming of forever.

In class . . . 🤓

I stare at the screen as tears roll down my cheek.

Sorry, Bella. Call you as soon as I can, she adds, as if she can see me.

She always knows what I need before I do. I love Luz, but she's so busy these days. The semester is in full swing. She's spending more time with her school friends, making new ones, and then, of course, there's Ari. Her life is full, rounded. I thought mine was getting there, too, but now I feel incomplete, a pile of raw ingredients that amount to nothing much.

I text Julien, my best friend from high school, but he doesn't respond. It's nighttime in France, and he must be out, having fun. Without me.

I have nowhere to go. My parents, Miguel, and Jacques have a reservation at Nutrio tonight. It was—is—supposed to be the last hurrah before the newlyweds head off to Mexico for their honeymoon tomorrow. Even though she has mixed feelings about it, Maman has been looking forward to seeing where I work, that famous up-and-coming New York restaurant! She's checked out the menu and made me tell her about the best dishes to order. I'm not just embarrassed. I feel dead inside. How am I supposed to explain to them that my great dream has come tumbling down? What am I supposed to say? *You were right, Maman. I don't have what it takes after all.*

For a long while, my home is a bench in the park, not far from where Zach and I made out just a few days ago. Roller skaters do infinity loops in front of me. To my side, a guy offers to recite poems for two dollars. I'm left in the great wide open, with my lack of plans. The emptiness of my life.

Like most lonely people, I stare at my phone, hoping it will give me answers, even if I don't know what the questions are. There's one thing I want to do, though, and it can't happen soon enough. I find my message thread with Zach. One deep breath, and it's deleted. Then his number is gone, along with our brief past. I don't know where he lives, where he'll be working next week, or how I might be able to find him again. I'm okay with that. Because if I still had his number, I'd be too tempted to text him now. I'd want him to be here for me, to hold my heart, to wrap me in his arms. I'd want him to be Ben.

Of course, I think about Ben. I've thought about him every moment since the wedding, and every second since Chef practically threw us out of the restaurant. I waited outside for him after I grabbed my things and walked away, my head hung in shame. I don't know who saw me or what they heard—I just couldn't face anyone. I gave up after about half an hour of standing on the other side of the street. Ben must have gone out through the back alley. He didn't want to hear what I had to say, couldn't face seeing me. And why would he? I hurt him, and not just once. I got him fired. I will never forgive myself.

I've always felt so sure that this is what I wanted. The great adventure in the big wild city. An epic love story. Life with a capital *L*. What happens now that I've lost everything? Am I supposed to keep going when it hurts at every turn? More tears come, and I don't wipe them away. In fact, I let myself full-on sob, loudly and messily. People walk by, some ignoring me, others looking at me kindly. One even mouths, *Are you okay?*

I nod but I'm not. What is it about New York that you can let your emotions hang out in the open, that you can cry in public and feel like it's the right thing to do? Just a few months ago, when I cried in Times Square, I was mortified. But now, it's just who I am. See, New York, you got to me. I thought I would grab you by the horns and make you mine. But you don't work that way, do you? You don't make concessions. You don't answer to anyone. Yet you let us be our most vulnerable selves out in the open, as if every street, every bench, every corner is our home. You're kind of wonderful and horrible that way.

A long time passes before I decide to peel myself off the bench. The threat of even more shame is what motivates me: I can't let my parents get to the restaurant and talk to Chef. They need to hear it from me.

When I get home, Papa's and Miguel's suitcases lie half-empty on the living room floor. There are stacks of summer clothes on the couch, piles of shoes next to it.

"Hello?" I call out.

"Margot?" Papa comes out of the bedroom holding three pairs of swim trunks. "Aren't you supposed to be at work?"

"What happened?" That's Miguel, who's in the bathroom filling his toiletry bag.

I can't breathe. Excuses and lies bubble up inside my chest, trying to escape. None of them will help me. None of them will change the fact that I screwed up my life so majestically.

"I got fired." I add nothing, no flourish.

"That chef," Papa says, shaking his head. He grabs his swimsuits from the arm of the couch, and makes space so we can both sit down. "You were right. He's a tough one."

"Nope." I stare at my lap. "I ruined everything all by myself."

"You want to tell me?"

Before I do, we text Maman, who's over here with Jacques in a heartbeat, her mouth agape, a litany of French curses spilling out. I tell them, well . . . enough of the story. The fight with Ben but not the full reason for it. I describe the screams, the clatter of pots, the olive oil everywhere. The investors who, honestly, seemed to enjoy the spectacle, even if Chef didn't.

At the end, my parents look at each other, and then let out a deep sigh in unison.

"Do you want to tell her or should I?" Papa says to her.

Maman seems to ponder it as they exchange another glance. I'm expecting a long speech, something I won't like, so I'm surprised when all she says is "You're too hard on yourself."

"But I'm really not. I lost my job. Papa and Miguel are moving to Miami in a few weeks. I can't find a place to live if I don't have a job, and I can't . . ." I don't even know what I was going to say. "I can't I can't I can't."

"Margot," Maman says with a heavy sigh.

"Please don't say I told you so."

"I wasn't going to. I understand how upsetting it is."

"But give it a few days, and you'll see. One door closes and another one opens," Papa says.

I look from one to the other, perplexed. This vote of confidence feels a little farfetched.

I stand up, needing to shake my legs. "Did you not hear what I'm trying to tell you? I got fired from my job. Chef basically had smoke coming out of his ears. And Ben lost his job because of me, too!"

I sit down at a dining chair, away from them, my face stinging from all the tears I've already shed. Jacques goes to get me a glass of water. I'm pretty sure he didn't have "major girl drama" on his list of things to do in New York. They all stare at me as I take a few sips.

"I ruined my life," I say, quietly now.

"Margot," Papa says calmly. "You're not listening to us. You ruined your day, sure. Your week as well, no doubt. But your life? Not even close."

"You have to make *some* mistakes at your age. It's—" Maman adds.

"It's practically mandatory," Papa continues for her.

My parents always act like an old couple, instinctively knowing what the other one wants to say, and finishing each other's sentences.

Usually I find it cute, but I don't think they understand the severity of the situation. "Where am I going to live? What am I going to do for money?"

Papa: "You'll stay here as long as you need."

Jacques: "I ate your food. It's amazing."

Miguel: "You'll get another job in no time."

I burst out crying, throwing my head in my lap.

"I know you're not going to like this," Maman says, "but maybe you need to go back to the classic recipe."

I look back up, intrigued. "What do you mean?"

"Remember the *mi-cuit au chocolat*?" Maman says as Papa nods enthusiastically at the mention of the chocolate lava cake. "You must have been ten, maybe eleven. You spent hours, days even, trying to create a new recipe. You wanted to put your own spin on it, and you experimented with every aspect. In one version you used olive oil, in another you sprinkled in cayenne pepper. At one point you reduced the cooking time so much that it was basically chocolate juice."

"That version was not all bad," Papa says.

I remember now. It was summer holiday and Papa was visiting. I can still feel my frustration, the repeated failures despite all my hard work. "I thought I could really make it differently."

My eyes well up at the memory.

"And then, after you'd gotten all that out of your system, you pulled out my recipe card, the one I've been using since I was your age," Maman says.

"And I still put my own spin on it!"

I made Maman's tried-and-true recipe, but I also made a pistachio cream sauce to go with it, rather than the classic *crème anglaise.*

"You sure did," Papa says.

"Some things don't work out how you imagine them, and so what?" Maman says.

"You can always pare everything down and go back to the essentials," Papa adds.

"This is what adult life is like for most people. We try new things and experiment, and eventually, after much trial and error, we figure out what really matters to us: the basic recipe ingredients. And then, when we know that, when we know ourselves, we can add on our own unique sauce to go with it."

I think about this for a long while, enjoying the comfortable silence.

And then I get an idea. It puts a smile on my face for the first time today.

Chapter Thirty-Two

I've spent the whole day in the kitchen. Just me, my thoughts, and total quiet. Well, as much quiet as you can have in a New York apartment. Sirens go past my window, someone is shouting on their phone, indescribable squeals trickle up to my little slice of the city. The grooms have left for their honeymoon. Luz is at school. Maman and Jacques are off exploring more of the Big Apple—today's itinerary includes everything from the *Fearless Girl* on Wall Street to the post-modern Guggenheim Museum on the Upper East Side.

It feels good to be alone. I'm not sure I've spent enough time with myself since I arrived here. I was always skipping—through the city with Luz or Ben, or around the restaurant kitchen, trying not to get yelled at. Here, I can let my mind wander while my hands practice their rehearsed moves: *la danse de la soupe à l'oignon.*

I find a Tupperware tucked in a drawer and scoop out the

mixture into the container. I haven't made onion soup from scratch in years. In fact, I can't even remember the last time I ate it before I went over to taste Ben's. I felt a little rusty as I went through the steps—texting Maman to double-check my instincts about the splash of red wine she adds, or the mix of cheeses she uses—but I kept telling myself that, for once, this isn't really about the food. I'm not sure what it *is* about yet; I'll have to wait to find out.

Carrying my precious package, I walk out the door and into the cold November air. The wedding was less than a week ago, but it feels like a different life, a different city. So much has changed in the space of a few days.

"That's the New York effect," Luz declared after she heard what happened. "One minute you're on top of the world and the next—"

She'd waited for me to react, to agree, to understand, but I'd just hung on to her words, hoping for answers, a path forward.

"I know it probably doesn't seem that way to you now, but it's what makes it exciting."

That's how I thought about New York over the last three months. *How thrilling! How bustling!* But honestly, doesn't it get exhausting after a while?

I walk up to Eighth Avenue to catch the L train, listening to an older man play jazz on the platform until the next Brooklyn-bound train arrives. A few stops later, I get off at Bedford Avenue in Williamsburg. Walking down the street, I notice that some of my posters are still up on the lampposts along the way. Maybe I'm just nervous and trying to slow down time, but I feel like I have to stop. Scraping with my fingernails, I peel each one of them off until this whole part of my dream is history, dumped in a New York City trash can.

No one answers when I press the intercom; all I hear is the sound of the buzzer opening the door for me. Climbing up the steps, I try to wave off the memories of when I last saw Ben, the look on his face when Chef told us to get the hell out of his kitchen. Once again, it's Karim—one of Ben's roommates—who opens the door when I knock. He looks at me quizzically, like he doesn't recognize me. This isn't a good start, but I power through.

"I was expecting a delivery," he says by way of explanation.

"I *am* here to deliver something." I point at the bag in my hand. "Is Ben around?"

Karim shakes his head. "He had a job interview."

"What restaurant?" I say, full of hope. Chef was so short-sighted to let him go. Someone with less temper and more vision will scoop Ben up in no time.

"I don't know if he'd want me to tell you . . . ," Karim says with a sigh.

I see news traveled fast about what a terrible person I am.

"I swear I want what's best for him. Just tell me it's somewhere good."

Karim looks away.

"Or at least tell me that it's not at one of the steakhouse franchises he's been talking about."

His face twitches. "For what it's worth, I told him he deserved better than handling a fryer for the tourist crowd in Times Square." He must see the despair in my eyes because he adds, "I'll talk to him again, but he needs a new job."

"Do you think I could wait for him? I really want to talk."

"He just left, and I'm going to head out soon."

"Right, well, could you give him this?" I hand him the bag. "And could you tell him that—" But there are too many things to say, private ones. "Actually, do you have a piece of paper and a pen?"

After he gives them to me, I sit on the top step in the stairwell. Karim offered for me to come inside to write my note, but I read the look on his face: he didn't want to betray his buddy. It's okay, anyway. I need time to think.

After some soul-searching, this is what I write:

Dear Ben,

I don't think I'll ever stop feeling sorry for how things went down between us. You were the first friend I made in New York, my only friend outside of Luz. Many of my favorite moments here happened with you. Because of you. You're so warm and kind, a gorgeous person inside and out. I wanted to be around you from the moment we met. I was just too focused on my fantasies to understand what that meant.

I learned so much in my few months here, but one of my biggest lessons has been that plans are pointless if they get in the way of life. I had such a specific idea of how my New York experience should go that I forgot to let the city take me by surprise. Because of that, I didn't just hurt myself, I hurt you, too, the person who's meant the most to me since I got here.

I know I lost your friendship—on top of everything else—but I wanted to tell you: Please listen to your heart. Don't do what I did. You deserve everything you dream of and more, even if it doesn't make sense, or if it's not part of a grand plan. I believe in you. I always will.

Love, Margot

PS: As you'll soon find out, your onion soup is better than mine. No contest here, but I'm trying. I really am.

As soon as I step inside Nutrio, I see the absolute last person I was expecting. Ari is sitting around the table for family meal, with most of the staff. I'm surprised, but it doesn't take me long to understand that he's not just here to hang out.

He's the first one to talk to me. "Hey, Margot."

His smile is kind, if a bit contrite. He and I have history, good and bad. But I don't begrudge him for coming back here. We all have to make the decisions that are right for us. In the moment anyway.

I have to push past the discomfort; I came here for a reason. "Hi, everyone, I wanted to stop by to say goodbye. I'm sorry I left like . . . you know, the other day."

Raven comes out of the kitchen then, and I let out an internal sigh of relief that Chef is not with her. I'm not ready to face him yet.

"It's good to see you," Raven says. There's a softness to her voice, to her face. Then, quieter, she adds. "I wish you could stay. You're one of the good ones."

My throat tightens. "Thank you."

It wasn't so long ago that she was willing to make bets with Ari about how long I would last. I didn't appreciate then how much things come and go. Change is inevitable in a place like this. Both at Nutrio and in New York.

She gives me a hug, and then, one by one, my ex-colleagues get up to do the same, including Ari. I manage to keep it together long enough to get through all of them.

"Chef's going to be out any minute," Raven says after I've hugged the last person. She gives me a look, checking to see if I understand what she's saying. I do, but I need to talk to him, too.

Without asking permission, I go around the back and find him in the office. The door is open, and I enter after a quick knock. He might throw me out any minute—who knows what kind of mood he's in today—so I have to be brief.

"*Bonj*—" I catch myself. I don't need to impress him anymore. I don't even want to. "Hi."

He looks up and frowns, but then it turns into a smile. "Margot! I'm glad you're here."

"What?" I must have heard that wrong.

"Please sit down. I want to talk to you."

I do but I can't help glancing at the door, like I'm going to have to make a quick exit because something is terribly wrong here.

"I've always felt guilty about how your mom and I left things. I was hoping to talk to her when she came for dinner, but they canceled their reservation at the last minute."

"Um, yeah, that's because you fired me that day."

"I gathered," he says with a sigh. "And I don't like to realize that I keep making the same mistake."

"Did you fire my mom, too?" I joke.

He raises an eyebrow. "You don't know the story?"

"What story?"

He tells me.

Maman and Chef weren't just colleagues. They were business partners who were about to open their first restaurant together. They'd been working the New York restaurant circuit for a few years at that point, and they felt ready to take the plunge, together as co-chefs. They worked relentlessly on their grand plan, and then Maman had me. After I was born, she switched to a catering job so she'd have a more flexible schedule.

"Eventually, things started to fall into place," Chef continues. "We agreed on a concept and a neighborhood, and started trying recipes while you napped in a corner of the room. We were so different: Nadia couldn't get away from classic French recipes and I was way more experimental. But that's why it worked. We complemented each other.

"By the time we started courting investors, you were a toddler and your mom hadn't worked in a restaurant for three years." Chef pauses; he doesn't want to tell me the next part. A flash of embarrassment crosses his eyes. "Well, the 'suits' didn't like it. They would ignore her in meetings or ask how she would manage running a restaurant as a single mother, ignoring her comments about how involved your dad was. They were acting like misogynistic pigs . . . ," he adds, with a sigh. "But I said nothing. I wanted the money. I'd dreamed of this restaurant for so long.

"After a lot of back and forth, we were offered the capital on one condition: that I take the reins, leaving your mom as a souschef." At this, Chef looks away, full of shame. "I took the deal. Nadia booked a flight back to France soon after."

I'm speechless. And then it hits me: it wasn't me Maman didn't trust all this time. It was New York. She'd experienced firsthand how easily you can get steamrolled out of here. Especially if you're a woman—and a mom at that—in a man's world. She didn't want that for me because she loves me, not because she didn't think I have what it takes.

I think about Papa, who supported her decision to move back to France even though it meant he wouldn't see me as much. He wasn't going to be one more man to quash her ambitions: if New York wouldn't let her be a chef, then she wouldn't let New York get in the way.

"That restaurant, my first one, it went bust within two years," Chef continues. "It was missing your mom's special touch and I wasn't organized enough to run it on my own. And then, when I tried to open my next one, it was twice as hard to get funding."

"Am I supposed to feel sorry for you?"

He chuckles. "No. What I'm trying to say is that I got another chance, and I want to give you one, too. I shouldn't have fired you, and I shouldn't have worried so much about what the investors were going to think. The job on the line is yours. Go grab a jacket and start over tonight."

That man is full of surprises, but I'm not here for them anymore. I don't want to work for him, not now and not ever.

I nod and get up. "No, thank you. And honestly, your baked Camembert isn't all that. I've tasted so much better in France. You don't have to put a different spin on things that are already perfect as they are."

Chef jerks back but he doesn't seem angry, more like impressed. "So what are you going to do? It'll be tough no matter which restaurant you land at in the city."

I shrug. "I've learned so much over the last few months. It's been the experience of a lifetime, and I'll always be grateful for that. And even though I didn't want it to end like this, it taught me a valuable lesson: no one has just one perfect future, or just one dream. I thought this was mine and maybe I was wrong. Or it wasn't the right time. But like you said, I deserve another chance. Just not here."

And this isn't just about work. If Zach hadn't let me down, I'd never have seen that we weren't actually meant for each other. Turns out there are no dream guys. Especially not if you have to put your future on hold for them.

Chef nods. "Good luck to you."

"Good luck to you, too."

When I get back to the dining room, Ari is waiting for me.

"I'll walk you out," he says.

One more wave goodbye at everyone, and I step out of Nutrio for the very last time.

"Chef called me," Ari says as soon as we're on the street. "My new job wasn't all it was cracked up to be, so I figured I'd try here again. I didn't come back to steal Ben's job."

"I didn't think you did. It's not your fault he got fired. It's mine."

"*Chef* got Ben fired. He's impulsive and moody, but he does value talent and hard work. He hired me back. Wouldn't get off the phone until I'd agreed. He sounded desperate." I think he can see the snark on my face. *Way to make it all about you, Ari.* "Anyway, what I'm trying to say is that I've already spoken to Chef. He didn't say it, but I think he knows that he's better off with Ben in his kitchen. There are many line cooks out there, but talented ones with zero attitude? That's not so common. Ben will be back here in no time."

"Really?" This is best the news I've heard all day. "I couldn't bear the idea of leaving New York without at least trying to fix some of my mistakes."

"You're leaving?"

I haven't said it out loud to anyone yet, but I've known for a couple of days. I need some time away from plans and dreams. I want to take a breath and hit pause for a minute. And a New York minute won't be long enough for that.

Ari looks back inside the restaurant. They're waiting for him. The show is about to start; all the performers must be in place.

"Hey, Ari," I say, feeling his attention slip away. "Since I'll be gone, you'll have to take extra good care of Luz, okay? And if you ever mess with her and break her heart, I'll come back here and slice you up in so many pieces you won't even fit on a sushi platter. Do you hear me?"

"I do," he says with a smile. "Loud and clear."

That's it, then. I'm done here.

Chapter Thirty-Three

Luz and I are sitting on the bleachers in Times Square, bottom right, though I had a hard time convincing her to come here. Yes, I know it's super touristy—the food carts crammed together, the abundance of live cartoon characters, and the neon lights from the ground up all the way to the sky—but that's what I am now. A tourist. To think I ever thought this was the most romantic spot to meet the love of my life. Wrong on all counts, Margot.

"I can't believe you're abandoning me," Luz says, staring ahead at a human-sized Woody from *Toy Story*.

"Hey," I say with mock hurt. "You abandoned me first. What with your new boyfriend and everything."

"Admit it: you like him now."

I laugh. We both do. I'm not sure I'm done crying yet, but I don't want my last moments with Luz to be tainted with too much sadness.

"I'm not ready to admit anything," I say.

We burst out laughing again.

"I'm so glad we got to be together," Luz says, wrapping an arm around my shoulder. "And that's all that matters."

I sigh. This part hurts. "I'm going to miss you so *so* much."

"Not as much as I'll miss you. Promise you'll be back."

I hold my hand up. "I swear! There's still so much I haven't seen, that I haven't done. A girl I love told me that nothing is forever in New York. Everything is for right now. This is goodbye . . . for now."

"That girl sounds incredibly smart and beautiful," Luz says deadpan.

"And completely full of herself," I add.

"There's something I want to tell you before you leave," she says, a sheepish look on her face.

"About New York?"

"No, about Ari. We're . . . even more serious now."

I wait for her to say more, but she just looks away and . . . ding, ding, ding, the ball drops.

"You did?"

A bright grin takes over her face.

"I'm going to need more details than this. When? Where? How?"

She raises an eyebrow, then takes a deep breath. "You really want to talk about it?"

"Um, yeah."

"But you—"

"But my love life is such a complete and total disaster? True that."

I stare at her, silently demanding answers.

"Fine," she says dramatically. "Last night, in his room, and I don't even know what the last question is supposed to mean. You do know how it works, right?"

I flare my nostrils, not in the mood to take her snark. Ari is not Luz's first, but something in the look on her face tells me this is different. Not that I'd know. Or will know anytime soon, based on my current situation.

She sighs, caves in. "It was very *very* good. I will take no further questions at this stage."

"You met him thanks to me. Let's keep that in mind for your wedding."

She rolls her eyes and we switch topics. We have so little time left together and still so many things to say. Then, Luz catches me up on her classes—she's loving learning about architecture from the seventies—and the students she's still getting to know. Everyone is so creative and driven: making art, making their own clothes, making waves on social media. Shaping their future careers already.

"You don't mind that I'm telling you this?" Luz says, when she's been talking for a while.

"Why would I? I'm happy for you. Actually, it's more than that. I'm proud of you. I can't wait to tell everyone that I know this super talented interior designer who's decorating the homes of the rich and famous all over the city."

"And I can't wait to tell everyone about this incredibly talented French chef who runs this amazing restaurant, wherever you end up landing."

"In my mom's kitchen," I say with a chuckle. "Right where I started."

I'm going home. As soon as the idea started to form in my head, I knew it was the right decision. I never really appreciated Maman's restaurant before, the recipes passed down through generations, the garden she grew to have fresh everything at hand. She always wanted to teach me her ways and I was too busy waiting for the new and exciting to understand what she was trying to do: honoring tradition, showing up day in, day out, striving for beauty and excellence. The French way. Ben helped me see that in more ways than one.

Maybe someday I'll go study at Le Tablier, for one of their yearlong courses. Or maybe I'll come back to New York and try my luck again. But one thing I know is that I'm not going to miss what I have in the moment, waiting for something better. And then not seeing it when it stares me in the face.

"Margot!" Luz says with a frown. She doesn't like when I get down on myself.

"Luz!"

We laugh. We *have* to laugh, otherwise this is too heartbreaking, leaving her here. She promised she'd come visit me, too, but when or how, we have no idea.

"What's on for the rest of the day?" she says at last, changing the topic.

Luz has to get back to classes this afternoon and I'm booked on a flight with Maman and Jacques two days from now. It was my choice, but the deadline feels crushing: a handful of hours before all of this is over.

"I have a hot date," I say, getting up. "The city is waiting for me."

I spend the rest of the day taking it all in, one more time. I walk around Central Park for a while, then swing by Levain for a late "lunch": a walnut chocolate chip cookie I eat on the same blue bench Ben and I sat on all those weeks ago. Afterward I make my way back downtown, wandering down the charming little streets of the West Village, then through the shops in SoHo, and even farther down to Tribeca. I'm gazing in shop windows on Broadway when my phone rings.

"Jacques wants to buy a Yankees cap even though he's never even been to a baseball game," Maman says in French. "Isn't that wrong?"

"No, I think it's New York. You can pretend to be whoever you want to be."

"D'accord, vous avez gagné." I can almost see her rolling her eyes at him while admitting defeat. "Are you having dinner with us tonight?"

"Oui. I'll be back soon."

When I saw Maman again after my conversation with Chef, my legs felt like jelly. I was still so enraged on her behalf, and yet, I completely understood why she never told me. The world can be hard on girls—women!—who dare to go after their dreams. Maybe she didn't want me to know just how hard for a little while longer. That night she told me about her own life in New York, the whole story: from great recipes to bad dates, and from weird work experiences to thrilling wins. I didn't know what I was going to do yet, but I realized this: I still had so much to learn from her.

We hang up as I reach One World Trade Center, the most prominent skyscraper on the southern tip of Manhattan. There is no line at the front. On a whim, I get a ticket and go right up to the hundredth floor, onto the observatory deck.

Feeling a little woozy from the fast elevator ride, I slowly make my way around, silently squealing every time I recognize a landmark. The Empire State Building! The Chrysler Building! The Brooklyn Bridge! I know this city. I was here. I belonged, even if it wasn't for very long. And then, as I finish my lap around the observatory, I spot her. New Yorkers' most beloved French lady. I can't leave without saying *au revoir*.

Outside I head west to the Hudson River, and walk along the waterfront, all the way down to the Staten Island Ferry terminal. My heart pinches as I board the ferry, alone. No, not alone. Ben isn't here, but the city is with me, always. The joys, the fears, the thrills, the disappointments. Maybe this is my great New York love. Not a guy I met one night, but this infuriatingly fascinating place, forever keeping you on your toes, and changing the rules on you.

The boat inches closer to the statue and I wrap my scarf tighter around my neck to fend off the November wind. And when she comes into view, I do what anyone would do when they realize front-on the kind of magic New York brings out: I squeal so loudly that my voice carries around, bouncing off the water.

See you next time, Liberté. Here's hoping I'll feel your shining light all the way across the Atlantic.

Chapter Thirty-Four

My last day in New York is a lot like all the other ones I've spent in the Big Apple over the past few months. I'm busy, rushing from one task to the other with little time to catch my breath. I FaceTime with Papa and Miguel, who answer from their lounge chairs with mojitos in their hands and straw hats on their heads. I pack my suitcases, which is no small task. Not only did Maman bring over so many of my things I'm now taking right back, I might have gone overboard during my shopping trips with Luz. And Maman can't help me on that front. She, too, is going home with a jam-packed suitcase, full of Converse sneakers, vintage Levi's jeans, and boxes of Oreo cookies, her Achilles' heel.

Little by little, I tick things off my to-do list. I manage to run out during Luz's lunch break to give her yet another last hug. I pop by one of my favorite cafés for my now usual—a chai latte and an acai bowl with banana and almond butter. I never did try a pumpkin spice latte; couldn't bring myself to do it. In fact,

I'm leaving New York without an ounce of cinnamon coursing through my body which, according to Luz, is a significant achievement.

I tidy up my room and the whole apartment, letting Maman tease me about how I'm so much neater in the States. And because I don't already have too much to do, I try a new cookie recipe I was just reading about, and leave the dough in the freezer, so Papa and Miguel have a treat to look forward to, a parting gift from their daughter.

On our way to the airport, I press my face against the taxi's window, trying to drink every last drop of the city. I have no regrets. This isn't the last time I'll see New York, I'm sure of it. But I'm excited about my next adventure: going back home and truly enjoying it. Learning my roots all over again, instead of feeling like there's something much better out there.

"Ça va aller?" Maman says after we go through check-in and security. *Will you be okay?*

She's been eyeing me funny all day. I think she's worried that this is too much change, too fast, but nothing is forever. Everything is for right now.

"Maman, you'll literally be ten rows ahead of me. I'm not going to get lost on the plane, I swear."

She looks back at me as they board. Because I booked my ticket at the last minute, I'm in the last group to get on the plane. Moments later, it's almost my turn, when my phone beeps.

Salut

It's from Ben.

I freeze, my heart at a standstill. I was so sure I'd never hear from him again that I didn't think that I was leaving him behind, too. For one crazed moment, I wonder if it's too late to go back. One word from him is all I need. I stare at the screen, my breathing out of control. What do I do?

Look up

I don't. I can't. I'm too confused, too scared. He never responded to my letter. Who knows if he even tasted my onion soup. Not that this is what matters right now, but I can't help it if I always have food on the brain.

"Margot."

It's his voice. His soft, mellow voice, coming from above me. Finally, I look up, and Ben is there right by the entrance of the gate leading to the plane taking me back to France. Smiling his beautiful smile.

"I read your letter," he says as I attempt to process what the hell is going on. "And then I thought, why *don't* I follow my dream? What's stopping me, really? You know, other than practicality, money, and my carefully thought-out plans."

"What are you doing here?" I say, finally able to get words out. I mean, it's pretty obvious. They don't let people inside airport terminals for no reason. But I need details, to know about everything that has kept us apart over the last couple of weeks.

"After I got your letter, I called Le Tablier. I'd been reading over the application letter and I had some questions. I think I just wanted to talk to someone there, to feel like this could be a real thing."

"And?" I ask, my breath hitching.

"They said they'd just had a last-minute cancellation for the winter course."

"You're going to Le Tablier?"

He purses his lips and his eyes twinkle, like he's holding back a smile. "I told them no. I couldn't do it. It was too soon, too rushed. I even tried to get cute, *merci mais non merci*. And then, right after I hung up, Luz texted me. She said you were leaving, that you were done with New York for now. Just in case I wanted to know. I couldn't believe it at first. And then I realized what was happening: it was a sign."

"I like those," I say, feeling my heart pound in my chest.

"It happened so fast. I'm sorry I didn't respond to your messages. I had a lot to think about."

I don't care about that anymore. "Where are you going to live?"

"Friends of friends of my parents are lending me a room for a few weeks, while I get on my feet. I'm doing the course part-time so I can work on the side."

"You're going to love it so much."

"I know. I can't wait." He looks down for a moment. Then he takes a deep breath before his eyes meet mine again. "I'm excited for this new adventure, but I'm also scared."

"I could give you my French number," I say. "In case you want some company. I'll only be two hours away on the train."

Ben comes closer and grabs my hand. I let him. Of course I do. "And make it so easy for me to get in touch? Margot, that is so not romantic of you."

I shrug. "Romance is overrated. And so is—"

But I never get to finish my sentence, because Ben is pulling me to him, and then he's kissing me.

I know I said I was done with wild dreams, but I might just have an idea for what I'm going to do for the rest of the flight. And all the days after that.

Bye, New York, and thank you for the best gift ever. Because this, my friends, is going to be one epic love story.

AUTHOR'S NOTE

I started thinking about this novel in late 2019, when New York was the vibrant, thrilling, and awe-inspiring city I had always known. Writing it through much of 2020 and 2021, I realized that, while I had no way of knowing what the Big Apple would be like on the other side of the pandemic—or if the pandemic would ever end—I couldn't rob Margot of the magical experience of moving to New York for the first time. Consider this novel a love letter to the coolest city I've ever met. May she bounce back even brighter and shinier than she ever was. If that's even possible.

ACKNOWLEDGMENTS

Many thanks to Laura Barbiea, Sara Shandler, Josh Bank, Hayley Wagreich, Romy Golan, and Josephine McKenna, all at Alloy Entertainment, for being such wonderful partners.

To the legendary Wendy Loggia and the whole team at Random House and Delacorte Press: I'm so honored to work with you. Thank you to Nancee Adams, Amber Beard, Emma Benshoff, Lili Feinberg, Colleen Fellingham, Becky Green, Beverly Horowitz, Alison Kolani, Kimberly Langus, Casey Moses, Alison Romig, Tamar Schwartz, and Caitlin Whalen for all you do in bringing books out into the world. It never ceases to amaze me how many talented people it takes to publish a novel, and I'm very grateful for this incredible team.

Huge thanks to Rachel Ekstrom Courage for the warm and enthusiastic support. It is much (*much much*) appreciated.

Thank you to Loubna and Fabien Pichard of the St Tropez restaurant in New York City, as well as Sandrine Jabouin and Clara Kasser for your precious help in the course of my research.

To my 21ders author family, it has been such a joy to write and publish alongside you. Big hugs in particular to Alysa, Alyssa, Anya, Caroline, Christina, Erica, Kate, Nicole B., Nicole C. Shakirah, Sylvia, and Yvette for all the writing power and friendships forged forty-five minutes at a time.

I'm forever indebted to my longtime friends, whose kindness, encouragements, and general badassery mean the world to me. To name just a few: Allison, Amélie, Assetou, Beth, Cécile, Clara, Émilie, Emma, Kate, Kirsty, Marie, Pip, Solenne . . . Argh, it's so hard to stop. If you know me personally and have ever asked about my work, read some of it, or perhaps bought a book of mine: thank you thank you thank you.

All of the French *bises* and Australian hugs to my family: Françoise, François-Xavier, Typhaine, Louis, Patrick, Marie, Lyn, Andrew, Kerry, Ryan, Zach, and Ben.

To my beloved Aggie, thank you for all the cuddles and *so* much love. This book wouldn't exist if I hadn't kept my butt on the couch just so I wouldn't disrupt your naps (and accidentally done a little writing in the process).

To Scott, for cooking pretty much every meal so I could focus my attention on imaginary cooks working in fantasy kitchens, and for absolutely everything else. You know what you did, and how much it means to me.

Lastly, I want to extend my deepest gratitude to all the bookstagrammers, bloggers, reviewers, booksellers, and librarians. Thank you for sharing your love of books and for promoting the act of reading. This also goes to all the readers. What an amazing treat it is that you spend time losing yourselves in a stranger's mind, taking stories on your own journeys, and giving them brand-new lives.

Bonjour, Paris!

Turn the page to preview this charming

romance from Anne-Sophie Jouhanneau!

CHAPTER ONE

I RUN THROUGH the airport in shapeless tracksuit pants, my hair flying behind me. A screaming toddler stands in my way, and I leap over him in a somewhat graceful *grand jeté* before *pirouetting* past a man who's struggling to carry his giant suitcase.

"Faites attention!" a woman yells at me after I almost step on her foot. *Be careful!*

The thing is, I can be careful or I can be late, and being late is not an option right now. This American girl needs to get to the other side of Paris *tout de suite*.

"Sorry," I say as I race through the Charles de Gaulle terminal, my backpack banging into my shoulder.

The reason I'm late is that there was a crazy storm in New York last night, and my flight was delayed by four hours, then six. I stopped counting after that so I wouldn't pass out from the idea of missing my first day of school.

Well, not *school,* exactly. School is a piece of cake compared to what's waiting for me here.

I bump into a group of children straddling the entire width of the terminal hallway and almost fall flat on my face, but I manage to turn it into a *pas de basque.* Thank you, muscle memory from approximately a million years of ballet classes.

I'll admit, this is not how I imagined my first hours in Paris. I had a picture-perfect vision of what was supposed to happen: I would get off the plane on a warm, sunny morning, my wavy brown hair bouncing and shiny, even after the seven-hour flight. I'd swing my tied-up pointe shoes over my shoulder and declare something cute in French with a perfect accent—the result of months of practice— before strutting elegantly toward the best summer of my life: an intensive ballet program at the prestigious Institut de l'Opéra de Paris. *Le dream, non?*

Instead, I "gently" shove past a few people to snatch my suitcase off the luggage carousel, then search the signs above my head for the word *taxi.* That's when something truly wild happens.

"Mia?"

Um, what? How does someone in Paris know who I am?

"Mia? Is that you?"

It takes me a second to recognize that voice. I turn around, and there she is, my nemesis. Or she would be, if I believed in nemeses.

"Whoa, Audrey! What are you doing here?" I realize

it's a stupid question only after the words come out of my mouth.

"The same thing as you, I guess," she answers, looking surprised. When I booked my ticket, I was surprised by how many flights there are to Paris every day. I guess we were on different ones, both delayed by the storm. In any case, I can practically hear her wondering, *How did Mia get accepted into one of the most exclusive summer ballet programs in the world?*

'Cause I worked my buns off, I want to say.

I'm not going to lie: Audrey is one of the best ballet dancers our age in the tristate area, but, hey, so am I. I know because we've competed against each other in every major event in the dance circuit since we were basically babies. I live in Westchester, which is outside of New York City, and Audrey lives in Connecticut, so we don't go to the same ballet school (thankfully!), but several times a year, I watch Audrey snatch roles, receive accolades, and almost always come out *just* ahead of me.

"*You* got into the Institut de l'Opéra de Paris?" Audrey asks with a perfect accent, one eyebrow raised in suspicion. I can tell she regrets her question, because she adds right away, "I mean, what level did you get in?"

I clear my throat, buying some time. There are five levels in the program, and students from around the world get placed according to the skills they demonstrated in their application video.

"Four," I say, holding her gaze.

Four is great. I was *so* excited to get level four. Honestly, I was happy to just get in, especially after being rejected from the American Ballet Theatre's summer program in New York. I've worked my entire life to get into a program like this. Ballet has run in my family for generations—or so the legend goes—and I know my grandmother would have been pretty sad if I didn't get into any school, though nowhere near my own major disappointment.

"That's great," Audrey says. Her hand tightens around the handle of her suitcase, the only sign that betrays her true reaction. Yep, I'm good enough for level four.

"And you're in . . . ?" I begin, even though I can guess the answer.

"Five," she answers coolly.

I nod. Force a smile. Of course she is. It's fine, really. Audrey's technique is flawless; even I can admit that.

"Are you coming?" she asks in a clipped tone, starting to walk ahead of me. "We should share a taxi. It doesn't make sense to take two cars to the same place," Audrey adds like she's talking to a child.

"Right." I hate to admit she has a point. "But we're probably in different dorms?"

I pull up the dorm address on my phone, which Audrey reads over my shoulder. She lets out a deep sigh. "That's where I am, too. Please don't tell me they put all the American students together."

"Seems like it," I say as we make our way to the taxi stand, not bothering to hide my annoyance. There are over a hundred girls and boys aged fourteen to eighteen attending the ballet summer program, and the dorms are scattered all over the city. The minute I received my admission packet with the address of where I'd be staying, I thought I'd won the Paris lottery. Now I'm not so sure about that.

"Boulevard Saint-Germain," I tell the driver once we're seated in the back of a metallic gray car with leather seats. Even the taxis in Paris are chic.

The man frowns at me in the rearview mirror, and I don't know what else to do but frown back. I have no idea what's happening. My thoughts feel like they're trapped in a cloud. Even if I had slept on the plane, Audrey's presence would be enough to throw me off my game.

She shakes her head, then hands the taxi driver her phone, which is open to the map with our dorm's address. My newbie mistake hits me right in the face. I've researched Paris so much that I should have remembered that Boulevard Saint-Germain is one of the longest streets in the city. It snakes across most of Rive Gauche, the side of Paris south of the Seine. Basically, it's like telling a New York City cab driver that you're going to Fifth Avenue.

Audrey gives me a pointed look that seems to say, *Lucky I'm here*.

Her phone rings just as we get on the freeway: a FaceTime call from her mom. I've never met her, but I know who she is—a retired principal dancer who spent her entire career in Moscow with the Bolshoi Ballet. As I listen to Audrey go on and on about how her flight delay almost ruined her life, I realize that I haven't even told my parents I'm here yet. I send a quick text saying that everything's fine. Dad responds immediately.

> Good luck at orientation! Show them who's boss! Love you.

I smile and respond.

> I'll try! Love you too.

And then nothing from Mom. I keep staring at my phone, hoping, wondering, wishing. She's still mad at me. Grandma swore she'd get over it by the time I left for Paris, but clearly she hasn't.

Ever since I was little, dancing has been my whole life. To my mom, however, it was just a hobby, something fun I did on the side, an extracurricular activity to keep me busy on weekends. I kept telling her I wanted to become a professional ballet dancer, and that I would do whatever it took to make it happen, but she always shrugged it off, like it was something I'd outgrow. Luckily, between Dad and Grandma Joan (Mom's mom), there was always someone to drive me to classes, help me sew costumes for my shows, and cheer me on during important performances.

But things got really tense with Mom when I started talking about applying to this program.

"You didn't get into New York. Why would you try again in Paris?"

I'd just received my rejection letter from ABT and was doing my best not to show how devastated I was. I always knew how competitive it would be, but I figured that, after a lifetime of dedicating myself to my art, I had a real shot. But Mom didn't agree with me. "So many girls want this; there just aren't enough spots for everyone," she'd said with a sad face. It hurt a lot to realize that she was right.

"Paris is every aspiring ballet dancer's biggest dream," I'd said.

To be honest, that's not exactly how I felt at the time. Even though it's true—the Paris program is just as well regarded as the New York one—I only ever dreamed of attending ABT, and of joining their company one day. But that wasn't going to happen this summer, and I couldn't allow myself to accept defeat. Everyone knows everyone in the ballet world, and borders don't really exist. If I made it in Paris, then I'd find my way into ABT eventually. They couldn't get rid of me so easily, even if I had to cross an ocean to prove it to them. At least that's what I told myself.

Mom shook her head. "It's your last summer of high school. Don't you want to see your friends, go to the pool, to the movies, and just, you know, do other things?"

"They have pools and movies in Paris, too."

She ignored my snarky tone. "Mia, there's more to life than ballet. You need to have a plan B. Everyone should have one, especially when they're only seventeen and chasing an impossible dream."

She'd never put it so plainly before. An impossible dream? Thanks for believing in me, Mom.

Despite everything she'd said, I kept rehearsing for my video, checking the requirements—an introduction to explain my experience and credentials, a showcase of each of the key steps, then a personal routine of at least two minutes. Grandma Joan even surprised me with a new leotard in a beautiful shade of dove gray.

"It'll be your Paris leotard," she said as I dashed to my room to try it on. It fit perfectly and complemented my blue eyes.

"I haven't even been accepted yet," I told her as I adjusted the straps over my shoulders. My hands shook as I imagined myself practicing *pliés* in a light-filled Parisian studio.

"But you will be," Grandma said, her voice firm. "How could they ever say no? It's in your blood."

"Mom!" Mom said to Grandma Joan as she walked into my bedroom. She cast a skeptical glance at the Degas poster hanging over my bed. "Can you please stop saying that? It's not even true."

Grandma sighed, then turned to me. "Of course it's true. You come from a long line of ballerinas, Mia." She gave me a wink. "You believe me, don't you?"

Grandma Joan has told me the same story since the day I put on my first tutu. The first part of it is definitely true: My great-grandmother was French. She met an American man in Paris when she was twenty-three, fell in love, and moved to the U.S. soon after their wedding. But before that—and this is when things get a little murky—she practiced ballet. Like her mother before her, and her mother before her, all the way back to the late 1800s, when my great-great-great-grandmother was a *danseuse étoile,* a principal dancer, the highest, most prestigious ranking in the Paris Opera. Supposedly, this was around the time Edgar Degas created his world-famous paintings of ballerinas.

Grandma insists that Degas painted my great-great-great-grandmother, and that she was the subject of one of his masterpieces. The nonspecifics of this family legend drive Mom crazy. She doesn't believe this story, and whenever Grandma Joan brings it up, she'll happily point out that no one actually knows which painting our ancestor might be in, or even remembers what her name was. *If* she was a ballet dancer at all. Mom never lets me forget that it's most likely made up, and that there's no way to know for sure. She doesn't want me to believe in fairy tales.

But I do.

The myth itself is proof enough that ballet is my destiny—how could anything as strange as this get passed down from generation to generation if it weren't true? This story has always been part of me, of how I dance. When I'm performing, I sometimes imagine my ancestor twirling across the stage, spotlighted by gas lamps, while Degas sweeps his oil paints and pastels onto canvas and paper. I like to think she was part of his inspiration, that he watched her spin in a sea of color and light.

I wore my new leotard for my audition video, which Camilla, my best friend from ballet school, helped me film. She'd decided to only apply to local summer programs, and swore it had nothing to do with the fact that she didn't want to be away from her new boyfriend—an aspiring musician named Pedro. I think Mom wishes I had a boyfriend as well, but my dating experience so far has only proved that no one can make my heart flutter the way ballet does. To go with my leotard, I put my hair up in a tight bun, my face fully made up. And two months later, I got into the Institut de l'Opéra de Paris, just like Grandma had promised.

I close my eyes for a moment, and when I reopen them, one of the most famous churches in the world stares back at me.

"Notre-Dame!" I squeal to Audrey, who doesn't react. I press my face against the window, soaking in its beauty, the two towers disappearing off behind our taxi, the arched structure revealing itself in the back, and the grand majesty of it all. My first look at Paris! But I don't have time to revel in the moment, because our taxi makes a right turn, and, a couple of minutes later, we pull off to the side of a wide street packed with cyclists, buses, and pedestrians.

"Finally," Audrey says, looking out the window.

The driver slams his horn as a bike zooms past, and I'm definitely awake now. The cyclist turns back and yells what I can only assume is an insult. Though, because it's in French, it sounds almost pleasant to me. Our driver just shakes his head in response as he parks in front of a white stone building, about six stories high, with small double windows all with matching gray curtains—our home for the summer. Thanks to my Google Street View research, I know exactly where we are—a stone's throw from the embankments of the Seine, and the lively student neighborhood called Saint-Michel.

Inside the building, the hall is very quiet. According to my admission packet, my room is on the third floor, and I pull my suitcase up the curved stairwell one step at a time as Audrey rushes ahead with her duffel.

"I knew it!" she calls down the stairs. When I catch up, she's standing in front of a door, shaking her head.

A handwritten sign reads: *Audrey Chapman & Mia Jenrow*

I take a deep breath. Roommates. Ugh.

In the room, two single beds with metal frames are tucked against opposite walls, which are painted in dirty beige. There are also two tiny closets and a small wooden desk barely big enough for a laptop. The window looks onto the building on the other side of the inner courtyard, letting in very little light, even though it's now the middle of the day. Okay, so it's not as glamorous as I'd imagined.

Without a word, Audrey pushes past me and claims the bed by the window. She quickly pulls out fresh clothes and makes a dash to the communal showers. I grab a striped tee and a flowy navy skirt and follow suit. Ten minutes later, we're both back in the room and ready to go when I notice the cardboard tube peeking out of my suitcase. I stop in my tracks.

"What now?" Audrey asks, standing by the door. Our flight delay means that we have to leave immediately if we want to get to orientation in time.

I don't want to have to explain to her that inside that tube is my favorite painting in the whole wide world. I'd promised myself I would hang it up as soon as I got to Paris. It'll only take a minute.

"You should go ahead. I . . ." I pick up the tube and open it. "I need to do something."

Audrey gives me a funny look, her big brown eyes framed by thick but perfectly curved eyebrows. I'm sure she's going to run out the door and not speak to me for the rest of the summer. Instead, she retrieves the few pins from the corkboard above the desk and kicks off her shoes. "Quick," she says.

I'm too shocked to respond as I join her on my bed. A moment later, I smile as I take in the image I've woken up to for as long as I can remember: *Ballet Rehearsal on Stage,* the Edgar Degas painting featuring tulle-clad ballerinas rehearsing on the stage of the Paris Opera. It's so striking; I can practically sense the tension before the curtain lifts.

"It's a superstition—" I begin.

Audrey cuts me off. "I get it. I put my ballet clothes on the left side of my body first. The left strap over my shoulder before the right, the left leg in my tights, my left shoe . . . I can't dance if I don't do that."

I grin. Audrey and I may have never exchanged more than a few icy words before, but this is promising.

"It's a nice painting," Audrey admits.

With the Degas dancers watching over me, my Paris adventure can finally begin.

CHAPTER TWO

THE SUDDEN KNOCK startles us both. Our bedroom door opens, and in bursts a petite girl with brown skin and long black hair.

"Mia, Audrey, *finally*!" The girl's voice is bright, with a strong British accent. "I'm Lucy. Everyone else has left for orientation already, but Anouk and I wanted to wait for you."

Lucy steps aside, and in walks a very tall, pale, blond girl. Anouk waves and gives us a sweet smile.

I'm overcome with gratitude. These girls are total strangers, and they waited for us—who even does that? "So nice to meet you!"

"Anouk was in the program last year, and she knows Paris really well," Lucy says, motioning for us to rush out the door. "Come on, let's go."

"We'll take the ten and then the five," Anouk says in an

accent I can't place. Then, at my confused expression, she adds, "The métro lines."

"Oh, right!" I say. We might be late, but at least we won't be lost.

"Oh, and here," Lucy adds, fishing something out of her tote bag. She pulls out two croissants wrapped in paper napkins along with two mandarins. "We saved you this from breakfast this morning, in case you didn't have time to grab anything."

I hadn't realized how much my stomach was grumbling. "Thank you!" I say, accepting my half from her and immediately biting into the pastry. Whoa. The buttery flavor is delicious, and I wish I had more time to enjoy my first taste of France. "You two are my favorite people in the world right now," I say in between two mouthfuls.

Audrey mumbles a vague "thanks" as Lucy hands her the food. It's kind of rude, of course, but Audrey's not here to make friends.

I wish I could be that disciplined, too, but I *like* friends. Friends are . . . nice. I throw my bag over my shoulder and slip on my shoes. "Ready," I say.

Q&A WITH AUTHOR
ANNE-SOPHIE JOHANNEAU

In this novel, the city of New York feels like a character in its own right. Can you talk about how you brought the city to life?

My last novel, *Kisses and Croissants,* was very much a love letter to Paris, where it is set. I loved experiencing it through the eyes of a newcomer and exploring my favorite neighborhoods on the page. This time around, I wanted to honor another favorite city of mine, the one I've called home for over a decade. New York City is such a special place: vibrant, diverse, culturally rich, and like nowhere else I've been. I wrote this novel throughout the pandemic, during a time when New York was bruised and battered, but I never stopped believing that my beloved city would weather the storm. At a time when it was challenging to enjoy everything it has to offer, I took great pleasure in offering Margot the best of New York, glory, lights, and all. It was also important to me that Margot's adventures go beyond the obvious spots in Manhattan, as there's so much more to the Big Apple. In fact, Margot visits all five boroughs—from Yankee Stadium to the murals of Bushwick, and from a trip on the Staten Island ferry to the restaurants of Queens—which allowed me to explore my own city more than I had in a long time, even though it was mostly in my head.

Margot mentions that her parents have always loved each other deeply, if not romantically. Can you talk about her family?

When writing a young adult novel, you have to think about the adult figures in your main character's life. What makes this stage of life so interesting to me is that teenagers are starting to explore all the facets of adulthood—discovering independence, taking on responsibilities, planning for their future, working, embarking on relationships, etc.—but they still have to contend with the adults in their lives, who sometimes can't help but treat them like children. I kept playing with Margot's family dynamics to figure out who would be there for her in New York. It made sense that she had family there, someone she trusted. In an early draft, Margot came to work at her aunt's restaurant. The story evolved over time and she ended up with a chef for a mom and a French-American father who lived in New York. The next step was figuring out how Margot's parents had met and ended up living on different continents. I was drawn to the idea of two people who chose to have a child together without being a couple. Margot grew up with love and support from both sides of the Atlantic. Her mother gave her

her life passion and her dad has been this wonderful presence in her life, opening up a world of new possibilities for her.

How did the wedding part of the story come about?

I played around a lot with Margot's motivations for coming to New York. She wants an adventure, and then there's her fateful meeting with Zach. Deep down, she also feels like she's missed out on exploring a part of her identity by not having visited the U.S. before, at least not since she can remember. There's a lot weighing on this move for Margot, and she has been looking for signs all the way. When her dad announces that he's getting married, it's just one more reason this move is meant to be at this particular moment. Aside from that, I *love* weddings, real and fictional, and always enjoy a wedding scene or plotline. So it was also an indulgence on my part. I knew Margot and Luz would make fun bridesmaids, even if the actual wedding day turns out to be a bit too dramatic for Margot's taste.

Did Margot *really* think she and Zach would find each other a year later?

I grappled with this a lot, and I think Margot needed signs that a big, bold move to New York was the right choice for her. She'd been wanting to do this for years, but taking the leap was another story. So when she meets Zach, and when they agree *not* to swap numbers, it means that she *will* have to be in New York then, because she can't take the risk of not seeing where their encounter might lead. I rewrote the prologue more than any other part of the novel because I had to make sure we felt the chemistry between Margot and Zach and understood their reasons for leaving their future up to fate. Margot latches on to the fantasy of what could happen with Zach even more than him as a person.

Let's talk about your research process. How many bowls of onion soup did you eat during the course of writing this novel?

Strangely, none! I've never attempted to make it myself, and I wrote much of *French Kissing in New York* during the pandemic, at a time when it wasn't as easy to eat out. Though now that I researched various recipes, it seems like something I could make, even with my somewhat limited cooking skills. I spent a lot of time researching the menus of various restaurants—both in France and in New York City—to figure out the type of food served at Nutrio, and interviewed several people who work in the restaurant industry. I also vividly remember writing the cake-testing chapter and having long brainstorming sessions with myself about the kinds of bakeries Margot and her family should visit. I ended up craving cake so much that I ordered delivery from a well-known bakery—which doesn't actually appear in the final draft!—and devoured my treats right at my desk at home. All in the name of research, of course.

Who was your favorite character to write? Who was the most challenging?

I love Luz so much! She was one of the first characters I developed—after Margot—as I knew right away that I wanted Margot to have the best possible companion throughout her New York adventures. Margot and Luz have had this deep, sisterlike connection for years, and that was just one more reason Margot couldn't wait to move to New York. Writing their scenes together was so much fun, and I wish more young adult novels explored friendships. They're so incredibly important at this stage of life.

Zach was pretty tricky. Margot has idolized him so much in her head over the course of a year, and it would have been hard for him to live up to those expectations. Even though he ends up disappointing her, it was important to make sure that he was a worthy adversary for Ben. Zach is flawed, but I wanted to make sure he didn't seem too villainous. He had to be someone for whom Margot would want to move mountains, even if she makes a different choice at the end.

Were you always Team Ben?

To be honest, I can't resist a good love triangle. I know they tend to get a bad reputation because they're hard to pull off, but I so enjoy watching a character being torn between two completely different love interests. It often gives such great insights into that character and their many facets. Margot is a different person with Ben than with Zach, but she carries both sides in her equally: the beauty of the fantasy and the comfort of what's real. Having said that, I think Ben is such a warm, wonderful person and anyone would be so lucky to have him as a boyfriend ;-)

What NYC restaurants are on Margot's must-eat-at list?

I wanted Margot to go everywhere and eat *everything*, but that would have turned the novel into a guidebook, ha! So I had to make some tough decisions about what to include and what to leave out.

Here are some favorites Margot visited in between chasing Zach around the city:

Shake Shack for a burger and cheese fries

Van Leeuwen for a scoop of their Earl Grey Tea or Brown Sugar Cookie Dough Chunk ice cream

Breads Bakery for their chocolate babka

Ippudo or Momofuku Noodle Bar for ramen

Tacombi for tacos and other Mexican specialties

Lombardi's for pizza (there can never be enough pizza)

Murray's Bagels for, well . . . bagels, slathered with all kinds of cream cheeses

Magnolia Bakery for the banana pudding

Now I'm hungry!

ABOUT THE AUTHOR

ANNE-SOPHIE JOUHANNEAU is a bilingual French author of young adult fiction and nonfiction, including the YA romance *Kisses and Croissants*. Her books have been translated into eight languages from French and six from English. After living in Amsterdam and Melbourne, she settled down in New York City with her Australian husband, where they spend much of their free time visiting French bakeries (and even some American ones).

asjouhanneau.com